AUTUMN'S RAGE

AUTUMN TRENT SERIES: BOOK FOUR

MARY STONE

D1736136

Copyright © 2021 by Mary Stone

All rights reserved.

No part of this book may be reproduced in any form or by any electronic or mechanical means, including information storage and retrieval systems, without written permission from the author, except for the use of brief quotations in a book review.

❀ Created with Vellum

To my husband.
Thank you for taking care of our home and its many inhabitants
while I follow this dream of mine.

DESCRIPTION

Revenge has no deadline...and endless rage.

Dr. Autumn Trent returns to Virginia after successfully assisting the FBI's Behavioral Analysis Unit yet again. Part of her heart remains in Florida with her long-lost sister whose trail has evaporated, but she moves forward to focus on her work as a forensic and criminal psychologist.

Intent on doing just that, she heads to Virginia State Hospital, where the prodigy of The Preacher awaits her return. Justin Black becomes the least of her worries when a new case practically falls in Autumn's lap.

Murder has its grip on the mental institution, and all signs point toward one suspect. Even though the case appears to solve itself, Autumn thinks the team is being led astray. Uncovering the truth is only half of Autumn's battle. She must first catch the killer before the killer catches her.

Autumn's Rage, the fourth book in Mary Stone's Autumn Trent Series, is a topsy-turvy ride through twisted criminal minds that will take your breath away.

1

"Good morning." Evelyn Walker smiled warmly at the man sitting on the sterile looking steel-framed bed. She picked up Gerard Helmsey's tray from her cart and approached his side, keeping a close eye on his every move. "Are you ready to take your meds for me?"

The epitome of compassion, care, and tidiness, Evelyn's dark curly hair was neatly tucked behind her ears. Cheerful brown eyes graced a plump, pink-cheeked face that many labeled as cherubic. It was fitting. The nurse made great efforts to spread positive energy to each and every patient under her charge.

"Don't look at me," Gerard mumbled, turning his face to the wall.

Evelyn had expected the reply. This particular patient usually offered her and everyone else only two comments. "Don't look at me," and "Screw a goat."

She greatly preferred the former.

As a nurse at Virginia State Hospital—Virginia's only Adult Maximum Security Treatment Program—Evelyn wasn't fazed in the slightest by Gerard's response. She was familiar with each of the patients and their habits, as well as their reasons for being in the establishment.

Gerard's backstory moved her deeply, and no matter his response, Evelyn treated the graying, lanky-limbed forty-six-year-old with kindness. Despite being a mentally disturbed criminal, he was also a victim and a human being who deserved the chance at recovery just like any other diseased individual.

Evelyn struggled to push the images the crimes this particular patient committed before he first arrived at the facility from her mind. Certain patients came to her hospital with lives full of details that were more difficult to digest than others.

Could she ever forget that Gerard Helmsey had forced three women to have sexual intercourse with a goat before throwing their bodies into a meat grinder?

No.

At the same time, Evelyn also couldn't forget that his own uncle had forced—on a daily basis—an eight-year-old Gerard to perform this same act of beastiality with numerous farm animals for seven years straight.

Young Gerard's abuse and horror had only ended when his uncle passed from a sudden heart attack, leaving him under the sole care of his unaffectionate aunt. *She* refused to acknowledge the maltreatment ever occurred.

Evelyn was convinced that Gerard hadn't ever had a friend in his entire life. Furthermore, she held a firm belief that friendship was the first building block to any mental patient's recovery.

Humans needed to know that someone genuinely cared before the motivation to get well could ever begin to blossom…or exist at all.

Gerard Helmsey was still a person, regardless of the atrocities he'd committed.

sit, he maintained a position of obvious comfort in his luxury leather desk chair.

Evelyn continued to appear pleasant, even though she knew what was coming.

"I believe I have made my viewpoint on the subject of interaction with patients incredibly clear in the time that I have been this hospital's director." His voice had taken on a lecturing tone she loathed. His unabashed sternness smothered his words in severity.

Dr. Philip Baldwin hadn't been the medical director of Virginia State Hospital for an entire year yet, but the majority of the staff disliked him to his core. To the contrary, Evelyn had been on staff for five years and counting. She was a favorite of the patients and her co-workers alike.

"The troubled minds we deal with here, Evelyn, require a much more formal code of conduct than you persist to display. Your 'Susie Sunshine' act is going to stop. I will tolerate it no longer."

Dr. Baldwin waited, as though Evelyn might need a few seconds to absorb the gravity of his words. She didn't need even one.

"I don't find anything wrong with bringing a cheerful attitude into the hospital's environment. This place is depressing enough as it is." She held his gaze direct and steady, her posture as tight as a bow. Her firm refusal to show her distinct discomfort powered her unwavering stance, even as she watched his face transform into an angry glower.

"Those people—"

"Those people in those rooms are thinking, feeling individuals. Not just specimens for us to observe and study." She lifted her chin. "And since we're on the subject, how do you expect to observe and study patients who are so drugged they can barely remember their first name let alone the crimes they committed and why."

She was so getting fired.

The clock on the wall seemed to be counting down the seconds until her termination while the doctor stared at her with disbelieving eyes filled with a rage that made her wonder if he should be the one locked behind bars.

"They are *sick criminals*, Evelyn," Dr. Baldwin countered with increased volume. "And you *know* that. Deranged. Murderers. Rapists."

Well...if he was going to fire her, she might as well say everything she wanted to say.

"They're still human beings...not science experiments. They deserve a chance at getting better." Evelyn stamped a foot, immediately regretting the show of anger. The asshole behind the desk would assess the act more closely to a toddler throwing a temper tantrum than an adult expressing her disapproval of his actions.

Dr. Baldwin ran a hand through his dark, wavy hair in frustration. "Those human beings are not going to magically get better by being buddies with Evelyn Walker. You are a nurse. You are *not* their friend. I want you to do your job, make your rounds, and absolutely nothing more. Understood?"

Her chin lifted even higher. "I understand what you're saying, yes."

His eyes narrowed. "You understand, *and* you *will* follow my protocol, Evelyn. Be honest with yourself. These patients aren't leaving anytime soon, and there are damn good reasons for that fact."

"All the more reason to show them kindness and attempt to keep their humanity alive. We're all they have now."

How could he not discern that truth? How could he not care?

Dr. Baldwin took a deep, dramatic breath through his nose and released the air from his mouth in an overly long and equally dramatic exhale. "You will get in step with my program, Evelyn, or you will face disciplinary measures. That is all. You may go."

Dismissed, Evelyn turned on her heel and exited the asshole's office.

She still had her job...for now.

Finishing out the day proved difficult, though she was determined not to let her mood be brought low by that heartless man and his overwhelming arrogance. She still couldn't believe how shortsighted he was. How coldhearted. How obnoxiously arrogant in his belief that his way of taking care of patients was the only way.

He only sat in a chair and talked about their feelings or flicked a wrist and wrote out new prescriptions by the dozens.

That egotistical bastard didn't have to walk into a criminally insane man's room by himself, get close enough to give the hands that had committed atrocious acts the medicines they were told to take. He didn't need to wade into the middle of a fight or find a way to administer a sedative when a patient went berserk.

No...Dr. Philip Baldwin didn't have to get his hands dirty with patient care, yet the unbelievably insensitive man thought he had the right to tell those who did how to do their jobs.

Well...screw him.

Evelyn smiled even brighter for the rest of her shift. Spoke in an even more pleasant manner to every single person she met.

But it was all a façade that weighed heavy on her shoulders as the day went on. One person could only handle so much, and between the standoff with Dr. Baldwin and the routine care of numerous mentally unwell individuals, Evelyn's energy drained to a severe level of low.

She, apparently, looked even worse than she felt.

"You okay, hon?" Brenda Daly leaned over the scarred surface of the nurses' station, her brow furrowed in concern. Brenda was a fellow nurse who also harbored an immense disdain for Dr. Baldwin. She'd worked at Virginia State Hospital for ten years and was only thirty-four, but her graying blonde hair, added to the numerous wrinkles lining her face, proved the physical toll the job extracted.

"I'm sure you've been informed about my glorious little meeting with Baldwin?" Evelyn stacked her patient charts together in a methodical manner despite her troubled thoughts. It was one of the things that made her such a good nurse. She could physically do her job no matter the worry swirling through her mind.

"News travels fast." Brenda's sheepish reply bordered on the apologetic.

"That man is not fit for his position. He shouldn't be allowed to deal with anyone or anything with a pulse. He's cold...heartless. Philip Baldwin would be better off conducting research in a sterile lab by himself." Evelyn released her pent-up vexation by slapping the charts down on the desk.

It didn't help.

"I couldn't agree more." Brenda gave an affectionate pat to Evelyn's shoulder as the latter prepared to leave the station for her final rounds. "Hang in there, Ev. The patients love you. You're an amazing nurse. *That's* what matters."

Evelyn fought the urge to cry.

You still have patients who need you right now. Hold it together.

"Thanks, Brenda. I'm going to finish up." She gave a small

wave and pushed off with her cart and its damn squeaky wheel.

Three steps later, she slipped on the freshly mopped tiled floor, her legs scissoring into a split that her thigh muscles were no longer toned enough to handle. Caught by her cart with a rough thud, Evelyn made a sound that was half groan and half chuckle.

This just isn't my day.

"So sorry, Evelyn." The nearby custodian's apology was immediate and sincere as he wrung his hands together before helping her to her feet. "Meant to put up the wet floor sign."

She took inventory of her legs, hoping to God almighty and the baby Jesus that she hadn't split her pants in the process. "I'm fine. No worries. Par for the course."

As she began pushing the cart again, this time limping a little, she held her head up high.

I will finish out this day just like every other. No slippery floor or asshole medical director will bring me down.

Evelyn headed for her next patient's room. Justin Black.

She liked Justin. He was one of the very few residents who she believed had a chance at full rehabilitation. Of course, he would still have to stand trial for his crimes even if the doctors were able to heal his mind.

That was a hard truth. But Evelyn had empathy for the young man. He had, after all, been raised by The Preacher— Douglas Kilroy. And worse yet, he was Kilroy's biological relative. DNA was inescapable.

Nature...

Nurture...

The poor child had been born into a world where the firm and unforgiving cards were stacked against him to towering heights.

After a polite knock, she opened the door to Justin's room

and entered with only her clipboard. No meds needed this evening. Justin received all his doses during the morning rounds, and he always dutifully swallowed the pills without a hint of fight.

"How has your day been?" Her naturally warm smile returned, firmly in place regardless of the day's upset.

Dr. Baldwin couldn't outlaw smiling.

"Good." Justin held his knees to his chest. "My meeting with Dr. Trent is tomorrow. I'm very excited for her to help me get better." He began to rock, a slow rhythmic movement that could gain speed depending on his level of agitation.

She was used to this habit, one of his coping mechanisms.

"The BAU agent?" Evelyn scribbled on her chart. "That *is* exciting. Anything I can do for you? Your dinner was okay?"

"Acceptable." Justin grinned, and Evelyn joined him. His rocking slowed, an encouraging sign that he wouldn't escalate.

"Good to know." She was pleased to catch Justin in such high spirits. The dark-haired young man was in peak physical condition, and she held high hopes for his full recovery.

All we have to do is fix that mind.

As she continued to chat with him, Justin calmed…almost serene. Evelyn was convinced in her heart of hearts that Justin Black was going to get out of this place. Her instincts supported this upbeat certainty as she included his visible positivity in her observational notes.

Turning to leave, Evelyn shot Justin one last grin. "Great luck at your appointment tomorrow."

He smiled back at her, but just as she grabbed the doorknob, he called out, "Nurse Evelyn." His voice changed with the words, and Evelyn swiveled to meet Justin's gaze. The tiny hairs on the back of her neck bristled as she looked into now vacant eyes.

"Be careful out there, Evelyn. The world is a dangerous place."

Why did his smile suddenly seem like a malicious leer? Why wasn't he even blinking?

Forcing herself to refocus and pull away from his magnetizing sapphire gaze, she left the room, giving the door a swift pull.

Click!

She sighed with relief. Automated locks were a godsend on occasion.

Maybe Justin Black wasn't such a likely candidate for rehabilitation after all.

She decided to forego her routine last glance through the observation window of the door and pushed the aluminum cart hastily down the hallway.

That horrible smile.

I was wrong. I was wrong about Justin.

Of course, she couldn't let his behavior derail her. How ridiculous would that be, considering her place of employment? She had been privy to far too many disturbing things to be this terrified of one young man's smile.

And yet...her fear was palpable.

Darkness.

Evelyn stared out the sole window of the nurses' station. Barred like all the rest, the ancient panes gave view to a dull, inky evening sky. Virginia winters, especially in January, ensured that by the time Evelyn's shift was over, the sun had completely abandoned the day.

She decidedly disliked this time of year.

Following her normal routine, Evelyn entered the employee restroom, locked the door, and peeled off her uniform. Fresh jeans and a soft sweater provided a sense of separation from the previous ten hours.

The germs, dirt, stress, and sadness stayed in the hospital where they belonged.

She walked to the punch out clock, typed her code, and retrieved her coat and purse from the nurses' closet.

Home. Forget Baldwin's lecture. Forget Justin's smile. I'm going home.

Evelyn walked to the stairwell exit, which was her habitual custom for making her way to the parking garage. Stretching her legs helped relieve a bit of the pent-up tension amassed in her muscles throughout the day.

Each landing was lit by a single low-watt bulb screwed into the ceiling…on any *normal* evening. Tonight, of course, the lights were out. She fiddled with the switch by the entry.

No luck.

Was this some type of joke? Was she being Punk'd? What else could possibly go wrong in this godforsaken building?

Just some faulty wiring. Not a new problem for this ancient dinosaur of a hospital.

Evelyn went up and down these steps so often she was confident that she could maneuver them blindfolded. Lights be damned. She was going home.

She traversed the first flight of stairs, beginning to breathe easier as she stepped onto the landing.

"Just get out of this building," she lectured herself in a harsh whisper. "Bad days happen. Tomorrow is a new—"

A hand clamped over her mouth.

Even before adrenaline hit her system, Evelyn launched an immediate struggle against the powerful grip. An arm curled around her throat like a snake and lifted her off her feet. A punch to her temple followed, annihilating her strength to battle.

She inhaled the stink of the man as she was forced to lean

against her attacker, her vision dark around the edges. She tried to strike out, tried to claw at his eyes, but she could barely lift an arm as he dragged her backward.

Through her mental fog, Evelyn remembered her personal duress alarm, her only weapon against a hospital full of mentally deranged criminals. She wore the device for every second of every shift...and she always removed the life saver when switching clothes at the end of the day.

Purse. It's in your purse. You have to...have to...

Her right hand dug in the satchel hung across her body while her left pulled at the relentless grip of her assailant's arm. The temple blow left her mind dazed, her body feeble.

Evelyn's instincts screamed that none of that mattered. *You must fight!*

Regardless of what her mind desperately wanted her to do, she was no match for the physical strength overwhelming her.

The attacker drug her through a doorway and into a dark utility closet.

Grab something...hit...you can hit...you have to...

Realization hit her like a fist. She wasn't in a closet at all.

Cables. Gears.

She was on top of an elevator car.

Understanding intensified her panic and horror, and Evelyn desperately lashed out, trying to injure her assailant with her arms, fists, clawing nails. She kicked and scuffled. Opened her mouth to scream.

Two gloved hands wrapped around her neck.

Act! If you don't, you will die right here, right now!

No matter what she did or how hard she struggled, the hands squeezed without mercy, preventing the slightest bit of air from reaching her lungs.

You're going to...going to...

Evelyn Walker's world went dark.

2

The Booby Trap really wasn't so bad when Dr. Autumn Trent considered that the world was full of war zones and natural disasters.

And cults. Baby-snatchers. Severed hands in swamps.

She gazed around the Florida strip club, focusing in on the oversized disco ball spinning rays of neon light onto the stage below. If she tilted her head just right, she could even make herself believe that it resembled a high-fashion runway.

But in The Booby Trap, the models were naked, and they didn't walk so much as they gyrated around tall metal poles.

Autumn spotted a platinum blonde holding on to a glittery pole with nothing but her thighs. The, um, talented woman hung completely upside down, breasts flailing as she lip-synced to one of Autumn's favorite songs..."Sweet Dreams Are Made Of This."

Impressive.

Even as Annie Lennox wrapped her in the warm embrace of her voice, Autumn fought a sudden desire to turn and run through the door. She didn't. She gave herself a mental shake instead.

None of these women mattered. Nor did the men leering at them. Boobs and butts didn't factor into her being in this building at all. She was here for one thing and one thing only...her sister.

But damn...how did Sarah end up working in a place like this?

Not now.

Autumn didn't have the time or patience to crawl down that mental rabbit hole. Now, she had a mission. Find Sarah. Save Sarah. Once that was accomplished, Autumn could ask all the questions she wanted.

She glanced at her watch. The airplane heading back to Virginia would take off at the crack ass of dawn. She didn't have time to overthink why she was here. She didn't even have time to think about why she was in Florida in the first place.

Dead women. Missing babies.

Aiden Parrish had asked Autumn to consult on the case just moments after she learned that her sister might be in Central Florida. Though she believed wholly in science, she also knew that some things couldn't be explained. And just as Autumn could feel a person's emotions through a simple touch, she knew that meaningful coincidences could occur through the magic of synchronicity.

Two birds, one stone.

Or so she'd hoped.

Autumn and the team had managed to take the bastard who was killing pregnant women down. Heck, Autumn had jumped from a helicopter in the attempt to save a baby. So why was she afraid to walk into this cozy little establishment and ask for her sister?

She even had her two best friends as backup.

A quick glance at Special Agent Winter Black confirmed her premonition that the scene would be entirely too ridiculous to fuel the jealous flair the woman had displayed just before entering this lovely establishment. Winter's lips were pressed together, and Autumn knew the dedicated FBI agent was fighting off a strong fit of nervous laughter.

To Winter's right, Special Agent Noah Dalton's head was moving around like a dodgeball as he apparently attempted to avoid looking at any and all naked body parts in the vicinity. His girlfriend was less than six inches away from him, after all, *and* she was armed.

While noble, Noah's efforts were in vain. Breasts were everywhere. All different sizes and colors—even a few oddly nonsymmetrical pairs.

She assumed Winter would have to give her boyfriend a free pass for this train wreck.

Autumn would have found the view embarrassing and humorous had she not known that her little sister was somewhere amongst the bare-skinned ladies. That fact effectively kept her straight-faced and sober.

She let the initial shock pass and refocused on her mission. A purple-wigged waitress, who at the very least had a bikini top on, leaned against the bar and eyed them with cautious reservation.

"Let's sit," Autumn ordered, choosing a wide cushioned booth shaped like a crescent moon.

Winter and Noah obediently followed her. The trio slid across cracked vinyl seating that was so sticky it made her wish for an entire crate of Lysol spray to fall from the sky.

Autumn fought the overwhelming urge to grab the nearest Booby Trap employee by the arm and gain any knowledge of Sarah that might be readily available.

She wouldn't seize anyone, of course. But being aware that she had the ability to get answers to questions she hadn't yet asked was sometimes a curse she could hardly bear.

Autumn's abusive father had gifted her with a traumatic brain injury when she was only ten. Following the consequential brain surgery required to save her, Autumn awoke to an alien world where she possessed a sixth sense she'd never asked for nor wanted.

A simple touch to or from another human sent instantaneous currents of information from the individual's mind into her own. The thoughts and emotions often overwhelmed her when she was young, making her reluctant to physically connect with *anyone*.

She hadn't viewed her special ability as a positive until her college days, when a certain high-stakes incident showed her how her "superpower" could be used to help a planet full of broken souls. The experience had also made her innately curious about how the mind worked and what led some people to lives of crime while others never ventured down that path.

Because she wanted to learn everything she could about the mind, Autumn followed her bachelor's degree with a master's in criminal psychology before deciding to earn her Ph.D. in forensic psychology. A Juris Doctorate made her feel as if her education was well rounded.

Upon her graduation, her degrees made her a marketable commodity that helped her land her first job with a six-figure salary. And now, the FBI wanted her on their team. With the Bureau, her unusual "talent" could be harnessed as an advantageous yet silent instrument of justice.

And even with all that education behind her, she still hadn't asked about her sister.

Pull it together.

The waitress wasted no time walking straight to their table. Her hips swung with considerable flair as she approached them. "Take your order?" Vivid violet eyes—surely the result of colored contacts—flitted from Autumn to Winter to Noah, where they lingered long enough for Winter to narrow her own vivid blue eyes.

"We're actually here for...Ginger Snap." Heat crept up Autumn's neck as she mentioned her sister's stripper name. The waitress, whose name tag fittingly read *Violet Star*, just stared at her. "Could you let her know she has some visitors?"

Violet chomped on her gum, giving the trio a suspicious glare. "No order?"

Autumn glanced at her friends. "Three colas would be great."

"You want *sodas*?" Violet adjusted her bikini strap. Her gaze turned dubious, then hateful. "What are y'all? Cops or somethin'?"

Technically no, but close enough. You're a sharp one, Violet Star.

No response was needed as Violet put two and two together. Purple eyes wide, she shimmied away, disappearing behind a door that Autumn imagined led to the manager's office. The agents barely had time to grin at each other before Violet was back with a man who was nearly as round as he was tall.

Curly black chest hair popped out of his cheap satin button-down shirt like a bush. He was mostly bald but still had the George Costanza hairline growing thick and proud. Graced with multiple gold chain necklaces, a ludicrously large gold bracelet, and several gold rings, the man perpetuated his own stereotype remarkably well.

"I'm Charlie. The *manager*. Can I help you folks with somethin'?" Charlie gave them a dark-eyed glare that indicated he had intentions to help them with absolutely nothing.

"Just getting some refreshments, Charlie. Hot day out there." Winter batted her eyelashes, gazing up at Charlie with innocent, brilliant blues.

Charlie rolled his eyes. "Yeah, well, this ain't really a soda kinda joint, and I'm sure that's pretty obvious. Why don't y'all roll outta here and find yourselves a McDonald's? Soda for days, that place." Autumn caught the glint of his golden front tooth decorating his grin.

"Okay, Charlie, ya got us." Noah bowed his head, as though confessing to a priest. He gave the manager a sheepish, guilty glance. "We don't really want sodas. We've got a slight obsession goin' on for Ginger Snap."

"All three of ya?" Charlie raised a thick black eyebrow as he peeked at Autumn and then Winter. He licked his lips.

"All three of us. Could we *please* visit with Miss Snap... er...Ginger?" Noah pressed his palms together as he begged.

Charlie turned to Violet Star. "Go get 'er."

Autumn bit her tongue until she tasted blood.

This was the moment. She was going to be face to face with Sarah *in the flesh* for the first time since—

Ginger Snap sashayed to their table.

Autumn had known there was a possibility that she wouldn't quite recognize her baby sister, even if she and Sarah were still similar enough to confuse that drunk jackass at the trailer park a couple nights before. The man had been convinced that Autumn *was* Sarah, but a fifth of whiskey could twist a lot of things around in a man's mind.

However, this woman was *one hundred percent* not Sarah. Smooth ebony skin and creamy chocolate eyes blasted the fact without a single spoken word.

She was, however, wearing a long, red wig.

Charlie smiled, presenting them with the object of their obsession.

"How many Ginger Snaps are there in this place?" Annoyance dripped from each of Winter's words before she turned an icy glare at the manager. "You have to recycle your stage names, Charlie?"

Realizing he hadn't just pleased three paying customers after all, Charlie's face turned surly. "Lotta people got a thing for redheads." He side-glanced at Autumn. "Evonne fills in when the original Ginger bails…and that's all the damn time. Guess you already figured that out for yourself. Fuckin' redheads."

Autumn's shoulders slumped. Evonne was a beautiful woman.

But she wasn't Sarah.

Charlie leaned down, giving Autumn a friendly eyebrow wiggle. "You got any dancing experience, honey?"

Autumn stared blankly back at the repulsively hairy beast before her. Disappointment rendered her speechless.

Winter, on the other hand, was shooting fireballs at Charlie with her eyes, and Noah had managed to turn what started as a very loud laugh into an incredibly convincing cough.

"How about this, Charlie? Ginger got any friends we could talk to?" Noah pushed back to the issue at hand.

Charlie's face scrunched with confusion. "*Talk* to?" He threw a hand up and snorted. "Fork over fifty bucks and you can 'talk' to Ginger Snap's bestie, Elvis's grandma, and the Queen of friggin' England. For exactly fifteen minutes."

Noah's wallet was on the table in a hot second.

"You'll be wantin' Angel Devine. She's tight with Ginger." Violet waved a hand, indicating they should follow her.

Evonne huffed, clearly offended by the dismissal.

"You're very pretty," Autumn assured her, earning a wink from her sister's fill-in before following after Winter, Noah, and Violet Star.

The waitress led them down a narrow hallway that

reeked of certain blatant, obvious human smells that Autumn refused to identify. The velvet red carpet was bunched in places, ripped in others, and seemed to be a thousand years old.

Violet drew back the curtain on a room to her right and ushered them in. "Only one chair. Guess you're taking turns." She shot Autumn a cold smile and pulled the curtain shut behind her.

Noah promptly sat on the metal folding chair. "How's anybody supposed to enjoy anything on this dang contraption? Reminds me of high school detention."

Winter placed her hands on her hips. "How often were you in *there*, Dalton?"

Autumn chuckled, but Noah didn't have a chance to defend himself before the topless platinum blonde with the impressive thigh muscles whipped through the curtain.

She appeared to be taken off guard by the extra persons in her assigned "one-on-one" space but recovered like a champion. "I like to watch too." She shrugged and grinned devilishly at Autumn and Winter before straddling Noah like a horse without the slightest warning. "I'm Angel Divine, sweetheart. What's your name?"

The question was asked amidst the forceful grinds of her nether regions against Noah's body. Angel's one-hundred-percent real boobs flopped generously in Agent Dalton's face, which had turned a shade of red that rivaled Ginger Snap's wig.

"Vanilla," Noah gasped, taking on the safe word Aiden Parrish used on a case not too long ago.

Winter turned away, her shoulders shaking with silent laughter. Autumn almost joined her but instead took pity on the stunned and horrified man trapped in the detention chair.

"Angel, we're actually here to ask you about Sarah."

Autumn's use of a common name found on actual birth certificates snagged Angel's attention.

The stripper stood, abandoning her attack on Noah altogether. "Sarah? Is she okay?" As if actual conversation made her feel naked, she folded her arms across her breasts.

"Well, that's what I hoped *you* could tell *me*." Autumn's pulse raced as she absorbed Angel's concern—no touch needed.

"Oh. Well...she was *really* freaked out cause one of her Johns told her there were cops searchin' for her in the trailer park a few nights back or somethin'. I tried to calm her down. I mean, if a cop wants to find you, they're gonna find you, ya know?"

Autumn glanced at Winter and assumed they were both thinking the same thing.

You'd be surprised how untrue that actually is.

"Anyway, the police never showed up again, but she was still freaked. I had a feelin' she might run. She didn't show up for work today so...I guess I was right." Angel's face was somber as she cocked her head and studied Autumn. "Ya know, you look a *lot* like Sarah. How crazy is that?"

Autumn fought back tears of frustrated disbelief. She had not only managed to be unsuccessful in finding her sister but appeared to be the sole reason Sarah purposely went off radar. Again.

I thwarted my own damn plan. I ruined this.

Angel, not yet aware of the rather obvious fact that this threesome of customers could possibly *be* the "cops" searching for her friend, stared down at Noah. "You still want me to finish this for ya? You paid in full, hon."

Noah flew out of the chair like a rocket missile. "I'm good. Thanks. Have a nice, uh, day...night...whatever." He kept his eyes low and exited the tiny room with remarkable swiftness.

Winter wrapped an arm around Autumn and guided her through the narrow doorway and out toward their SUV.

"Thanks, Angel. You get an A for effort," Winter called over her shoulder.

Autumn knew Winter's attempt at humor was forced. Connected as they were, the disappointment flowed between them in gut-wrenching pulse-waves.

"This doesn't mean you won't find her. You know that, right?"

Winter meant for the words to be comforting, but Autumn no longer believed finding Sarah was in her near future. According to the truths flowing from Winter's arm around her shoulder, neither did she.

3

You have to go in there. Pull yourself together like a big girl and go do your damn job.

The next morning, Dr. Autumn Trent stared at Virginia State Hospital from the confines of her car. She knew, professionally, that what had transpired last night in Florida changed nothing as far as her work expectations were concerned.

But the events of the evening before had altered her internally in a manner she viewed as utterly irrevocable.

She closed her eyes and laid back against the headrest. Her bright red hair hung in auburn curtains over the driver's seat as she pondered the reality of her failure.

She'd found Sarah and lost her simultaneously...just like that.

Before she had time to beat herself up much more, Autumn's phone rang through the silence of her Camry. She jumped—alarmed out of the memories of The Booby Trap visit—and hastily grabbed the device.

Blocked.

She scowled, tossed the phone back in her bag, and

thumped both hands down on the steering wheel. Forcing back the tears she'd been fighting since leaving the Florida strip club, Autumn turned off the car engine.

The time had come to stop obsessing about Sarah. Refocus. But how?

The sting of the loss was still sharp.

Drowning in disappointment, Autumn had been forced to return to the hotel, pack her bag, and catch the early morning flight to Virginia. Only to end up immediately back to work at this hospital with Justin Black and his exhaustive mind games.

She wasn't sure she had the energy.

Fifteen minutes of sitting in her Camry and staring at that building from the shadows of the parking garage, and she hadn't even been able to bring herself to open the car door. The act of pulling her shit together, smiling, dealing with other people's problems—not a single cell in her body cared.

But she tried to remember Winter. They were more than co-workers. They'd become very close friends. Justin was Winter's little brother, and while Autumn couldn't seem to help Sarah right now, she could still attempt to help the Black siblings.

So, you're back to square one. Maybe that's for the best.

Autumn exited her vehicle, squared her shoulders, and forced herself to regain her composure and professionalism.

She walked with more confidence than she felt toward the formidable brick building where she showed her credentials to the security guard and waited while her belongings were searched. After his nod of approval, she gathered her things and headed straight for the nurses' station.

"Hi, Brenda," Autumn greeted, noting the nurse's nametag. "Dr. Trent, here to meet with Justin Black."

Brenda smiled politely and used the back of her hand to

brush some stray hair away from her sweaty forehead. "Would you like his chart?"

"Yes, please." Autumn accepted the folder and flipped through to read the recent notations.

This wasn't good. Since her last visit, Justin had experienced a meltdown of sorts while visiting with his attorney and required sedation. The incident had taken place while Autumn was in Florida.

"How is Justin doing today?" Autumn's pleasant tone was unable to soften the absurd fact that she was inquiring about a violent serial killer's current mood.

The nurse frowned, pushing back another strand of gray-blonde hair. "His regular nurse, Evelyn Walker, was a no-show for her shift this morning. Very unlike her. Justin was incredibly upset." She leaned forward, lowering her voice to a conspiratorial level. "And then there was an incident in the rec room after breakfast."

Autumn's eyebrows raised. "Oh?"

"Many of the patients were present. Apparently, Justin whispered a few choice words to one of the other guys, and just a few minutes later, that same patient attacked a guard. He bit half the guard's ear off." Brenda clucked her tongue. "The entire room went chaotic. Several patients, including Justin, had to be sedated."

Autumn smacked a hand to her forehead.

The hits just keep on coming.

"When he woke up, he seemed confused. He told me I was mistaken and that he hadn't said a word to anyone." Brenda's expression conveyed her doubt.

"Has anyone reviewed the camera footage?" Autumn knew there should be a recording of every event that took place in the hospital's recreational room.

Brenda's frown deepened. "Well, you may or may not

know that our esteemed medical director decided to take most of the cameras out of the facility." She held up a finger. "The red room is one of the few areas where one remained, but the camera stopped recording for twenty-three minutes...the exact amount of time that the group was in the room."

Autumn stiffened, sensing Brenda's worry, which compounded upon her own.

There was no way in hell that the timing was a coincidence. Too precise. But how could any patient—criminal—pull off that kind of rigging in a maximum-security hospital?

She handed the chart back to Brenda, scanning over the station area. A large box with Justin's name on top sat next to an empty desk chair.

"What's with the box?" Autumn nodded toward the bin.

Brenda rolled her eyes. "Justin's fan mail. He's *quite* the sensation."

Autumn stared at the admittedly large container. She'd studied many notorious criminals and knew that they often developed a fan base. Sometimes, they even received marriage proposals while in prison.

Justin was an attractive individual, sharing Winter's black hair and striking blue eyes. The adoration really shouldn't have surprised her, but Autumn still floundered at the idea.

Fans of incarcerated individuals who'd committed crimes of such disturbing natures were often mentally unstable themselves. This instability led them to obsession, and obsessed humans were unpredictable under the best of circumstances.

Autumn recentered and approached the security guard stationed at the entrance to the patient rooms hallway. "I need to meet with Justin Black, and I'd prefer for him to be brought to the conference room."

The guard nodded. "Do you want him shackled?"

Autumn hesitated, but not for long. "Yes."

"Fifteen minutes, ma'am. I'll bring him to the third-floor conference room." With a little salute, he walked speedily down the hall.

"Thank you." Autumn barely got the words out before a disturbance in the dayroom caught her attention.

An elderly man with unkempt gray curls hurled books from the dayroom bookshelf at a small, freckle-faced, and much younger patient. The nonresponsive human target sat frozen in a blank stare as each hardback struck his increasingly blood-covered face.

"Talk! Talk! Talk!" the older patient screamed with each book he threw. His victim, nevertheless, remained silent.

Autumn wasn't sure the injured man was even aware of what was happening to him. There wasn't five full feet between them, and he was essentially being beaten at point blank range with leatherbound missiles. But his eyes showed no comprehension nor pain.

Yet another patient—young and well-muscled—joined the chaos, flinging himself onto the book thrower and screaming in a high-pitched wail while he punched the old man's face once...twice...three times.

No longer able to hurl anything, the defeated elder pled his case in between the punches. "He won't talk! Make him fucking talk! He's going to kill us all! *He's going to kill us all!*"

The screaming and the punching continued, as did the blood pouring out of numerous lacerations on the freckled patient's face.

Autumn walked toward the room, unsure as to what she would do to stop the brawl, but certain that it must be stopped. She was pushed aside as three orderlies, two nurses, and a doctor rushed past her. The orderlies pried the hysterical book thrower and the muscular puncher apart while the frantic nurses administered sedation shots.

"He's going to kill us all! All! All!"

The doctor attempted to stop the blood flow from the still-silent freckled patient's face, and numerous others spectated from their positions in the large room.

Autumn discerned that some of the "audience" of patients seemed horrified, while others appeared just as confused as the bloody-faced man. Many of the patients were smiling—some even clapping and giggling.

As the situation calmed down, Autumn turned to head for the elevator, and nearly screamed when she locked eyes with a young, hazel-eyed boy with shaggy brown hair. He observed her through the glass of the dayroom window with haunting concentration.

He was wearing a suicide gown—a garment resembling a poncho, made of highly durable material that prevented patients from ripping the fabric and using the cloth to harm themselves.

He smiled at her, his gaze vapid. She smiled back as her heartbeat pounded wild inside her chest.

I wonder what his story is...

But there was no time for that quandary today. Fifteen minutes were almost over, and she had a date with a different troubled soul. She took off down the hall, reminded of her purpose for being in the facility.

The quiet of the elevator was soothing. Autumn hit the third-floor button and sighed with relief as the doors shut. The car jerked a few times, causing her slight alarm, but then rose smooth.

Seconds later, another jerk nearly tossed her against the wall, and then the elevator stopped moving altogether.

Terrific.

She was stuck between floors.

Autumn raised her eyes to the elevator ceiling and detected a brownish liquid seeping between the tiles. She gagged as the scent filled the car.

That smells like actual shit...

She homed in on the substance.

"That *is* shit."

Autumn covered her mouth with one arm and reached up toward the tile, her terror rising as her mind screamed for her to mind her own business. Ignoring the warning voice, she gave a push...then another...

The tile fell, along with the arms and torso of a dark-haired woman.

A *dead* woman.

Autumn slammed her palm against the call button so hard she was surprised the plastic didn't crack.

"Yes?" came a pleasant female voice.

"This is Dr. Autumn Trent. I'm stuck in the elevator between floors two and three. And..." Autumn closed her eyes, "a woman's dead body just fell through the ceiling."

"A *what?*" Not so pleasant now.

Autumn forced herself to remain calm. "You need to call the police immediately. My phone has no signal in here. And please send someone to get me out of this elevator."

As soon as fucking possible.

Autumn knew she had no authority to declare an official time of death, but the importance of establishing that the woman was deceased appeared necessary. Visually, she had no questions about the status of this body, but she knew many doctors who'd been sued for not doing something as simple as checking for a pulse.

Taking great care not to touch the body, Autumn gingerly pulled the woman's sweater collar aside. She placed her fingers to the carotids—*definitely, definitely dead*—and then glimpsed the dark bruises ringing the woman's neck like fine jewelry from hell.

This was not an accident.

Knowing that she was sharing the elevator car with a cadaver had been disturbing enough. Homicide raised her horror to a new level.

Only a few minutes passed before the scraping metal clangs of the elevator door being pried open reached her ears. But Autumn swore to herself she'd been in this ghastly, reversed jack-in-the-box for centuries.

Once the door was braced open by the maintenance crew, two muscle-bound orderlies each grasped an arm and pulled her up through the small space the elevator had managed to clear of floor three before halting.

Autumn's stomach scraped against the tiled edging as her body entered the third floor, and a brief flash of terror shot through her mind as she pictured the elevator dropping and neatly slicing off her legs.

Numerous employees had gathered around the spectacle. Two nurses helped her up and guided her away from the door just as another started sobbing. "Evelyn!"

I'm afraid I must inform you that Evelyn won't be replying. And if she does, you might wanna call your friendly neighborhood exorcist.

Autumn shuddered.

The guard who was to meet her in the conference room with a shackled Justin Black approached and confirmed Autumn's assumption that Justin had been taken back to his room.

No mind games today, Mr. Black.

Police officers arrived and set about establishing the crime scene before anyone could contaminate it. One of them, informed that "the hot redhead doctor" had been the lucky individual stuck in the elevator with the dead woman, walked to her.

His face was grim. "We're going to need you to stick around for a bit, Doctor."

Autumn nodded her consent but headed for the conference room a few doors down. She had an extraordinarily fun phone call to make.

4

Returning to the quiet atmosphere of the FBI's Richmond, Virginia Field Office after the massive pandemonium of the Florida case hit Special Agent Noah Dalton as a bit bizarre.

Dealing with a psychopath submerged in his own god-complex wasn't exactly abnormal in this line of work. But processing all the kidnapped infants, murdered mothers, and distraught partners affected by the madness had been uniquely taxing.

The murderer had covered his tracks incredibly well, hiding the babies on his own private island with his weird-ass cult of followers. He'd had a lot of assistance from the local wildlife too. The alligators of Florida's swampland happily made the dead women's bodies disappear. Noah didn't envy the brave divers who were still going into the swamp, looking for women the gators had stashed on the bottom for a much later snack.

Of course, the bad guy had messed up. They always messed up, even if only by trusting another individual who wasn't quite as careful and intelligent as themself.

Noah could have done without being bomb-blasted into the marina, but overall, he approved of the team's effort and execution. One hundred and eight children were saved from the Eden cult and were in the process of being returned to what was left of their families.

However, the case had left Noah and his co-workers with a ton of paperwork. As an employee of the FBI, Noah fully understood the importance of accurate documentation.

As a guy, Noah wanted to go grab a beer, some nachos, and forget about Florida for a few hours. Or maybe just forget about Florida forever.

He'd already groused and grumbled more than anyone else currently in the office. Winter kept her head down and ignored him altogether. The burden was split amongst the entire team, and Noah was aware that he needed to man up *and* shut up.

The reams of repetitive record keeping might be exhausting, but Noah begrudgingly admitted—to himself and no one else—that they were necessary.

Adequate, faultless documentation had the power to make or break a case, not only for upcoming trials but for the appeals that were sure to follow any conviction.

Noah knew of one prisoner serving a life sentence for two murder convictions who did nothing else but study law books with every minute of free time he had. The man was searching for some sort of judicial error that might have occurred in his case, leading to his particular verdict and sentence.

An error regarding a jury instruction or involving the presentation of evidence, or even a single tiny rule that wasn't followed precisely in terms of things like warrants, submission of evidence, or chains of evidence could toss all the hard work they'd accomplished on a case out the window. Just one microscopic oversight that led to a conviction gave a prisoner the right to appeal the court's decision.

He had no doubt that one day the persistent bastard would find a technicality and walk. And for that reason, Noah made sure to dot every I and cross every T on each specific case he worked.

He'd never be able to live with himself if a perp walked free simply because he hadn't filled out a damn form correctly. His only deep motivation to face the grueling task was based on a firm determination to keep justice from being overturned.

As he reviewed yet another form, his cell buzzed. He glanced at the screen. Aiden Parrish. Noah groaned. Whatever Aiden needed...no. Just no.

But after swiping the message open, his intrigue was piqued.

Come to Virginia State Hospital ASAP. Tell no one where you are going.

Noah wasn't a rocket scientist, but he knew that by "no one," Aiden clearly meant Winter.

He gazed at her, absorbed in work at her desk. She'd haphazardly thrown her shiny black hair into a semblance of a bun and bent over her paperwork in deep concentration. Was he supposed to outright lie to her?

Shit.

His thumbs jabbed out a reply: *On the way.*

Noah walked as casually as possible toward Winter's desk. "Aiden wants me. I'll be back."

Winter's head went up and down slightly in a semblance of a nod, but she was too engrossed to even make eye contact. Noah seized the opportunity to get the hell out before she had a chance to register his words.

The walk to his truck and even the drive was welcome after sitting in that godforsaken desk chair.

Better than some of the chairs you've sat in lately.

Noah flushed. The embarrassment from the night before was still fresh, but he had an inkling that no matter how much time passed, Winter and Autumn would never let him forget that particular seated experience.

Time to work, Dalton. Save your mortification for later.

He parked in the hospital visitor lot and strode up the sidewalk. Cool confidence returned when he spotted Aiden in the lobby, along with Autumn and Special Agents Mia Logan and Chris Parker.

Mia's pleasant smile and open expression was a stark contrast to Chris's frown and brooding demeanor, striking Noah as amusing. But nothing was as funny as Parker's doo-bop doo-wop blond hair precisely arranged atop his giant head.

He looks like a friggin' highlighter.

As soon as he reached the group, Parrish was on him. "Were you able to get away without any issues?" The SSA's cool blue stare instantly hit a nerve.

"How 'bout we stop playing games?" Though Parrish bristled at his tone, Noah didn't soften his words or lower his voice. He'd grown used to pissing off Aiden Parrish by now. "No. Winter doesn't know that anything is wrong at the hospital where her brother and best friend currently are."

And I'm fucking exhausted. Too exhausted to cater to the SSA's enormous ego.

Aiden's calm expression didn't change. "Good. Winter not knowing is for the best. For now. No need to worry her before we better understand the situation."

Noah massaged the tight muscles in his neck. "So, you gonna tell *me* about the situation?"

Parrish shot him a sharp glance. Noah's mood was clearly not appreciated in this moment, and he knew, like it or not, that SSA Aiden Parrish should be addressed with polite civility.

Parrish outranked him. On occasion, Noah despised this fact.

Autumn stepped in to diffuse the tension. "The situation is a dead body that I was lucky enough to have fall through the ceiling of my elevator car."

Noah snapped to attention and listened carefully to Autumn's story. There would be plenty of time to bicker with Parrish in his foreseeable future.

"I assumed an accident had happened. The elevator jammed between floors, and there was this feces odor." Autumn rubbed her goose-bump-covered arms. "Shit... actual shit seeped through the ceiling tiles."

Noah swallowed a gag, not wanting to imagine being in Autumn's shoes.

Autumn raised a hand over her head, mimicking her previous actions. "A couple pushes on the tile and...boom. Dead woman falls halfway into the car, right in front of my damn face. But the kicker is that she was clearly murdered. When I checked her neck for a pulse, I found the very obvious strangle marks." Her expression had gone severe.

"So. Not an accident." Noah's sympathy for Autumn's "discovery" immediately tamed his edginess.

Autumn grimaced. "Definitely not an accident, but at least they got me out of there."

"They?" Noah questioned, scanning the room. The lobby was crowded with law enforcement and hospital employees.

"Some orderlies and maintenance guys. Pulled me through to the third floor, which is where I'd been heading." Autumn's bright green eyes were grateful, but her face was pale and drawn. It was obvious that the scene had shaken her to her core.

"I'd like to head to the crime scene." He gave Parrish a little sarcastic salute. "If that's okay with you, of course."

Parrish's eyes narrowed the smallest fraction while the rest of his face was carefully blank. "What an excellent idea, Agent Dalton. You may go." The man was ridiculously skilled in the art of showing no emotion whatsoever.

Noah fought the urge to punch Aiden Parrish in his smug supervisor face. Instead, he gave a pleasant nod to Autumn, ignored Parrish, and headed for the door marked "stairs."

Elevator rides were overrated anyway.

He didn't even break a sweat running up the three flights. Noah stayed in excellent physical shape and could have easily ascended another dozen more.

An FBI agent never could foresee when running would be necessary, but they all knew that a good sprint could be the defining difference between catching or losing the bad guy. Maintaining a healthy physique was a job requirement.

Noah pushed open the stairwell door and joined the madness of the third floor.

The crime scene was evident, having been taped off and secured. A female officer approached him, her face stern and distrustful.

"I'm Adrienne Lewton, the local police chief. I figure it's only fair to tell you right off the bat that I don't need the FBI to get involved in this. I know one of your own found the body, but my department has the situation handled." Her gray-blue eyes expressed the obvious resentment she'd incurred over the FBI's presence.

Noah held up both hands. "Special Agent Noah Dalton. I assure you, we're only here to help, Chief Lewton. Nobody is going to step on your toes."

His promise was solid. The FBI was a powerful organization, but they couldn't just throw the door open and take over a case.

"You are correct, though. One of our agents found the body, and the Behavioral Analysis Unit was already working with a resident here in the hospital. We have good cause to get involved." Noah studied Adrienne's facial response.

She was young for a police chief—he guessed mid-thirties —and therefore probably hadn't had her position for a long period of time. In addition, Noah knew all too well that women in any branch of law enforcement still fought constant sexism.

Adrienne deserved the same respect given to her male co-workers, and she apparently wasn't shy about demanding due veneration. Noah applauded her boldness. He had a deep appreciation for strong women. The proof was in the pudding on that matter.

His girlfriend was a badass.

However, history had displayed a clear favoritism for the male species, in this career and practically every other. Time had brought drastic change and improvement toward the caveman attitude, but Noah knew there were still dillhole male cops—males in general—who frowned at the idea of a female supervisor.

"I understand. You guys have some irons in the fire here." Adrienne forced a stray strand into submission with the rest of her short, light brown hair.

"Exactly." Noah was relieved. This police chief would be a tough cookie, but she appeared to be very logical as well. He surmised that she would make decisions based on what was best for the case no matter how much she didn't want the FBI around.

"Okay. Your team can *help*, as you said, but make sure you and all the other agents don't forget that this is my case. I'm in charge here. Got it?"

Adrienne's stare reminded him of his third-grade teacher, and he offered her a quick thumbs-up. "Got it, Chief."

Adrienne's crime techs dusted the scene for fingerprints while Noah stepped toward the edge of the yellow tape. He scanned the scene before him. The dead body of the female nurse had been removed and now lay zipped inside a body bag on a gurney against the hall wall.

"I know it goes without saying, Agent Dalton, but don't touch anything." Adrienne's warning was stern.

And unnecessary. Noah was well aware that one misstep, no matter how small, could derail an entire investigation.

A whiff of feces assailed him.

Poor Autumn. What an effing mess to walk into. Or...have dropped on you.

His friend had experienced quite the letdown less than twenty-four hours ago. He'd already been concerned for her, and Winter seemed more than convinced that Autumn was "not okay at all."

So, how was Autumn doing now? She'd seemed composed and pulled together in the lobby, but that was almost a prerequisite of the job.

If an FBI agent started losing their shit in front of civilians, all hell would break loose.

Noah repeated his scan, as he always did, to make sure he hadn't missed anything. But aside from the noxious body fluid that still remained, even after the dead body with strangle marks around her neck had been removed, nothing else seemed out of order.

Well, except for the elevator. That beast wouldn't be operational any time soon.

No blood. He knew the techs would scour the entire scene for every clue—a strand of hair, a drop of saliva. The smallest details nearly always told law enforcement the most crucial information.

Granted, most people could figure out pretty quickly if the human before them was dead or alive. But only highly trained specialists could perform adequate searches through the fibers of a sweater or the miniscule granules of an invisible substance on a shoe.

The fact that the murder had occurred in a hospital full of criminals was going to make this case a million times more difficult. The majority of the hospital's "patients" were here for far more gruesome crimes than simply strangling a nurse.

This would be like trying to find a hymen in a whorehouse.

The madness was just beginning, Noah knew. He had hoped for at least a few days of quiet upon returning to Virginia. Living with Winter sure as hell didn't mean spending loads of time with her. Not the kind of time a developing relationship needed.

They were both dedicated to their jobs and the relentless nature of such careers.

He admired Winter's drive. He was proud of her and proud to be *with* her.

But Noah couldn't deny the ever-present fear that had settled and taken hold in his gut. Would the stress of being FBI agents serve to push them apart somewhere down the line?

Assuming there still *was* a line after Winter became aware that he'd purposely withheld information about being called to the exact facility in which her mentally ill brother was being detained.

He'd only followed a direct order from his superior by keeping his mouth shut, but Winter Black wouldn't give a damn about those semantics. She would consider herself betrayed regardless of how valid his reasons had been.

This exact type of situation fell into the dating your co-workers "gray area" that Noah feared.

But currently, he didn't fear anything quite so much as the impending wrath of his girlfriend.

5

Autumn mentally groaned as Noah marched away toward the hospital stairwell. She was well aware that Aiden and Noah weren't the best of friends, but after what the entire team just went through together in Florida, the coolness between the two men seemed ridiculous.

Get over yourselves. You're not four-year-olds, and this isn't a playground.

Autumn absently massaged her temples.

"Could I speak with you for a moment? Privately?" Aiden gestured toward an empty waiting room.

Autumn didn't bother to ask why. "Of course."

Why not? What could you or anyone else possibly have to say that is more upsetting than the events of the last twenty-four hours?

"You must be exhausted, Dr. Trent," Aiden stated as they sat on the cushioned chairs beside each other.

Autumn smiled wanly. "What, from *this*? No big deal. Why would a dead woman falling into my stalled elevator car as I made my way to talk to a probable psychopath who also just happens to be my best friend's little brother in a state hospital full of deranged, cold-blooded killers bother me?"

She'd meant to be funny and allay Aiden's concerns but nearly burst into tears instead. She kept them at bay by reminding herself that she'd promised SSA Parrish that her emotions would not affect her job performance.

"Exactly. That's a lot. You're allowed to have human reactions, you know." Aiden gazed at her with such intensity that Autumn wished she could sink through the floor and disappear forever. She didn't have the energy for this conversation.

"Yes, Aiden, I know. I'm fine." She forced herself to smile again.

Aiden shook his head. "I don't believe any of us are 'fine' after the Florida case. Obviously, we're in the business of dealing with disturbing shit, but that was some *disturbing shit.*"

Autumn noted that he also appeared exhausted—more so than he already had before flying to Florida. The nonstop case hopping was taking a toll on everyone. Despite his authority, experience, and stupidly expensive suits, Aiden was a mere mortal.

And he didn't seem able to hide behind his concrete walls when they spoke.

Most of the team assumed he didn't have any emotions to begin with, and Autumn understood why. The man was steel cold and infamous for his serious nature.

"Well, okay then. I'm as fine as the rest of you. Fair?" Autumn hoped they could change the subject to anything that didn't involve emotions and well-being.

Aiden cleared his throat and pressed his fingertips together. He was nervous. The fingertip movement was one of his very few tells. She wasn't going to like what he was about to say next.

"I know about your trip to find Sarah. I'm sorry that didn't work out for you."

Nope. She didn't like it at all.

Autumn tensed as grief flooded her. The pain was too fresh. If the conversation turned to Sarah, she would lose her composure entirely.

Too much. Too much. Too much.

"Winter filled you in?" Autumn couldn't imagine that Noah was the bean-spiller. He enjoyed knowing something the SSA didn't too much.

Aiden leaned back and rested his head against the waiting room wall. "Only out of concern for you. As your boss, she figured I should know in case…"

Autumn whipped her head toward Aiden. "In case what? In case I'm too weak to handle that *and* my job at the same time?"

"In case you seemed down, which you do. I'm only saying that I understand why you would be. Nothing more. I'm supposed to monitor the welfare of my team. Part of the job." Aiden turned and stared out the window.

They both knew that he monitored Autumn a bit more closely than the rest of the team.

"I'd prefer to focus on Justin. I haven't met with him since before the Florida case, and then *this* case…" she closed her eyes against the image of the nurse falling through the ceiling, "practically landed at my feet when I tried to go to him."

Aiden stood and began pacing the room. "I'm pleased they've placed him here. You're under no time frame to have him declared competent to stand trial. Really, the longer he's in Virginia State Hospital rather than prison, the better."

That had been Autumn's conclusion too, and she was glad Aiden felt the same. Still, she wanted to understand his thoughts on the subject better, so she raised an eyebrow. "And why is that?"

"The hospital better enables you to research his case, his mind, his history. I want you to learn as much as you can about Justin. Your insight and background in forensic and criminal psychology gives you an advantage. You will pick up on details from before and after his crimes that most people wouldn't."

Aiden's faith in her abilities was simultaneously nerve-racking and heartwarming.

"Justin is extremely intelligent. I might need more than an advantage to go deep into a mind like that, especially since we have to be careful with how I investigate him prior to his trial. Don't want to be accused of leading the witness or any of the number of details a defense attorney will attempt to latch on to."

And Justin would attempt to create those mistakes. Autumn recalled his piercing blue eyes and the way he seemed to stare straight into her brain.

He would have made an amazing psychologist.

"*You* are extremely intelligent, Dr. Trent." Aiden's voice softened. "Remembering that would serve you well."

She looked away, focusing on a bird outside the window so he wouldn't see her embarrassment. "I have to admit that I am excited to study Justin." The science nerd inside of her broke out, and her skin warmed for the first time since stepping into that elevator. "Having direct access to a serial killer who was raised by a serial killer is a gold mine. A sad and twisted gold mine, but still. Can you imagine the insights he'll provide to the nature versus nurture argument?"

Aiden stopped pacing abruptly, turning his full attention onto her. "I believe the resulting data will be informative and interesting."

Autumn frowned, wondering if Aiden had misread her intentions. "I'll do everything possible to *help* Justin too. He's not a lab rat. I'd like to offer him therapy, anger management, and several other counseling services…if the Bureau will let me."

"Autumn," Aiden began, his expression concerned, "you really shouldn't get your hopes up when dealing with Justin Black. He very well may be past any 'help' you could offer outside this establishment."

She was instantly angry, and she doubted Aiden would need to glance at her mood ring to figure that much out.

He held her gaze, steady as ever. "I know that's not what you want to hear, but you're not a fairy godmother who can wave her wand and make the world better. This is real life, not a Disney movie. Bad guys, *especially* the type we deal with, don't often have a magical change of heart."

The anger grew with each word of the lecture, and she shoved the desire to scream back down in her gut. "Yes, Aiden. I'm a professional, and according to you, I'm 'extremely intelligent.' Never once have I thought I can *fix* Justin Black. But I can, and will, *help* him."

Aiden appeared to have been turned into stone. "He's your best friend's little brother. That has an effect on you whether you'd like to admit it or not."

Unbelievable.

"None of that changes the fact that I'm an educated, trained doctor." Her molars ground together. "Winter's connection to Justin and me doesn't mean I'm going in with blinders on."

Aiden didn't appear at all fazed by her indignation. Before either of them could get another word out, a dark-haired man strode into the waiting room, his murky green eyes set on Autumn's face.

"You." He pointed at Autumn, his upper lip curling into what appeared to be disgust. "Are you the one who started this debacle?"

Autumn envisioned snapping his pointer finger straight

off. Whoever this man was, he was attacking her at the wrong time. This treatment coming right on the heels of her upsetting conversation with Aiden triggered a deep anger he didn't want to mess with.

"I can assure you," she stepped toward the pompous asshole, "that the person who 'started this debacle' is the one who strangled that poor nurse to death and dumped her body in a damn elevator shaft."

The man's eyebrows shot up, softening the glower as confusion took over. He blinked several times, his gaze flicking back and forth between her and Aiden. "Strangled? This isn't just a terrible accident?"

Autumn gave a sharp shake of her head.

He immediately lost a bit of his gusto at the startling piece of information. "I'm Dr. Philip Baldwin, the medical director of this hospital." As if the simple act of remembering who he was made Baldwin bristle again, his gaze rotated from Autumn to Aiden with renewed resentment.

Autumn was familiar with the name. Dr. Baldwin had a wide-reaching reputation for being an arrogant control freak. He certainly wouldn't be happy that the FBI was invading his turf.

"Dr. Autumn Trent." Autumn didn't offer a hand or a smile.

"And I'm Special Supervisory Agent Aiden Parrish. Good to meet you, Doctor." Aiden stood still beside Autumn. No handshakes for anyone today.

"Perhaps you could tell me, Agent Parrish, why my hospital is being flooded with officers and agents?"

Autumn wanted to throw up her hands. Seriously?

Though the question had been aimed at Aiden, she refused to be dismissed so easily.

"This hospital is flooded with officers and agents," she used the same tone she would have used had she been instructing a child, "because one of your nurses has been murdered."

"I've gathered that much, Dr. Trent," Baldwin countered, narrowing his eyes. "Have you considered the possibility that you could have used a bit more stealth or perhaps a touch of common sense before calling in the entire cavalry?"

Aiden stepped toward the seething man. "I would appreciate—"

"What exactly should I have done differently, Doctor?" Autumn fired back. "What would you do if a dead body dropped out of the ceiling right in front of your face? Sing Kumbaya?" She wasn't yelling yet, but that was coming soon if this prick didn't back off.

Dr. Baldwin's entire body grew still. "I simply believe that the matter could have been handled with a bit more dignity and decorum for the good of my patients. My job does not entail teaching you how to react to alarming circumstances. Usually, *Doctor*, you pick that up before they grant you the fancy Ph.D."

Autumn used every ounce of self-control she had left to not Krav Maga the crap out of this jerkwad doctor's face. She took a deep breath to settle her raging fury.

"The authorities are acting with wisdom. They're following protocol, as did I. I'm guessing *you* don't know that much about law enforcement procedure. If there's a killer in 'your' hospital, you might want to take into account that your patients' safety is at risk."

Dr. Baldwin hesitated, almost as if he hadn't considered that little piece of information before. He exhaled through his nose, making a whistling sound that grated on her nerves. "Fine. I'll allow you all to stay."

Aiden chuckled, but his expression held no humor. If a laugh could be identified as sarcastic, this one could have been.

"But…" the doctor held up a haughty finger, "I demand to be kept in the loop about *everything* that happens here. And any disturbances to the daily routine of my hospital shall be kept to a minimum." He turned on his heel and walked away.

Autumn and Aiden regarded his retreat in stunned silence.

"That guy will definitely be a problem during this investigation." Aiden kept his eyes trained on the doctor.

"That guy is a problem, period." Autumn was uncertain as to how such asshole individuals ever made their way into positions as sensitive as medical director of any hospital. Dr. Baldwin should never have set a pinky toe, let alone a foot, in a maximum-security treatment facility such as this.

Aiden nodded his agreement. He appeared to be equal parts amused and pissed off by the doctor's blatant disrespect.

Or maybe Baldwin's that upset because he has something to hide.

They left the privacy of the waiting room, and immediately the nurse with graying blonde hair walked straight toward them. Her eyes were puffy from crying, and she had a fistful of used tissues clenched in one hand.

"Brenda, hi. This is my supervisor, Agent Aiden Parrish. We're so sorry for your loss. Is there anything we can do for you?" Autumn almost placed a hand on Brenda's arm to comfort her but stopped herself.

If I intake any more sad or bad or mad juju today I might actually go insane.

"I'm fine. It's just…Evelyn was a *good* person. She didn't deserve this." Brenda's distress was obvious. She was not "fine."

"Of course she didn't," Autumn agreed in a soothing voice.

"But I truly believe that you, the FBI, should know that

Dr. Baldwin and Evelyn had words yesterday. Angry words." Brenda's frightened eyes told them more than her voice.

Angry words. A bad argument. *She's scared.*

Did Brenda think Philip Baldwin was capable of murder?

Autumn glanced around them to confirm that the medical director had left the lobby. "Did you happen to hear what exactly they were arguing about?"

Brenda teared up again and pressed the tissues to her cheeks to catch the tears. "Evelyn loved her patients. She tried to befriend all of them. She believed kindness was a huge part of her job."

Autumn understood immediately.

Apparently, Aiden did too because his jaw flexed in agitation. "Let me guess. Dr. Baldwin wanted her to conform to *his* idea of what a nurse should be."

Brenda blew her nose as she nodded. "But Evelyn isn't... wasn't easy to push around. She wasn't afraid of Dr. Baldwin. She had no intention of following his rules."

"Do you have any idea how the conversation ended?" Autumn didn't want to push too hard. Brenda was already in a fragile state.

"Just that he warned her there'd be consequences if she didn't comply."

Autumn and Aiden exchanged a glance.

"Did he state what those consequences would be?" Autumn asked.

The distraught nurse only shook her head.

"Thank you, Brenda, for this piece of information." SSA Parrish offered her a polite smile and handed her his card. "Your assistance could prove very useful as we investigate. If you think of anything else that might help, big or small, don't hesitate to contact me directly."

Brenda stuffed the card in her pocket before scurrying away.

"Brenda's input doesn't tell us much for certain. Baldwin is obviously a dictator asshole," Aiden pulled his phone from his suit pocket, "but that doesn't mean Baldwin *did* this. Still, the lead is worth checking into."

Autumn had gathered as much.

They rejoined Mia and Chris on the other side of the lobby, and Aiden wasted no time assigning their tasks.

"We're going to divide the list of patients between us. Assessing some of the patients' states of mind would be a wise idea and could possibly provide information that only the residents of this hospital would know. Yes, they're dangerous, mentally unsound criminals, but they have eyes and ears. They may inadvertently help solve this case."

Autumn and Mia nodded, but Chris had obvious qualms with this method of investigation because he threw up his hands.

"We're going to need a patient list. Backgrounds, criminal records, medications. We need to know who we're talking to before they start blabbing out ridiculous, false information."

As he ranted, Autumn wondered if his disapproval stemmed from not having thought of the interviews first. Although the chances were good that he was simply being his usual disagreeable self.

Chris Parker would have a qualm with Mother Teresa.

"Right you are, Agent Parker. I've already taken it upon myself to obtain such a list, starting with the patients our victim had direct contact with the day she was killed. The information was emailed to me, and I've divided the patients I want interviewed into three groups. Three patients for each of you." Aiden gave his phone a few swipes, and all their devices began beeping instantaneously.

Autumn scrolled through her assignments.

Not a soul on her list was a simple "disturbed murderer" or "serial rapist." The highlights of her patients' backgrounds made her nauseous, horrified, and fascinated in turn.

She'd been assigned to the sickest of the sick.

She attempted to catch Aiden's eye, but the SSA had already moved on to his next order of business and walked away.

The most dangerous of the criminally insane had been gifted to her by Aiden Parrish. Had he done this intentionally?

And if so, was her "special" assignment a display of his trust...or a test?

6

I couldn't take my eyes away from the window. Various authorities—mostly local police and FBI agents—buzzed around like obnoxious flies. Back and forth from the scene of the crime, all of them making seemingly endless calls, exploring the hospital's perimeter.

And removing Evelyn's body from the site.

Evelyn probably hadn't deserved to have her light snuffed out in such a brutal way, but the woman just didn't know when to shut up. She'd made herself a target by running her damn mouth nonstop.

Always so argumentative and obsessed with befriending mentally unstable criminals.

Who did that? Why would anyone even want to?

She may have still been alive right now if she'd just kept her nose down, done her job, and minded her own business.

The deed was done, regardless. Evelyn Walker had walked right on over to the other side. No use fretting about the situation now.

Her death would serve a greater purpose in the long run,

and that was my comfort. Of course, she would never know how she'd *been* of service, but again...

The deed was done.

Although things hadn't exactly gone as planned.

Taking the nurse off guard had been easy. Evelyn stuck to the same exact routine every single day, and once she clocked out, so did her awareness of her surroundings.

Such a mistake.

I always knew what was taking place around me. Always. That was the only way to live if you wanted to ensure that you *kept on living*.

Maybe her shifts with the crazies wore her down too much to care. But those interactions should have drove home the point to her in a very real way that there were psychopaths out there.

Lots of psychopaths.

Carry some mace in your hand instead of your purse. Check your locks.

Don't enter a dark as night stairwell with the awareness level of an ADHD-ridden toddler.

The more I pondered the situation, the better I felt. Evelyn wouldn't have lived out a long, productive life even if I hadn't strangled the breath out of her. She was simply too careless.

At least her life mattered now. In death.

Strangling her had been as unexpectedly cathartic as it had been easy. No muscle strength at all, that one. Went out like an old lamp.

Still. They weren't supposed to find her body so quickly.

I'd been so sure...so sure...so sure...that I had at least a couple days to carry out the next steps in my plan.

How was I supposed to know she'd shit herself enough to leak through the damn elevator ceiling? Defecation was a normal after-effect of dying, but seriously? The woman must have had twenty pounds of fecal matter stored in her intestines.

Should I have known that? Put a damn diaper on her or stuffed her ass in a bag?

Gritting my teeth, I shook those thoughts away and went back to berating myself, thinking through all I'd done wrong so that I wouldn't make the same mistakes again.

I should have taken into account the age of the elevator itself and better learned why all the pulls and cables worked. Old Ev probably got herself stuck in a gear somehow. Pushed that shit right out.

But I still held that taking such a giant dump at a time when I desperately needed her to be discreet was rude and uncalled for. Not very ladylike behavior.

Downright discourteous.

Popping in on an actual FBI agent had also been unbelievably inconvenient. A normal person would have screwed that crime scene up so fast authorities wouldn't have been able to make heads or tails out of the mess.

The average Joe or Joanna would have screamed, made ridiculous attempts at escape, disturbed the body—purposely or otherwise—and generally acted the way people did when they had the shit scared out of them.

No pun intended.

But a trained professional, especially such a whippy one as that redhead doctor, had known how to preserve the whole damn box. Hadn't contaminated an inch of that elevator.

She hadn't even *screamed.*

What kind of insanity had that woman stumbled across in her lifetime to make her so impervious? Had to be some heavy shit.

Again, no pun intended.

The woman's grit was irritating.

All the orderlies and maintenance guys—hell, even some of the officers—had chattered about how hot the redhead was. The jibber-jabber reminded me of an old ladies' sewing circle.

The sexy doctor needed to watch her step. A lot of men were cramped into this building full of nuts, and I knew for a fact that most of them, given the chance, would jump her in a heartbeat.

Not me. I wasn't like that. I respected ladies.

And besides that, I was busy. *Goal oriented.*

But everyone else had the gumption in them, in my opinion. You couldn't work in a place like this surrounded by evil loons and not have a little of the madness rub off on you.

That wasn't my problem, though. Let the hot doctor handle her admirers—or be handled by them. Made no difference to me.

I simply needed to reassess the situation and keep going.

My schedule was thrown completely off-kilter by Evelyn and her happy bowels, and I did not appreciate when events didn't go as planned. But I couldn't exactly bring her back to life and kill her again as punishment.

I'd have to do some reconfiguring. The goals remained the same.

The damn authorities were still rushing around out there, although now they reminded me of the ant farm I had as a kid. So busy, these nimrods. Every last one of them had intense, miserable expressions on their faces.

I wondered how many of them actually hated their jobs. Why waste your life being so upset all the time?

Happiness. Why did it allude so many? And how...*how*... could you make someone happy when they were far past listening to reason?

I knew that answer. You couldn't.

Whatever. None of them mattered. They didn't even

know what they were searching for. Hide and seek with blindfolds on, that's what those people were playing at.

Wouldn't recognize the answer if it was two damn inches from their face.

But...they were doing what they were supposed to do. I didn't fault them for that. And as long as all these official's eyes and ears were going to be on the hospital, I might as well somehow work the matter to my advantage.

I could take on a challenge. I was more than up for the task. *Nothing* would ever deter me.

I just needed to give myself a moment to think.

My plans would most definitely need some altering, but I could already envision the next few days playing out as I morphed with the circumstances.

Ride the waves. You had to ride the waves in life. Go with the flow. Fighting them was futile and only ever resulted in drowning.

I wasn't going to drown. I had an end goal that I refused to lose sight of.

No matter how I got there, I *would* make my way to the ultimate ending.

The ending always made me smile.

7

W inter Black grimaced and sat up straight in her office chair. The intense fire burning through her back made her start to question the accuracy of her own age.

Maybe my birth certificate isn't real. Would that really be so shocking after everything I've been through?

The day had been long and the paperwork relentless, but Winter preferred to get all her notes copied over from the Florida case while the events were still fresh.

Fresh and disturbing.

Memory was a fickle bitch, especially when you considered the fact that the human brain was capable of purposely blocking out unsettling experiences altogether.

Repressed memories—clinically assigned as dissociative amnesia—enabled an individual to forget all recall of certain traumatic events. Most commonly, the stored away memories were connected to childhood abuse of some sort.

But not exclusively.

Any person at any age could repress a troubling occurrence. And while the memory was still capable of affecting behavior and emotions through a silent subconscious influence, the individual might have no recollection whatsoever of the damaging experience and its continuous impact on their day-to-day life.

Winter had a plethora of incidents piled up from her childhood that she wished her brain would store away in some dark, untouched closet of her mind. All too often, memories would assail her at very inopportune times.

Revisiting her youth at all was something she generally steered away from. But Winter, like every other mortal on the planet, wasn't always in control of what random recollection her mind decided to throw at her on any given day.

And the profession she'd chosen as her life's purpose had created its own ever-growing stack of disturbing happenings.

The Florida case, with all its madness and baby snatching, was definitely a story that could fade away from her psyche with her absolute blessing. But not until every damn detail was recorded in full.

If a single one of the assholes involved in the Florida case got off on some ridiculous technicality, she'd never forgive herself.

The murderer's smug face flashed through her mind.

Death instead of a lifetime wearing prison orange meant that egotistical bastard got off way too easy.

She yawned.

Dammit.

As committed as she was to putting every single member of the baby-making cult in prison for as long as possible, she needed to get home and get some sleep. Good sleep in her own bed, with Noah breathing steadily beside her. The image held heavenly appeal.

Motivated to leave, Winter made a half-hearted attempt to organize her desk.

Organized-ish. Good enough.

Another long day would be ready and waiting in the morning. Time to get out of here.

She walked toward the breakroom to grab a water from the vending machine and spotted Sun Ming working late as well. Sun appeared startled. Winter figured the agent hadn't expected anyone else to have lasted this late into the evening.

"Guess we're burning the midnight oil together, huh?" Winter tried to be nice to Sun most of the time. Or at least relatively civil. But Sun frequently made that a very hard task to follow through with.

Sun gave a single nod, and Winter took the eloquent response as the most communication she would get from the prickly agent. She didn't give a crap, though, about endearing herself to the woman.

But Winter *did* give a crap about Noah, who she assumed was also running on fumes by now. "You have any idea what case Noah got called away on? I was so busy, I barely registered he left."

Sun twirled her chair toward Winter, a catty little smile on her face. "I guess I figured Noah would have told you that much himself."

Winter clenched her hands into fists. Throttling Sun would be an amazing stress reliever.

Just walk away. Walk away. Go home. Sleep.

Turning on her heel, she stopped when Sun chuckled. "Maybe you should ask Autumn where Noah is."

Winter froze. Sun just couldn't resist stirring the pot. Perhaps the time had come for her and Agent Ming to get a few things straight.

"I'm right here." It was Noah's voice...the most welcome sound in the world.

She turned toward him, relieved. His tie was askew, and his hair was sticking out haphazardly. But just the sight of him righted her universe.

Winter *still* struggled to believe she'd made her way into a healthy, adult relationship. Noah was so stable and made her incredibly happy. They were solid in a way she'd never expected.

But her life had played out like a disaster movie before Noah ever arrived on the scene, and forgetting her past was hard. And she didn't always know how to communicate her feelings.

The Preacher—Douglas Kilroy—murdered her parents and kidnapped her brother when she was only thirteen. He attempted to kill her as well, but instead, she'd been left with a traumatic brain injury requiring immediate major surgical intervention.

Her grandparents took her in after the murders, and she'd been blessed with a wonderful life under their care.

But Winter's psyche was altered following the brain surgery. She occasionally experienced brutal headaches, accompanied by a tell-tale nosebleed that caused certain objects and areas around her to glow red. Often, the aura led her to clues, hints, answers that she never could have known without her "supernatural power."

In most cases, the nosebleeds also indicated that she was about to blackout entirely. But the blackouts gave her insightful and sometimes terrifying visions.

The "gift" was an asset at times, especially in her chosen career path, but more often than not, Winter considered herself cursed.

Cursed people didn't get a happily ever after.

Neither did her baby brother.

Kilroy raised her little brother—only six at the time of his kidnapping. The elder serial killer molded and warped Justin's young mind, producing a protégé to carry on his work. Now, that little boy was a grown man, locked away in Virginia State Hospital for his own deranged serial killings.

Justin hadn't deserved the childhood he'd endured, and Winter carried the guilt of his demise on her shoulders every second of every day.

She couldn't have saved him then. She knew that. But far worse was the fact that she couldn't save him now.

Rehabilitation for Justin was becoming an increasingly unlikely possibility.

Winter appreciated Autumn's attempts to reach her brother, but the truth was in her friend's eyes every time they spoke of him.

Justin Black was past saving.

Why should she end up with a good life, career, and relationship? She didn't deserve to be this happy while her brother sat ruined behind barred windows.

She hadn't even made a solid effort to visit Justin on a regular basis. Witnessing him as this *monster* that he'd become was horribly painful. In her heart, he was still that innocent six-year-old boy who wanted to cuddle.

The loss of their bond was so thoroughly disheartening that she'd avoided visiting as much as possible. And when she considered that Justin didn't have anyone else, not even their grief-stricken grandparents, willing to go to him...

How would he ever get better if he was convinced that the world had given up on him?

Selfish. Not stopping in to check on her baby brother more often had been selfish as hell. Maybe going to that building and viewing him in such a state was uncomfortable...nearly unbearable.

But Justin was trapped in the hospital every day while Winter had a world outside of those brick walls. Justin had nothing. How unbearable was that *for him*?

You definitely, definitely don't deserve to be so happy.

But she *was* happy. She loved Noah, and despite grappling with the plague of unworthiness, she knew he loved her too.

Sun's mind games had worked, however. Winter was suspicious now, and the effect was irreversible.

She grinned and attempted to be completely nonchalant, though she was burning inside for answers. "So, where ya been, Dalton? Local strip club?"

Sun remained only a few feet away, and Winter would bet money on the fact that Agent Ming was dying to witness an argument between the couple. The situation reminded her of high school.

Enough of this bullshit.

Noah didn't answer, and Winter began to suggest they go somewhere private when Aiden came striding down the hall and into the main office area, followed by Autumn.

A very pale Autumn. An entirely *too* pale Autumn.

What in the hell happened to her?

"Okay. Someone needs to tell me what's going on," Winter demanded as her concern for Autumn heightened her frustration. "Now."

Noah stepped toward her, apparently volunteering. "There's been a murder. At the state hospital."

All the blood seemed to flow from her head. "Is J—"

"Justin's fine. He wasn't involved," Noah assured her, placing a hand on her shoulder. "A nurse was strangled and dumped in an elevator shaft. Her body...her body fell through the ceiling of an elevator car. Right in front of Autumn's face."

Winter's gaze shot to Autumn. No wonder the woman was pale. "You were *in* the elevator she fell through?"

Autumn nodded and attempted to smile. It faltered on her lips. Clearly, the incident had taken a toll.

Noah ran a hand through his hair, rumpling it even more. "The local authorities are working to establish how long the body was in the shaft, determine suspects and motives, and identify a square one to start from."

Noah looked exhausted, and though she had empathy for him—for all three of them—she was ready to add one more stricken victim to their list of worries.

Herself.

"How could you not *tell me*? Clue me in? My brother is in that hospital!" Though her shouts were directed at Noah, they were meant for them all.

Sun was apparently going to get the show she'd hoped for, after all.

"And you? You just decided that I should stay out of the loop on this one? Just like that?" Winter's wrath turned to Aiden.

Noah tugged lightly at her arm, but she pulled away with a vehement jerk. He shook his head. "Of course you were going to be informed, but c'mon…you know how this works. You're too close to this case. Too close to the crime scene."

Too close? How ironic.

"I spent years not knowing what was happening to Justin. Years! And the whole time he was in the hands of a killer! But now, I'm too close?" She threw up her hands. "I'm done being kept in the dark. If a murderer is prowling around the exact hospital my little brother is locked up in, I should be made aware of that!"

Winter shot her glare back and forth between Noah and Aiden. Neither of them said a word. Autumn looked unsure of what to do…tackle her to the ground or pull her into a hug.

"Unbelievable! You two are a couple of assholes, you know that?" Winter kicked the nearest desk chair. "Noah…" she paused until he met her direct gaze, "tell me you're going to keep me informed from here on out. *Fully informed*."

Noah met her gaze, his dark green eyes full of apology. "That's not my call, Winter."

Rage cut through her chest like a hot knife. She turned to Aiden. "You? Are *you* going to keep me informed, then?"

Aiden stared back, his face emotionless. "I don't make the rules, but I do follow them."

Winter fought the urge to slap him. He'd been there. He *knew* the hell Douglas Kilroy had wreaked on her life because he'd witnessed the pain in person. Aiden knew finding Justin —helping Justin—meant *everything* to her.

She turned to Autumn, who appeared utterly miserable. Autumn had lived through her own hell. She'd lost a sibling as well.

No one understood what Winter was experiencing better than Autumn, yet her friend couldn't even meet her eyes.

Winter turned and walked toward the door.

The three people I trust most in this horrible world...

How dare they? She would never do the same to a single one of them. If she found out that Sarah had a *hangnail*, she would tell Autumn immediately.

And Noah...

Noah was supposed to be on her side, always. Her partner. Her rock.

She'd been waiting for the other shoe to drop in her romantic life, and here it was.

The betrayal. The absolute betrayal...

She knew they'd all convince themselves that they were doing the right thing and "protecting" her. What they were really doing was treating her like a fragile porcelain doll.

Don't tell Winter. She might break.

Screw them. Noah, Aiden, and Autumn were only proving, in unison, a truth she'd learned long, long ago.

Friendships, relationships, partnerships be damned.

You can't trust anyone.

8

Justin was tired of staring at the damn lock and planning his escape.

How long could he really be expected to sit in this room doing absolutely nothing aside from performing his ass off?

I deserve an academy award.

Granted, he'd had a bit of fun earlier today in the rec room. Convincing ole Roy the schizo that the guard on duty was actually a demon in disguise sent to kill him in his sleep had been way too easy.

Roy already believed many people in his life weren't who they claimed to be, so technically, the framework had already been set.

Justin warned him that if he didn't kill that evil guard now, he'd suffer terribly at midnight. Roy didn't ask *how* Justin knew this. He just straight up believed him.

Instantly.

Then Roy charged the guard like a damn locomotive and bit the screaming man's ear off. Blood sprayed everywhere and the expression on the whitecoats' faces when they ran into the room to "help" was absolutely priceless.

Priceless.

If it hadn't been for the fact that he had an act to keep up, Justin would have collapsed in a laughing fit. That was some funny shit.

Instead, he'd laughed on the inside, which was fine. He'd been doing that for years.

That psycho had freaked out way worse than he'd hoped for, and the resulting hell that broke loose provided the few seconds needed to snatch a pen.

Now, that pen was going to serve a very important purpose.

Justin examined the lock.

Every dumbass in the hospital was otherwise engaged with the whole murdered nurse debacle. As if running around like a bunch of idiots was going to solve anything.

Dead was dead. Move on, morons.

But whatever. The chaos gave him more than enough time to practice picking the lock before "lights out" took effect.

Practice makes perfect.

Justin never did anything half-assed. His murders were masterpieces. True art.

His escape from this never-ending *Looney Tunes: The Hades Version* episode would display the same skill and prowess as the rest of his accomplishments.

Legendary.

His numerous outside sources were coming through magnificently. Warping the media, creating "safe houses" for him to flee to, and in general growing more loyal as the hours passed.

If his followers continued to amass so rapidly, he'd have his own full-blown cult by the time he broke out. That had never been his goal, but he could admit the benefits of such a development.

Only the weak followed, and nearly all his fans were women anyway.

Filthy, disgusting women.

But how much fun would he have killing them off one by one while they dutifully led him to safety? The possibilities were endless.

Staying in contact with his peons wasn't even a challenge with his clandestine phone. Justin knew having a cell to connect to the outside world was risky, but he wasn't worried about the device being found. Not really.

What could they do to punish him? Lock him up?

Done, assholes.

He had already lost his freedom, albeit temporarily.

Many individuals are going to pay in full for that.

His recent overload of downtime had sent his mind deep down the rabbit hole regarding torture tactics. He had so many new, exciting ideas.

And given all the people he planned to kill plus the bonus idiots throwing themselves onto his path like sheep, he'd be more than able to try out some thrilling experimental inspiration.

Voices from outside his door—*familiar* voices—were approaching.

Winter was here, and apparently, she was showing her credentials to one of the many orderlies, Albert Rice.

Justin made a habit of memorizing names, faces, voices. He was always more than aware of his surroundings. Information and observation were two vital tools sorely underutilized by the average human being.

He walked to his cot, calm and resigned to the fact that his lock-picking practice session would have to wait. He hid the pen beneath the mattress and laid down.

Showtime.

The door opened, and sure enough, his sister entered the room, accompanied by a guard.

He hoped desperately that at least one guard would get in his way when he broke out. They were so obnoxious. Acting all high and mighty when most of them were just as sick as the convicts.

There was a reason they could work around these kinds of twisted, disturbing freaks.

Was he the only one who could do that math problem?

Winter's visit was a complete surprise, and he was incredibly pleased. But *that* attitude would screw up his script. He had a specific scene planned for his big sis.

Justin pulled his knees up to his chest and began rocking. He stared at Winter with wide, fearful eyes. "W-why are you here? Please don't hurt me!"

The shock on Winter's face as she registered that her "poor, misled little brother" was terrified of her was absolutely epic. He wished he could take a picture and frame her expression.

Maybe I'll just frame her actual face when I get outta here. Peel her skin right off while she's still breathing. Perfect gem for hanging above the fireplace. How's that for a conversation starter.

And he could always use her skeleton as a Halloween decoration. Waste not, want not.

"Justin...Justin, *please* don't be scared. It's just me. Just your big sis. Nothing to be afraid of, okay? I promise." Winter addressed him like he was still that six-year-old boy she'd abandoned.

Justin knew that was how she viewed him. She couldn't overcome the sentiment. Her "love" for him was instinctive, and she didn't know how to stop. Hilarious.

There were the rare occasions when a particularly clear flash of Winter as a kid...as his big sister that he adored...

assailed him. Some foreign softness would tug at his chest for mere seconds, and then pass away entirely.

The brief recalls made him furious. Justin didn't *want* to remember a day in his life where he'd loved anyone or anything. Including his sister. The sooner she was dead and six feet under, the better.

He'd been done with caring for her years ago. So many years. But she wouldn't accept that—*couldn't* accept that.

Winter was making a huge mistake by refusing to acknowledge who he truly was, and that error would be the death of her.

She's an unclean whore, anyway. Her death won't matter anymore than her dirty, pointless life.

Justin stuck a thumb in his mouth.

"Can you try to be brave? Could I just visit with you for a few minutes? Would that be okay?" Her face tensed with concern and sadness.

He nodded but remained wide-eyed. "Okay."

Winter approached him with extreme caution. She stopped when only a few feet lay between them. He noted how her blouse rose and fell nicely over her twin peaks. All the fun he could have with his sissy...how exciting.

I could totally kill her right here, right now if that damn white-coat wasn't pretending to care about her safety.

His sister was so genuinely concerned. He struggled to swallow his laughter.

"Justin, a staff member was murdered in the hospital today." She tilted her head and studied his face as though she feared the information might break him.

He shivered and rocked again. Faster now. "I really believed I'd be safe here. This was supposed to be a *safe place.* Safer than a prison cell. But now...now I'm not safe *anywhere.*" His eyes filled with tears.

I was never safe anywhere, and that's your fault, you bitch. The things he made me do...while you were off baking cookies with your grandma.

Justin's hands trembled with the desire to kill his sister. He hated her. He would always hate her. Every last damn atrocious activity he'd been forced into...

Her fault. He would hate her for all eternity.

Winter shook her head. "Justin, I promise you. *You are safe.* I will make sure you are safe. I'm going to do better. I'm going to be the big sister you deserve." A tear slipped down her cheek.

Idiot. Bigshot FBI agent who can't even hold her shit together. How is she buying this? How is she that stupid?

"I'm going to speak to Autumn and make sure I'm well informed on your sessions," Winter assured him fervently.

Justin hung his head in dramatic disappointment.

She really was that stupid.

Or maybe she thought he was stupid enough to believe her. Autumn wasn't allowed to share what they discussed in private. Duh.

"When I talk to Autumn...I mean, I know she can't share what we talk about. She'd lose her job. And that's not her fault, really. But I would be a *lot* happier if *you* came around more. So *we* could talk." He met her eyes, detesting how similar they were to his own.

Half-sister. That means nothing. You're the slutty half that needs to admit your sins. And pay for them. And die.

She was holding back an obvious tidal wave of tears. Justin eyed her quivering lips and imagined slicing the plump, pink flesh right off her face.

Would Winter still be pretty without a mouth? Would Agent Douchebag still want to screw her then? Doubtful.

"Listen to me, *please.* Your recovery means the world to me. I've been lax with visits, but I guess I was afraid to push you too much or too fast. I didn't want to just push you *away*." Winter clasped her hands, still staying a safe distance from him.

Could you really push away someone who wanted to kill you in the slowest, most torturous way possible? They were essentially on different planets. No push needed. What fantasy world was she attempting to live in?

Winter had clearly convinced herself that they had some type of magical bond—some imaginary relationship.

Maybe she was the crazy one. Maybe *she* needed to be locked in a room somewhere.

Justin liked that idea.

"Well, I guess." He rocked slowly and offered her a timid smile. "Maybe there's a silver lining to the tragic death of that nurse. If you and I can truly reconnect."

She shook her head like a bobblehead doll. Her excitement was abhorrent.

"Yes. We're going to make the best of this. We're going to reconnect. I'll make you my number one priority. I'll be here with you *every step of the way* while you get better." Winter stepped forward and surprised him with a fierce hug.

He allowed the embrace, greedily inhaling the scent of her black hair. A soft mix of floral and fruit...intoxicating. Slutty, obviously, but alluring as hell.

I'm beginning to understand why Douglas had such a hard-on for you.

Justin squeezed tighter, enjoying the way her breasts pressed against his chest. His sister was well endowed. Delicious. Scrump-diddly-umptious.

I'll fulfill your desire for you, Grandpa. I'll make sure she knows we're both taking her. You'll be with me.

That would, of course, have to wait until he had a decent amount of time to play. Certain tasks could be rushed when necessary, but torturing and enjoying Winter's body before he ended her disgraceful existence would be one dream he carried out with slow, careful precision.

She had a lot to pay for. And she was smoking hot. What a wonderful combination.

I'm going to have so much fun with you, Sis. So much fun.

He had his own hard-on now, but Winter was too emotional to notice.

The whitecoat escorted her out, flashing Justin a glance that clearly indicated *he'd* taken note of the impropriety.

But the guard hadn't said or done anything to intervene.

He's probably hoping I'll let him watch. I bet he'd even keep an eye out if I promised him a turn.

Justin smiled. While the idea of taking Winter right there in this room before passing her on to other greedy hands was appealing—*so appealing*—he had plans for her that didn't include this hospital or any dumbass whitecoat.

In fact, if anyone laid a hand on his sister, he'd have to kill them.

She was family, after all.

9

Autumn arrived at Virginia State Hospital ten minutes early, a bright smile plastered on her face. Challenge, test, show of trust—she'd concluded overnight that she didn't care.

If Aiden wanted to stick her in a room with Hitler, Stalin, and Satan, she would accept the task with grace. She'd spent a ton of time and a shitload of money earning her degrees. Dealing with the criminally insane was her *chosen* career.

Today's interviews were an expected part of her job and also the most riveting aspect of working in her field. Analyzing the inner workings of Aiden Parrish's mind was neither. And frankly, she didn't have the energy to waste mulling over the SSA's intentions.

Aiden arrived at nine sharp, followed immediately by Mia and Chris. Her fellow agents appeared completely calm, and Autumn was determined to not let her anxiety betray her.

Aiden ushered them into a quiet corner of the lobby. "Okay, Agents. No need to drag this out. You all have your assignments. We have the necessary warrants in place that will allow us to access needed patient background. The charts are pulled and waiting at the nurses' station."

Autumn glanced toward the desk area. Brenda Daly was observing them patiently.

"I'd prefer to get these interviews done by lunchtime, but don't rush. Every one of these patients had contact with Evelyn Walker the day of her murder. Their input matters more than our time frame." Aiden focused on Chris, who'd repeatedly expressed his opinion about this "asinine assignment."

Chris Parker didn't believe criminals in a mental hospital had a lot to offer the FBI by way of helpful information. Autumn surmised that his close-mindedness would be directly displayed in his corresponding lack of results.

He nodded toward the waiting nurse. "Let's get to it."

Autumn couldn't reach her stack of charts fast enough.

Brenda eyed her warily as she approached. "Your boss either considers you a genius or hates your guts." She passed the appropriate pile of folders to eager hands.

"I'm aware." Autumn grinned despite her racing heartbeat. No need for Brenda to be any more stressed than she already was.

Autumn hadn't settled on a particular order when she went over the shortlist details of her patients the night before. Every single one of her assigned individuals could star in their own horror movie series.

Autumn headed for the conference room, where two guards awaited her first patient request. Aiden had granted her sole use of the conference room in light of the level of insanity he'd allocated to her.

Of course, he'd managed to do this in a way that didn't quite acknowledge how severely he'd tasked her. And she'd returned the nonchalance without fail.

Time to work.

"Murphy Tobeck, please," she calmly requested of the nearest guard.

He raised an eyebrow. "Shackled?"

Autumn shook her head. "That won't be necessary."

"You might change your mind," he mumbled, and the two men exited to gather her first patient.

Autumn shook off the comment and studied Murphy's chart as she waited.

Although Murphy was a twenty-seven-year-old man, the sudden death of his father when he was thirteen had caused his seemingly permanent regression to the developmental level of a four-year-old.

He spoke, behaved, and generally functioned as a small child. While age regression wasn't necessarily uncommon, the studies addressing the specific prevalence of such behavior amongst hospital admitted patients was severely lacking.

Many hospitalized patients exhibiting regressive behavior were simply referred to as "agitated." The high frequency of "agitation" diagnoses on record suggested that the occurrence of acute regression was much more prominent than the medical community realized.

The cause of Murphy's regression had always been obvious. He was traumatized by the unexpected passing of his father, who had smothered to death after falling into a grain bin.

The fact that Murphy never "returned" to age-appropriate behavior made him a bit of an anomaly. Most patients were able to process their trauma through a mixture of cognitive behavioral therapy and medication.

Murphy had "processed" his quite differently.

He'd first developed a fondness for smothering small animals in his closet. As his physical age increased, so did the size of his furry victims.

But the closet remained a necessary part of Murphy's "hobby."

His mother had attempted to downplay the carnage when she found mice, then squirrels, then raccoons dead in her son's closet. Surely this was a stage that Murphy would grow out of, just as the doctors had promised he'd come out of his regressive behavior.

When he progressed to killing the family dog, his mother caved and sent him to an institution to "get better." The doctors released Murphy less than three months later, and his mother was confident the treatment he received had done the trick.

The regressive mannerisms were still present, but there had been no more nasty surprises in his closet for mommy. That was, until a year later when she found Murphy's ten-year-old brother dead on the small patch of carpeting previously reserved for his experiments.

He'd told his hysterical mother that his brother was fine. Daddy was lonely, and now he had family to keep him company in heaven.

Murphy added to his mother's terror by admitting that he was planning on doing the same to his eight-year-old brother as well. *"Just for fun, though."*

His sense of guilt was nonexistent.

He'd immediately been committed to a juvenile asylum. Shortly after this placement, the bodies of five missing teenage girls from different areas of the county Murphy resided in had been found inside an abandoned house three blocks from his own.

Each body was in a separate closet. This time, Murphy hadn't *only* smothered them—he'd raped them *while* taking their lives.

Physically, the boy had developed exactly as any other male. His new needs and desires had only heightened his enjoyment of witnessing the life drain from another living creature's body.

Murphy had immediately admitted to the murders, unable to comprehend why everyone seemed so upset about them.

Transferred from the juvenile facilities the same week he turned eighteen, the general consensus amongst Virginia State Hospital staff was that Murphy Tobeck was a "lifer."

While in custody, he'd attempted on three different occasions to shove his nurses into nearby utility closets but had never been able to successfully carry out his well-known plan.

A guard, orderly, nurse, or doctor always intervened.

And Murphy asked the same question every time they dragged him back to his room. "Am I going to get a time-out?"

Autumn scanned the room multiple times for any type of doorway that even resembled a closet. She certainly didn't want to offer Murphy inspiration.

One-hundred-percent closet free.

This made interacting with Murphy much less unnerving.

Without the availability of that key component to his favorite activity, Autumn believed any immediate threat to be minimal. Chaining the patients up wouldn't encourage the most agreeable of moods.

Then again, Murphy had made the list of interviewees based on his obsession with asphyxiation. There was a possibility that he had evolved and no longer required a closet. If this were the case, Murphy Tobeck could land himself on the suspect list regarding Evelyn's strangulation with little to no effort at all.

By omitting the use of cuffing, Autumn was aware that she could be placing herself in more danger than she'd like to admit. With guards and her Krav Maga skills at the ready, though, she was comfortable with the risk.

The twenty-seven-year-old squealed with delight as the guards brought him to the chair placed directly across the table from Autumn. This blond man-child was genuinely happy to meet her.

"Hello, Murphy. I'm Dr. Trent. Would you be okay with us chatting for just a bit?" Autumn smiled widely to assure him that there was no "stranger danger."

He returned her friendliness with childlike enthusiasm. "Of course! We could play too, if you want!"

Autumn stiffened but retained her grin. "We're just going to talk today."

His face went somber. "I know. We probably have to talk about serious stuff, right? You're a doctor. Doctors always wanna talk about serious stuff." His disappointment was evident.

Autumn observed as he pulled his legs up and crisscross applesauced them in his chair.

Twenty-seven-years old.

"Well, I do have a few questions to ask you, Murphy. But the first one isn't serious at all, I promise." Autumn grabbed her pen and prepared to take notes. Murphy's blue eyes grew wide with excitement. "My first question is, how are you doing today?"

He giggled and threw his hands in the air with unhindered glee. "I'm doing great. *So great.* Today is so sunny! This would be a great day for the beach."

Autumn humored him. "Have you ever been to a beach, Murphy?"

"No," he replied, his expression sobering. "But someday I'll go." He smiled at her again. Murphy was at least six feet tall, but Autumn instinctively wanted to cuddle him close like a preschooler.

She was beginning to understand how easy the mistake of letting her guard down around Murphy could be. He was so authentically sweet…but he would never leave this place.

Murphy was a developmentally stunted psychopath. He would never stop smothering and raping for pleasure.

He couldn't even understand why he wasn't supposed to do such things.

Evelyn Walker had noted in his chart several times that he'd happily told her how *fun* his killings were.

Autumn worded her next question carefully. "Murphy, I read that Evelyn is one of your regular nurses. Did you happen to speak with her yesterday?"

Murphy beamed at her. "Evelyn is the best nurse in this whole entire hospital! She's the nicest lady in the whole wide world! My favorite!" His adoration instantly troubled Autumn.

He appeared to have no idea that Evelyn was, in fact, dead. Murphy was clueless about the tragedy. And while she knew he could be faking, the idea was doubtful.

He was fundamentally a child. Children were known for telling the truth mostly due to the fact that their young brains hadn't perfected the ability to lie.

That usually came later.

What disturbed her most, was that based on his history, sudden loss could trigger an even more extreme regression. Returning to the infantile stages was a very real possibility for Murphy, as was a heightened desire to smother and rape as a self-soothing mechanism.

Instead of pondering whether he had evolved and murdered Evelyn, Autumn now worried that Evelyn's murder might trigger his evolution.

"And you spoke with her yesterday? You were on her patient rounds list." Autumn tried to focus on the case instead of Murphy's mental instabilities.

"I see her every day. Well, not today. Sometimes she gets a day off, but that's on Sunday. Evelyn goes to church on Sundays." Murphy held his hands together as if to pray solemnly but burst into giggles instead.

"Was she happy yesterday, Murphy?"

You are walking a fine line, Dr. Trent.

"Yes! Evelyn's always happy!" Murphy's smile slid away and melted into pure sadness. "I miss her. When is she coming back?"

Autumn swallowed the lump in her throat. "Well…" She hadn't even decided what answer to give him, but that didn't matter.

Murphy burst into sobs. "What happened? Tell me. Tell me!" He banged his man hands against the table. "Where's Evelyn? *I want Evelyn!* Tell me what happened to my nurse!"

The guards approached the table, and Autumn turned to assure them she was fine. But in that one moment of inattention, Murphy scurried up onto the table, his teeth bared like an animal.

An instant before the big man flung himself at her, his hands aiming for her neck, Autumn jumped out of her chair and backed against the wall. Murphy face-planted on the tile floor, and the guards moved in with lightning speed.

"Evelyn!" he wailed, fighting his holders with all his strength.

Autumn stood in silence while the guards held him down and a nurse rushed into the room to administer sedation.

Murphy no longer cared that Autumn was in the room. He screamed Evelyn's name repeatedly as they carried him out the door and down the hallway.

She breathed deeply as a pang of woe throbbed in her chest. The man's crimes were horrific, but his life story was tragic. Murphy would never go to a beach. He would never fall in love, tour Europe, or climb Mt. Everest. After today, he might not even talk or wipe his own ass again.

His "bedroom" would always have bars on the windows and a lock on the door.

But never a closet.

Though she knew the next patient was just as troubled, Autumn was relieved to start her second interview. The guards assured her that Walter Weber at least knew his own age.

But Walter had a different set of problems.

He presented with extreme ommatophobia, the fear of eyes, and severe chaetophobia, the fear of hair. These conditions, added to his lifelong struggle with schizophrenia, had eventually caused Walter to crack in a catastrophic way.

On a cold December evening five years ago, Walter had simply tied his family to their dinner chairs with rope, cut their eyes out one by one with an ice cream scooper, and yanked out every last hair on their heads with his bare hands.

His wife had survived the assault, though she was legally blind afterward. His two young daughters had not been so lucky...or unlucky, depending on how one chose to look at it. The six-year-old died from blood loss—he'd gone too deeply into one of her eye sockets—and the four-year-old's neck broke with one of Walter's hair yanks.

Walter had dropped each of the six eyeballs into a margarita glass and hid the "cocktail" behind a gallon of milk inside the family's refrigerator. Then he went to bed, while his wife struggled to find her phone and dial 911.

Doctors and nurses alike had emphasized repeatedly in his chart that Walter found his crimes entertaining. Whatever break he'd experienced had wiped away his ability to empathize.

Autumn conceded to let Walter be shackled. She appreciated her eyes and hair, and preferred they stay attached to her body.

Walter plunked down in the seat across from her. He appeared annoyed. His shaved head glistened in the glare of overhead fluorescent lights, and ironically, his own eyes were unharmed.

"Hi, Walter. I'm Dr. Trent. I'm here to ask you a few questions about—"

"The dead nurse in the elevator shaft," Walter growled before she could finish. "I didn't do it. Can I go now?"

"Not yet, Walter. I'm not here to accuse you of anything, I promise. But Evelyn did visit your room yesterday. I hoped you could give me some insight as to her mood." Autumn calmly crossed her hands on the table.

"Aren't you scared I'm gonna scoop out your eyes? Tear out your hair? You do know what kind of hospital you're in, right, Doc?" Walter asked the questions as though he were inquiring about the weather.

Autumn considered his queries. She *was* slightly uneasy, but that's what the chains were for. "I'm not worried about that at all."

He gave her a wink. "Good. They've got me on so many medications, I couldn't take those suckers out with a battle ax. Although I do hate them."

This was so interesting. She couldn't help but lean forward a bit. "Hate them?"

"Your eyes. They're green." Walter shuddered, his entire body trembling with the movement.

"What's so bad about green?" Autumn wished she had more time to pick through Walter's mind. She'd never met any patient with his combination of phobias and disorders.

"Green is too bright. Green is *offensive*." Walter spat on the floor to his left. "I've tried explaining that a million times to every shrink they slap me with. Green is asking to be removed."

Fascinating.

"Okay, Walter. I apologize for my green eyes, but I do believe we've gotten a bit off topic." Autumn attempted to rein the conversation in. "Evelyn Walker. Did you like her?"

"I don't like anyone." Walter's robot voice was back.

"Was she kind to you? In comparison to the other employees?" Autumn was determined to drag a real answer out of this man.

Walter rolled his eyes. "Yes. She was *too* kind. She was the most obnoxious nurse I've ever endured." He twiddled his thumbs in a circle, causing the chains around his wrists to rattle.

"Was she the nicest nurse you've ever endured?" Autumn knew she was borderline leading him with the question, but Walter was purposely being difficult.

"Sure. Nicest. Most obnoxious. She wanted to be everyone's friend. Like we were all gathered around a Girl Scout campfire. Naïve." He scanned the ceiling absently. "My oldest daughter was in Girl Scouts. The uniforms were hideous, but damn...the cookies. Is there anything more enjoyable than a Thin Mint binge session?"

Autumn was intrigued by the man's ability to speak of his daughter with such loftiness, but she tried to focus on Evelyn. This conversation was the verbal equivalent of treading water.

"Did Evelyn's excessive friendliness ever set you off? Was she ever just too much to handle?"

Walter emitted an echoing belly laugh. "Dr. Trent...it was Trent, right? I never denied my crimes. If I'd killed Evelyn, I wouldn't deny that either. But I had no reason to. Her eyes weren't even green, and she always put her hair up when she was in my room."

"How thoughtful of her," Autumn murmured in apt attention.

"Thoughtful?" Walter leaned forward, spittle flying from his mouth as he scoffed. "She was ridiculous. A ridiculous woman with ridiculous ideas."

"Some would say that obsessing over green eyes is a ridiculous idea." She blinked a few times for good measure. She was interested in how much it would take to set him off. "I wouldn't say that, of course, but some would."

"You're pushing your luck, Doc. You'll want to avoid that around me." Walter's eyes narrowed with hate and distrust, and Autumn saw the monster encased in medication that operated behind that stare.

She lifted her shoulders and dropped them indifferently. "Evelyn was her normal friendly and obnoxious self when you saw her yesterday?"

"Yep." Walter stopped his continuous thumb play, the good humor drained from his voice. "Your hair is red. One of my daughters had red hair. *Dark* red hair. Hard to tell where the hair stopped and the blood started." He threw back his head and laughed.

Autumn wasn't making much progress. The man had only confirmed what she already knew. Evelyn was a happy-go-lucky woman who cared about her patients—maybe too much. And Walter Weber displayed no particular interest in the murdered nurse's life or death.

Walter leaned in as far as his chains would allow. "You dye your hair, and not very well because it's obvious. Why don't you get colored contacts too? Do the world a favor?"

"We're done here." Autumn gave the guards a nod and turned her attention to the next patient chart. "Thank you for your time."

She knew Walter was bound and unable to hurt her. She

also saw no particular reason to consider him a suspect in Evelyn's demise.

But he was one of the scariest sons of bitches she'd ever come across in her entire life.

"I'd do it again, Doctor." Walter chuckled just before the guards pulled him from his chair. The sound was a low grumble that might have come straight from the depths of hell.

"Excuse me?" Autumn met his vacant yet horribly coherent stare.

"Take out their eyes. I wasn't trying to kill them, but I'd do it again. They all had green eyes just asking to be removed."

Autumn tensed as Walter grinned at her over his shoulder.

"Someday, I'm gonna find you, fuck you, scoop out your eyes, then fuck you again."

She turned back to her next chart, refusing to acknowledge him.

"Green is asking for it. Green is asking for it. Green is..." Walter's voice faded away as he was guided down the hall.

She rolled her head, trying to work out the tension building in her neck and shoulders.

One more. Just one more of these conversations today.

Autumn had saved the best...or worst...for last. Perspective was everything.

Gerard Helmsey. Forty-six. This patient had been physically and sexually abused as a child by his uncle, who gained custody of Gerard when his parents perished in a car wreck.

His uncle had forced him to perform acts of beastiality with various farm animals. Every day. For seven years. His hell had only ceased when his uncle passed away from a heart attack.

But the mental effect of such abuse would never cease.

As an adult, Gerard—undoubtedly warped and scarred beyond repair—had gone on to force three female victims to perform the same atrocity. He'd made them screw goats and thrown the women into a meat grinder immediately after.

His chart warned that he rarely spoke. And if you *were* lucky enough to drag any words out of him, he seemed to have only two catch phrases.

"Don't look at me," and "Screw a goat."

Autumn massaged her temples. All of these people in the same building.

How did anyone work here five days a week?

When he arrived, Gerard sat his lanky body cautiously down and avoided eye contact altogether.

"You're not gonna get anything outta this guy, Doc," one of the guards whispered as he returned to his post by the door.

Autumn straightened in her chair.

That remains to be seen.

"Hello, Gerard. I'm Dr. Trent. How are you doing today?"

"Don't look at me." He swiveled sideways in his chair.

"Okay. I'll stare out the window if you'd like. I'm only here to ask you a few quest—"

"Screw a goat."

Autumn battled a wave of frustration. Gerard had been one of Evelyn's last patients of the day. Considering his constant state of reclusive silence, he wasn't at the top of the suspect list. But he was one of the last residents known to have seen Evelyn before her fateful evening came to its conclusion.

He could confirm if anything had been off with the nurse. Maybe something had changed in her demeanor by the time she made it to Gerard's room. An argument, an altercation, a phone call…something significant may have happened shortly before her murder that could lead them to the killer.

But if she couldn't get Gerard to speak to her, what he knew or didn't know would remain a mystery.

"I know you have no reason to like or trust me, but I promise I'm only here because I want to help bring justice to a woman who helped take care of you. A woman I've been told was good to everyone…including you."

Gerard's chin sank slowly, not stopping until it rested on his chest.

Autumn licked her lips. "I'm talking about Evelyn. Will you talk to me for just a few minutes? Help me discover who wanted to hurt her?"

To her enormous relief and surprise, Gerard began to move, turning back to face her as if moving through quicksand mixed with molasses.

Good. Yes. Any reaction is better than no reaction.

"Did you like Evelyn, Gerard?"

He lifted his head, then let it drop. A single nod.

Autumn's heart raced. He was responding. "Was she kind to you?"

He lifted his head. "Friend." He said the word and lowered his chin.

He's sad. He knows she's not okay. They've all written him off as completely gone, but he isn't. He liked Evelyn.

The irony that she might get the most information out of a convict who had nearly been declared mute was astonishing.

"Was Evelyn happy yesterday, Gerard?"

He nodded again, a single dip of his chin.

"Did you ever see Evelyn upset? Perhaps there was a patient or nurse she didn't particularly get along with or—"

Gerard raised his head and stared straight into Autumn's eyes. Seconds passed as she felt him look straight into her soul.

Tell me. Please, just tell me.

"Baldwin."

Relief and disbelief swamped through Autumn's body. She leaned forward, feeling herself on the edge of a breakthrough. The only breakthrough of the day, to be exact.

"Baldwin? Dr. Philip Baldwin, the medical director? What about him, Gerard?"

"Bad," his brow furrowed, hatred coming alive in his expression, "man."

Her heart was like a rabbit in her chest. "Bad man...how?"

She waited for an answer. And waited. And waited. Silence was usually her friend during any interview or interrogation, but not this time. As the clock ticked on the wall behind her, Gerard's eyes glazed over, and his jaw became as slack as raw dough.

He began to rock slowly in his chair. "Don't look at me. Don't look at me. Don't look at me." It was a chant. A prayer. A little boy muttering his most fervent wishes.

Deciding not to push, Autumn gave the man a gentle smile. She was thrilled that there had been any dialogue to begin with. The guards were probably pissing their pants.

Her first piece of patient-shared insight pointed in one clear direction.

Baldwin. Bad man.

10

Autumn exited the hospital stairwell and closed the door with a firm thud. She was beyond grateful that the interviews were over. Her head ached and she was starving. She spotted Aiden in the hospital lobby and walked toward him at a brisk pace.

The SSA appeared entirely tranquil.

Not fair, Aiden. Not fair at all.

But the situation *was* fair. She specialized in this branch of psychology. Aiden didn't. And rattled as she was, she was also deeply intrigued by the three men he'd assigned her. The backstories, the pivotal moments and breaking points that had brought them to be locked away in this hospital, the—

"Ready to grab lunch? Mia and Chris already headed to the visitor's cafeteria. I figured you might prefer a change of scenery." Aiden's cool blue eyes divulged nothing.

I might prefer a change of memory.

The myriad of emotions currently spiraling through her psyche threatened to overwhelm her composure. Sadness mixed with fascination, added to empathy, and topped with horror.

She took a deep breath, allowing all the feelings to run through her.

Murderers were human beings. That was a fact that the general public happily ignored, and Autumn understood the reason why most did so. Discerning the humanity and light in the same souls whose actions proved he or she was capable of brutal villainy and darkness was, at times, nearly unbearable.

Despite the avalanche of activity taking place in her brain, Autumn refused to give Aiden anything less than a calm smile. "You're correct. I'm not eating here."

Aiden's eyebrows shot up. "Rough morning, Dr. Trent?"

She fought the urge to roll her eyes. "Let's go."

Aiden led the way out of the hospital and straight to his vehicle just inside the parking garage. Autumn climbed into the passenger's seat and drew a deep breath.

The toxicity inside of that building was unbelievable. Autumn wanted a long, hot shower and three days of laying on the couch with Toad and Peach. An entire weekend off to rewatch the *Lord of the Rings* trilogy with her sweet dog and sometimes grumpy cat.

Maybe that'll do the trick.

But she was more than aware there was no "trick." No magic potion. She wasn't Gandalf.

Those interviews…the patients and their backgrounds… were a part of her now.

Forever.

And instead of taking some downtime to distance her psyche from these patients, Autumn found herself enticed and wishing she could devote considerable chunks of time to studying each murderer's life experiences individually. Birth to present day.

There had to be a key moment in each of their paths where intervention could have stopped the madness. Or at least helped manage it before such dire crimes were committed.

Murphy had lost his father, and the trauma changed the course of his life. Autumn couldn't help but think of being forcefully separated from her sister. The loss still tore at her insides, and in many ways, she felt as though Sarah had died when they parted.

What turned Murphy into a killer while Autumn went on to study men like him?

What part of his brain was different from hers? How close had she come to being just like him? Were her loving adoptive parents the only difference?

Nature and nurture.

There had to be more, she just knew it. And she was determined to learn what that something was...and use it to steer at-risk children away from the path these men had gone.

These criminals were once innocent, squalling babes. What turned them into living monsters?

Any of these stories could have played out so very differently. The random injustice ate away at Autumn's heart.

Who would Murphy be if his father were still alive today? Or perhaps if he had received mental care the *first* time he smothered a mouse rather than being gifted with his mother's denial...

Would improved healthcare and treatment have kept Walter's schizophrenia under control and his daughters alive? He must have loved them before his break.

And Gerard...the abuse he endured...

Autumn remembered that desolate, helpless feeling of being a child at the mercy of a monster. Who would *she* be if she'd been forced to endure her father's mistreatment for the entirety of her childhood?

Eighteen years of abuse may very well have made "Dr. Autumn Trent" nonexistent.

It was unfair how some people were born into wealth and privilege, or even just kindness and normalcy, while others— by no choice of their own—came into existence bound to houses of horror.

And the lucky ones...how easily they labeled the others. Psychos. Freaks. Trash. Junkies.

Mere twists of fate...

And yet, many times what the person was born into wasn't as telling as what the person was born with. Numerous ongoing studies had proven through brain scans of convicted killers that there was a significant difference in the size of the amygdala when the criminal's scans were compared with the general public.

A psychopath's amygdala was significantly smaller than an ordinary individual's. Because of its control over the emotions, a shrunken amygdala could explain the lack of remorse or empathy that enabled a killer to carry out his or her deed.

A true psychopath didn't have to swallow their guilt for heinous acts they committed because they had little to no ability to experience guilt to begin with.

The scans also displayed another abnormality. Psychopaths had much lower levels of activity in the prefrontal cortex areas of their brains. This area corre-sponded with concentration, as well as impulse control and aggression.

They'd essentially been born with a defect of sorts, making them prime candidates for a future of killing. By no fault of their own, they'd entered the world with an invisible mark that may, or may not, allow them to become cold-blooded monsters.

The most interesting part was that there were many

people with similar abnormal brain flaws who never committed a single violent act throughout their lifetime. These individuals, though almost never clinically diagnosed due to a lack of cause for such examination, were referred to as "high-functioning psychopaths."

Surgeons, CEOs, lawyers, politicians...many were capable of becoming the next notorious serial killer plastered across the nation's news networks. Their success could, in part, be attributed to their incredible immunity to stress and fear.

But triggered at an early age by abuse, trauma, or abandonment amongst many other acts of cruelty and injury, their future likelihood to kill grew substantially.

The fact that some killers' brain scans were perfectly normal threw another log onto the fire. Regular people with unremarkable brains could also commit horrible wrongdoings. An infant with no defect whatsoever could become the next Ted Bundy.

The reasoning for why a diagnosable psychopath didn't become a killer when other "normal" specimens did was controversial. This was where the nature versus nurture debate came into play.

The two factors crossed at some hazy, undefinable point where a human's fate was decided.

Autumn believed that she could help stop those trains before they derailed. With early intervention and proper treatment, so many of those stories could play out tragedy free.

Her largest frustration lay in the fact that she couldn't possibly ameliorate the futures of so many anonymous minds. Human limitations burdened her every single day of her life.

Autumn attempted to shake off the heavy thoughts. She needed food. Water. Some time to breathe in air that wasn't drenched in sadness and despair and overwhelming discontent.

Agent Parrish had apparently known this before she ever set foot in the lobby, and though she still questioned his motives in assigning her those particular cases, she was grateful to be immediately whisked away.

Aiden chose a nearby deli. As soon as they entered the establishment, Autumn beelined for the restroom.

Wash your hands. Splash fresh water on your face. You're fine. You trained for this. Buck up.

She left the ladies' room somewhat refreshed and fast-tracked to the table Aiden had selected. *Now* she could deal with the impending conversation, or at least attempt to.

Aiden had granted her peace and quiet thus far, but Autumn knew that short reprieve was over. A waitress appeared, jotted down their order, and left them alone with two tall glasses of iced water.

The SSA gave his lemon a hearty squeeze. "Okay. Status update. Have you gained any useful information from the patients?"

Autumn met his gaze squarely. "Well, apparently, green eyes are highly offensive."

Aiden cocked his head. "Oh really?"

"Absolutely. Also, I will never look at goats the same." Autumn gave an overexaggerated shudder and dropped a straw into her glass.

"How exactly did you view goats *before* today, Dr. Trent?" Aiden kept a straight face and a monotone voice, unflinchingly holding her stare.

Autumn shook a finger at him. "You gave me the worst ones." She searched his face for acknowledgement of his guilt.

Aiden Parrish stared back at her with tranquil indifference and admitted nothing. "I gave you the most *complicated* cases because you are a doctor of psychology. You were best suited for the—"

"Worst ones," Autumn finished for him as she attempted to ignore the growling in her stomach.

Aiden gave her a slight grin. "For the most difficult patients, yes."

And the truth was, she wanted the very worst, most difficult cases. Craved them, even.

The brain fascinated her, and never more than when it didn't work properly.

"You can't pretend that you didn't find your patients intriguing." Aiden toyed with his napkin, daring her to challenge his statement.

"Walter Weber wanted to *take my eyes out*." Autumn kept her voice low, but her tone was vicious.

"Walter Weber wants to take everyone's eyes out. Don't consider yourself too special." Aiden was quiet while their waitress placed plates packed with sandwiches, huge pickles, fries, and salads before them. She added two small cups of soup and flashed Aiden a suggestive smile before heading to her next table.

Autumn chucked a crouton at Aiden's chest. "Parker would have been more than happy to take on the challenge, and you know it."

"The threat to Agent Parker's hair was too monumental." Aiden tossed a pickle in his mouth, ignoring the breaded assault.

Autumn sputtered out a laugh despite her agitation. Walter probably *would* have had a few choice words for Chris's magnificent haystack.

"That could have been an epic showdown. Wasted opportunity." She took an enormous bite of her sandwich, the rye and pimento creating an instantaneous pacifying taste sensation in her mouth.

Aiden squirted a tidy pile of ketchup next to his fries. "You were the most qualified, Autumn. I wasn't punishing you. I wasn't testing you. I matched you based on your ability."

Autumn sobered and gazed across the restaurant, sandwich in hand but momentarily forgotten. "Walter was disturbing, but Murphy. Murphy was just...sad. I'm not sure which is worse."

"Murphy's case is very unique." Aiden stirred his soup in a slow, steady rhythm, noodles and chicken chunks surfacing in quiet turns.

"The nurses in that hospital..." Autumn envisioned Evelyn's body dropping through the ceiling of her elevator car and forced the mental image away. "I don't know how they deal with that level of derangement day in, day out. I realize they're trained to take care of sick people, but I'm not sure nursing school prepared them for all of that."

"I would imagine they grow a bit desensitized. Calloused," Aiden mused, and the indifference in his tone had her glancing up to study his expression.

Speaking from experience, SSA Parrish?

"Evelyn didn't. All of that work and dedication yet she still managed to stay soft. Gerard Helmsey called her his *friend.*"

Tracing a finger down the condensation on her glass, Autumn waited for her words to take effect. Did Aiden remember enough of Helmsey's background to understand her meaning?

Aiden's head snapped up, and she could almost feel him reading the convict's history. "But Gerard Helmsey doesn't talk. He *spoke* to you?"

Autumn bobbed her eyebrows just once. She'd been pretty surprised at the time. "First of all, he does speak. He has two catchphrases which I'm very sure you were thoroughly aware of before assigning him to me. And he didn't say another word until I brought up Evelyn."

"Oh?" Aiden leaned back in his chair.

She had his full attention now. "When Helmsey said 'friend,' he appeared to be very sad. When I asked him if there was anyone Evelyn didn't seem to get along with, he said 'Baldwin' followed by 'bad man.'" Autumn's nostrils flared in disgust as she stabbed a tomato with her fork. "Baldwin. Bad man. The implication is clear. I believe—"

"Hold up." Aiden pointed his spoon at her. "I'm no more a fan of Philip Baldwin than you are, but it's important to note that only the *implication* was clear. An accusation of specific physical action taken against Ms. Walker wasn't given. Not even close."

Aiden appeared mildly frustrated by his own flawless logic, but Autumn accepted that he was correct. As much as she disliked Dr. Baldwin and his methods, Autumn knew they didn't have any evidence against the doctor.

Nothing solid, anyway. Yet.

Just that a nearly mute patient was willing to break his silence so he could share that Philip Baldwin is a bad man. No big deal. Happens all the time.

"The nurses, the orderlies, the guards...even the janitors," Aiden said with grave conviction, "all gave basically the same story, more or less. Evelyn was wonderful, if not a little too hellbent on befriending every patient in the place."

Autumn's eyes narrowed. "And Baldwin?"

"Every employee I questioned became highly uncomfortable when I brought up their all-knowing medical director. But...no one said one negative word about him other than they thought that he was too strict with protocol."

"We already knew both of those things." Autumn tapped her fingers on the table. "She was one extreme; he was the other."

"I suppose the task of keeping his staff safe while also juggling the mental health of the patients is a tight rope to walk on. You have to give the man that much." Aiden poked his fork at the remainder of his Caesar salad. "A man can be an asshole and still be a good person."

Autumn snort-laughed at the unexpected comment. "You think so? I've never met anyone even *remotely* like that."

"Well played, Dr. Trent." Aiden returned her grin and added a defeated nod of approval. "So, with what we have so far, who would you say is next on the interview list?"

"Baldwin. Definitely Baldwin." Autumn reached for her purse.

"Nope." Aiden threw money on the table before she could even pull out her wallet. "Got it."

"Oh, did we somehow travel back to 1955 when we stepped into this deli?"

Aiden laughed, but true to his stubborn nature, left the cash. "I'll join you for the interview. We both need to get a better handle on this guy."

Autumn stood and followed Aiden out of the restaurant. "Time for the shrink to get shrunk."

He chuckled as they walked and opened the passenger door for her. "That's a horrible line, Dr. Trent. Don't put that on your business card."

Autumn fake-glowered at him and buckled in.

When Aiden was seated behind the wheel, he stole a brief glance at her. "You ready for more fun?"

She didn't even need to think about it. "Always."

Aiden's ice-blue eyes bored into her. "Still excited about joining the BAU?"

Autumn gazed back, replaying the events of the morning in her mind like a dysfunctional highlight reel. "Yes." Her mindset was cemented in dedication. "I wouldn't say the job is *easy*, but I want to make a difference in this world. This position is the best place for me to do that."

"Excellent." Aiden turned his attention to driving, and Autumn enjoyed the last few minutes of peace before they went head-to-head with Dr. Philip Baldwin.

The bad man.

11

Autumn and Aiden had barely stepped into Virginia State Hospital's dismal lobby when his phone began buzzing. He silenced the device and turned to her.

"I have to return this call now. Do you—"

"Want to go start the interview with Lucifer alone? You bet your ass I do." Autumn entered battle mode and immediately resolved to go straight to the medical director's office by herself. "It's actually for the better. The interview will seem more like a casual drop in this way."

Aiden hesitated for a brief moment. "I'll be there to tag team in five minutes tops. Try not to get into a brawl before then, Dr. Trent."

Autumn was tempted to toss him the double bird. An older "sister" at her second...no, third foster home had taught her the gesture. Her younger self had found the maneuver to be of great amusement, even though using it had earned her a week's worth of solo dish duty.

She shot him an animated mock glare instead and headed for the stairwell door yet again.

Elevators were an unnecessary invention anyway.

Her somewhat labored breathing after making the three-flight climb challenged that sentiment. She really needed to restart her Krav Maga training.

Her mental to-do list was beginning to get out of hand.

Autumn wasted no time heading straight to the administrative wing once she reached the proper floor. Part of her hoped that Aiden's call would delay him longer than he'd guessed. She had a lot to say to Dr. Philip Baldwin.

The door to the medical director's office was shut, and her first knocks brought no response. Autumn frowned at the door and knocked harder.

Still nothing. She peered through the frosted glass insert and eyed a blurred figure inside. Faint sounds emanated from the room.

Someone was obviously in there, and she was ninety-nine percent sure that "someone" was Philip Baldwin.

Autumn gave the door a light push, and just as she'd hoped, it hadn't been latched completely. She stepped into the office and instantly caught sight of the doctor leaning back in his chair. He was wearing noise-canceling headphones and facing the side wall.

She approached with caution, not wanting to startle the already high-strung man, but her efforts were in vain. Baldwin turned his head a marginal degree, spied her standing before his desk, and ripped off his headphones after yelping like he'd been stung by a bee.

"How did you get in here?" he barked, slamming a fist on his desktop.

Autumn wasn't sure if the doctor was angry because he'd left himself so vulnerable inside a hospital full of the criminally insane or because she'd had the nerve to enter his holy sanctuary uninvited. "I apologize. But the door was open, and I did knock several times. You didn't answer."

Dr. Baldwin's sneer was vicious. "I am under no obligation to cater to you and your ill-timed visits. Do you barge into other people's private spaces on a regular basis, Miss Trent?"

Autumn returned his growl with a sweet smile. "*Doctor* Trent."

Baldwin gripped the arms of his chair. The man sure did seem to have an anger management issue. "Sure. Whatever you say."

"And I only barge in when I have important questions to ask. This just happens to be your lucky day, Dr. Baldwin." Her smile appeared to be infuriating him. She attempted to widen her grin.

"Dear god, you people don't know when to quit." Baldwin threw his hands in the air. "I've talked about the murder *enough*. I've already given the FBI access to the patients' files *and* the personnel records. What more do you want?"

Autumn, calm and collected, scanned the walls of Baldwin's office, deciding not to remind him that he gave access to the records and charts because he didn't have a choice. "There seems to be quite the lack of video surveillance footage in this hospital, Dr. Baldwin. Why keep the camera recordings so minimal?"

"*My* methods of running *my* hospital are none of your concern." His stare would have frozen ice in an instant.

Autumn glanced at the discarded headphones. The muffled squawks of two female voices resounded through the office from the cushioned speakers. They were joined by a male, and after prattling back and forth for a few moments, the individuals emitted dull laughter.

She raised an eyebrow. "Or did you possibly replace the video monitoring with an audio surveillance system?"

His angry scowl was replaced by surprise, but only for a brief instant. Looking down at his desk, he gathered scattered papers together. "What in the world do you think that would achieve, *Doctor* Trent?"

"Well," Autumn sat with bold prerogative in a chair directly across from him, "perhaps patients would speak more freely if they didn't have a camera pointed at them. That method could work well for talk therapy *and* for keeping tabs on your staff."

Philip tensed ever so slightly. Barely visible. But Autumn caught the micro-reaction.

She didn't give him time to argue. "Of course, Dr. Baldwin, the patients and employees would have to be *aware* of the recordings, for legal purposes. But the technique has promising possibilities." Autumn crossed her legs.

Baldwin's eyes narrowed. "You might want to save your opinions for when they matter."

Autumn wondered how exactly Dr. Baldwin had become so frigid and disdainful. Surely he had his own backstory of pain that had led him to be this man. "Let's talk about the conversation you had with the victim, Evelyn Walker, the day of her death. I've been told that your nurse was quite upset afterward."

Baldwin lifted his chin. "That was a work-related conversation. She was out of line. As her boss, my job requires doling out the occasional reprimand."

"Could you expound upon the reasons for that particular reprimand, Doctor?"

Poke the bear. Poke the bear until you get what you want.

"That's private information. In hindsight, I do, of course, regret the timing of the conversation." He pressed his fingertips to his temples. "But I will say that I am not sorry I instructed her on how to properly deal with the patients."

"How exactly *do* you prefer your staff to handle patients?" Aiden's voice boomed from the doorway. He stepped into the office and gave Dr. Baldwin a reassuring smile.

Autumn flashed Aiden a side-grin, but the medical director of Virginia State Hospital appeared uneasy at Agent Parrish's sudden presence. Good.

"Forgive my intrusion." Aiden gave the man's hand a hearty shake. "I was just passing by and gathered a little snippet about instructing employees. I'd love to learn more about how you run this hospital, Dr. Baldwin. I imagine the job is incredibly difficult."

Autumn admired Aiden's ego fluffing technique. She just hoped the bit of flattery would get the man talking.

"Well, Agent," Dr. Baldwin puffed his chest with visible pride, "the type of patients we deal with in this hospital are obviously not the common criminal, nor are they simply in need of counseling and a hug. They're sick. Ruthless. *Demented.*"

"Yes," Aiden agreed with exaggerated sympathy. "I've gathered that from their files. You have your plate full here."

Philip nodded vigorously. "Exactly. The decisions I make and my protocol are based on the simple fact that I'm trying to keep my staff *safe*. Their personal well-being is my responsibility."

"That is a large weight to bear. I can empathize." Aiden was sucking up in a way Autumn had never witnessed before.

The method was nauseating, but his tactic was working.

"My conversation with Nurse Walker was necessary for her *own protection* and to ensure she upheld hospital policy. The patients must view the staff *as the staff* and nothing more. No friendships. These criminals need to have a firm, clear awareness that this hospital is not the Holiday Inn." Philip's mood displayed a substantial improvement when he had the stage to himself.

Autumn controlled her vehement desire to argue his opinions. Dr. Baldwin's responsibilities as a mental healthcare provider certainly did not include forcing the patients to be as miserable as possible. Criminals or not, rehabilitation was a tunnel that needed to be well lit with guidance and care.

The people locked in these rooms were already drenched in desolate defeat, but she doubted that now was the time for an intellectual discussion on patient rights or the intrinsic nature of providers' moral and practical duties.

Focus on the case.

"We were just discussing the lack of video cameras in the building and the benefits of audio surveillance." Autumn smiled at Dr. Baldwin as she filled Aiden in. "Audio provides solid record without making a patient or even staff members uncomfortable the way a camera does."

Baldwin scowled at her, his triggered fury immediate.

What are you hiding, oh great and mighty Dr. Baldwin, that makes you so sore on this subject? Murder? Evelyn's murder? Worse?

"How about that last conversation with Nurse Walker? Surely you record what happens in your own office. I'd like you to play that recording, Doctor." Aiden's segue was so perfectly timed that Baldwin was reaching for his tape recorder before the SSA had finished the statement.

The medical director of Virginia State Hospital appeared to finally grasp what they were really there for. He stood with abrupt indignance and shook his head. "Agent Parrish, I've already respected your warrant for patient and employee files, but I would never hand over my personal recordings to the FBI without a warrant. I must respect my patients' and staffs' privacy."

Autumn swallowed an exasperated laugh. *Now*, Dr. Baldwin was concerned with not upsetting his patients and staff? Hilarious.

"If you don't mind, I'd like for you both to leave." He

gestured toward the door. "I have patients to care for, and quite frankly, I've allowed you to waste entirely too much of my time already."

Autumn was mentally armored for battle, but Aiden simply raised a hand and gave Dr. Baldwin a pleasant nod. "Thank you for your time, Doctor. We'll be seeing you soon."

Following her boss's lead, she headed toward the door, but the moment her hand touched the cool knob, she glanced over her shoulder.

Philip Baldwin stood stock-still beside his desk. His eyes were full of hatred while his hands curled into fists.

Did he want to choke her too?

She waited a beat...then two...then three before giving him a smile that held all the warmth of a Minnesota January. "I'll speak to you again soon."

Autumn closed the door before he could reply.

The good doctor was hiding something. Something terrible. And Autumn wouldn't give up until she found out exactly what it was.

12

Aiden Parrish sipped his latte and tried not to stare at Agent Parker's hair as he followed the man into the Richmond BAU conference room for their briefing on the morning's interviews. One piece of Chris's perfectly coifed blond helmet was sticking straight out to the right, and he obviously hadn't yet noticed the disarray. Apparently, neither Autumn nor Mia had volunteered to tell him either.

Chris was going to kill everyone in the room when he finally reached a mirror.

"Okay." Aiden sat at the round table and powered on his iPad. "We're going to compare notes and figure out if we've narrowed down any suspects as well as work on developing a solid profile for the killer. Agent Logan, I'd like you to go first."

Mia grabbed the manilla folder in front of her and scanned its contents. "The patients I interviewed didn't give me much. Neither did the guards and orderlies I spoke with. They all essentially just added more accolade to Nurse Walker's list of admirable qualities."

Aiden had guessed as much.

"Okay…" Mia stifled a yawn. "Roy Greiner, fifty-two, presents with schizophrenia and demonomania, as well as a severe case of Capgras syndrome."

"Demonomania? Capgras?" Chris raised a skeptical eyebrow. Aiden supposed that the man doubted the validity of any condition he wasn't familiar with himself.

"Yep." Mia touched a tiny hand to her pale forehead and closed her eyes for a moment. She was clearly exhausted.

And she didn't even get the worst ones.

Agent Logan picked up her coffee cup and took a gulp. "Demonomania is a type of psychosis in which someone believes that he or she is possessed by demons. Sometimes the mania causes an unnatural fear of devils…hell…the dark stuff. That's the type Roy has."

"So, he's scared of demons and hellfire." Chris tapped his pen on the table, clearly impatient. "That's not very original. Capgras?"

Aiden glanced at Autumn, who held a piece of her red hair out sideways, the corners of her lips twitching while the rest of her face stayed perfectly blank. He gave an infinitesimal grin, and she let the strand drop. They both returned their attention to Mia.

"Capgras syndrome, sometimes referred to as 'imposter syndrome,' is a condition that causes the individual to believe someone they know has been replaced by someone else. Hence the imposter part." Mia was clearly impervious to Parker's attitude, which was why Aiden partnered the two together.

"So, to paraphrase, he has extreme paranoia on top of insidious fears on top of endless delusions. I'm surprised he even leaves his room." Autumn's fascination was visible. She leaned forward, eyes glued on Mia, and Aiden guessed that she probably wished she'd solely conducted all the interviews.

"Well, he definitely does leave his room. Just yesterday, in the rec room, another patient convinced Roy that the guard was a demon, and he promptly attacked that guard. He bit half his ear off." Mia slowly accentuated each syllable.

"Wow. He straight Mike Tyson'd the guy." Chris spurted out a laugh. Aiden found the comment mildly amusing but remained stoic.

"Justin," Autumn informed them, her voice somber. "Justin Black was the patient who freaked out Roy."

Mia's eyes widened, and Aiden experienced the gut-punch sensation he'd had for quite a while about Justin.

The kid is bad news. He's past saving. He's a bona fide psychopath, and he enjoys being one. Winter will never get the ending she wants.

Chris cleared his throat with over-exaggerated volume. "Am I the only one who gets that we've strayed completely away from the case?"

Aiden kept his features carefully blank as he stared at the younger agent. "Cases occasionally overlap, especially at hospitals for the criminally insane. Sharing relevant information is not straying. Continue, Mia."

She flipped through her notes. "Roy did appear to be uncomfortable speaking with me. I'm not sure he believed I was actually an FBI agent. He definitely has enough paranoia and conviction to kill an innocent person."

"Both of which could easily be pieces of our profile considering where the murder happened." Aiden considered the prospects. "Did he suspect that Evelyn was an imposter or some type of demon as well?"

"I asked him about her directly. He seemed to relax at the mention of her name. She's someone he trusts is real, apparently. Roy said that Evelyn was a good nurse who 'fought the dark world with her light every single day.' He liked her." Mia let out a quiet sigh.

Chris threw up his hands, a laugh that was more like a snort bursting from his mouth. "Fought the dark world?"

Autumn inhaled a long noisy breath into her nose.

Mia continued to ignore Chris. "The others were...run of the mill...for the most part. Timothy Cotter and Matthew Warren. Both violent serial rapists in their twenties who were on Evelyn's rounds sheet that day. Either one would probably have raped and beaten Evelyn given the chance, but a non-sexual murder doesn't fit either of their histories, unless they've evolved. They did both vocally appreciate her kindness."

Chris snorted. "They appreciated her ass. You can't actually believe they gave two shits about her 'kindness.' They're rapists."

"They're humans," Autumn countered with a heated snap.

Aiden took a deep breath and attempted to fight his increasing agitation.

Did I stumble into a middle school debate class?

"What's important right now, Agents, is informing each other of this morning's experiences, possible suspects, and possible profiles. Argue on your own time. We have a dead nurse on our hands." Aiden shot Chris a stern stare. "Agent Parker, you may go next."

Resentment flashed in Chris's icy blue eyes, but he seized the chance to showboat his personal encounters with immediate eagerness. He swiped at his phone screen a few times, and iPads dinged as the group received scanned photos of his patients and their charts.

"I believe you'll all be better able to follow along with the information right in front of you." He shot Mia a smug sideglance, which she disregarded.

Aiden reminded himself that physically harming Chris Parker would cost him his career.

Still almost worth it...

"The first image is Avery Kingston, twenty-eight, single father of one boy. After his wife's death six years ago, he experienced a mental break, triggering his OCD and a manifestation of compulsive sexual obsession." Chris stopped for air, though Aiden was positive the man had more than enough—plus reserves.

Autumn and Mia inspected Avery's photo while Aiden drained his coffee.

"Basically, he raped five nannies and paid them for their silence. But the fifth one refused the money, so he shot her in the head." Chris shifted in his chair. "He progressed to raping any and every inmate he possibly could while in prison and was sent to Virginia State for...help, I guess. I barely *mentioned* Evelyn's name and the sicko started masturbating right in front of me."

Aiden raised his eyebrows. "Did he have a particular obsession with Evelyn?"

Chris lifted a shoulder. "Yes and no. The guard told me he's obsessed with basically all the nurses. He masturbates nearly every time one of them leaves his room. There is the possibility that he attempted to rape her, she fought back, and he gave her a different shaft instead." Chris looked around, clearly waiting for a laugh.

He didn't get one.

"Is this funny, Parker?" Aiden hated to let himself be triggered, but enough was enough. "If Avery *did* attempt and fail at raping her, then disposing of her would certainly have been in his best immediate interest. None of which is joke-worthy."

Unaffected. Always remain unaffected.

Before Parker could respond, Autumn redirected the conversation to the case. "There weren't any signs of attempted sexual assault on Evelyn's body. Her killer went straight for strangulation."

"Obsession could still very well play a part in the motives of our unsub," Mia mused as she stretched her arms over her head. "Strangling a human to death takes commitment. Commitment requires passion."

Aiden jotted down some details on Mr. Kingston. "Not enough there to make Avery an official suspect, but he should stay on our radar."

Chris rapped his knuckles on the desk, taking back the conversation. "My last patient somehow gave me even less than the sex loon, even though he's got *suspicious* written all over him. Robert Mooney, thirty-eight, declared incompetent to stand trial. Shot three cops in broad daylight two years ago. Claims that killing police officers has been his assigned mission since birth."

Mia's head whipped up. "Since *birth*?"

"Yes. He was waiting to act until he 'found the right cops.' Shows no guilt, and says his name isn't Robert, although he won't say what he thinks his actual name is. Claimed to not know Evelyn, even though she was in his room the day of her death within the last half hour of her shift." Chris held his hands up in frustration.

Aiden set his phone down. "That's suspect, but there isn't a lot we can do with that except to tag the denial. He appears to disbelieve many basic facts of his own existence. Claiming not to know Evelyn is more than likely a sign of his condition."

"But get this." Chris paused, clearly relishing the opportunity to drop a tiny bombshell. "He told the overnight nurse that Evelyn was mean to him that night. She'd called him 'Robert,' and apparently, she normally refrained out of respect for his feelings."

"Tag him. That may have set him off." Aiden wasn't pleased to admit a possible lead when the information came out of Chris's smug mouth, but the case wasn't about them. "Anything else?"

Parker seemed disappointed at the lack of praise and tossed his phone on the table. "That's it."

Aiden turned to Autumn, who looked eager to share her notes. "Your turn."

Autumn scanned over her pages. "I'll try to get through this quickly. I'm sure we're all overwhelmed."

Chris gave her an instigative smile. "I'm absolutely fine, Dr. Trent."

Autumn sent a sweet smile back to Chris. "Okay, Agent Parker is fine. Now that we've established that, I'll go over my patients as swiftly as possible."

Aiden noted the giant, forced yawn that Parker gave in response.

This is why you will never have my position, asshole. Why you will never be an SSA. "Unaffected" isn't in your vocabulary.

Autumn squared her shoulders. "Murphy Tobeck, twenty-seven. Diagnosed as an acutely age-regressed psychopath. Smothered first animals and then his own brother to death but also raped and smothered five teenage girls."

Chris whistled. "Busy boy."

Autumn ignored the interruption. "Murphy operates with the mannerisms and developmental abilities of a four to five-year-old. He *loved* Evelyn. Adored her. He caught wind during the interview that something had happened to her and broke into a screaming, crying tantrum."

Mia leaned forward. "Do you think it was remorse?"

Autumn considered the question. "I don't think so. He lunged at me during his fit. As much as he cared about Evelyn, he still has a very violent side when triggered. And obviously, he has an abnormally strong obsession for the victim."

As carefully controlled as Autumn was holding herself, Aiden had a hunch that she didn't *want* Murphy to be a suspect. She pitied the man.

Compassion was one of Dr. Autumn Trent's greatest strengths and greatest weaknesses.

Aiden stood and walked to the whiteboard. "He'll have to stay on our radar as well. Any mentally unstable killer who cares that much about a single nurse, considering there are dozens at the hospital, is somewhat suspect by default."

Autumn's mouth tightened, but she nodded her quiet agreement. Opening another folder, she gave a brief rundown of Gerard Helmsey's history of abuse and forced beastiality, followed by the repeat of his childhood experience with three female victims and a meatgrinder.

Agent Parker's jaw dropped hard while Mia covered her mouth with the tips of her fingers. The backstory itself was, of course, horrific, but Aiden experienced a private satisfaction at witnessing Parker's unchecked jolt.

"He barely talks, and when he does speak, he says one of two phrases, which include, 'Don't look at me,' or 'Screw a goat.' But," Autumn smiled triumphantly, "I got a few other words out of him."

Mia hunched over the table, fascination causing her eyes to practically glow. "Oh?"

"I asked about Evelyn, and he seemed to come alive. Slightly, at least. He confirmed that the nurse was happy the day of her murder, and he seemed to also perceive that something horrible had happened to her." Autumn's somber tone reflected what Aiden guessed to be a fraction of her emotion regarding Gerard.

"And?" Chris gave another dramatic yawn.

"He called her 'friend.' And without my mentioning the name, Gerard brought up Dr. Baldwin, calling him a 'bad man.' But then...he clammed back up." Autumn tapped her pen in apparent frustration.

Aiden wondered how much more Gerard would have been able to share regardless, but he knew she believed that the interview had been cut prematurely short.

"So, Baldwin is our suspect?" Chris's expression displayed his deep objection. "Because a goat screwing murderer mentioned his name? Or the goat screwing murderer is the suspect because he said three words about Evelyn?"

"No. We need much more than that. But Gerard's comment was the only time a specific name was mentioned in any of the interviews." Aiden met Chris's gaze. "That raises a flag, even if the flag is small."

"I spoke with Dr. Baldwin after lunch," Autumn added. "He didn't answer his office door, but lucky for me, he hadn't shut it completely. The guy is shady as hell."

Aiden nodded in agreement, filling the team in on their suspicions that Baldwin was using audio surveillance in his hospital. "Officially, we have nothing on him. But he refused to hand over any audio recordings without a warrant. So, Agent Logan, I would like for you to work on getting a warrant for all audio surveillance at Virginia State Hospital." He was more than ready to wrap this briefing up.

Chris turned on Autumn. "Do you really believe that barging into the doctor's office was a wise move?"

Irritation almost oozed from Autumn's every pore, but she kept her expression neutral as she stood and faced Chris. "The door was cracked, and I had every right...as well as *reason*...to speak with Dr. Baldwin."

Chris stood as well, dwarfing Autumn in an instant. "*You* are not even an official FBI employee. You need to remember that before you go stomping around on people's toes while representing the bureau."

Aiden observed the two of them facing off, reluctant to

intervene. If he stepped in now, Autumn would assume he didn't believe she could fight her own battles. And Chris and Mia... There were already quiet grumbles amongst the Behavioral Analysis Unit's agents that Autumn received "special" treatment.

"I conducted myself in a professional, calm manner which provided important insight into a case. I believe the FBI is okay with that behavior." Autumn stared up at Chris without a hint of fear.

"I *worked* my way into this BAU. I didn't just fly in on a fluffy 'teacher's pet' cloud," Chris hissed. "You are only at that hospital because of Justin Black's case. A dead body falling into your elevator doesn't give you the right to overstep your damn boundaries!"

Mia stood and grabbed her partner's arm. "Not fair. Autumn has brought us useful information from her interviews. We wouldn't even know that Baldwin is so possessive of the audio recordings if she hadn't walked into that office. And without her interview of Gerard, we wouldn't have reason to even *glance* Baldwin's way."

Chris shook his arm away from Mia and spun his fury onto her. "I'm pretty damn certain that two highly trained FBI agents such as us could have gotten the same fucking information out of that animal screwing psychopath!"

"Enough!" Aiden barked as he stepped into the fray. "Are you in charge here, Parker? The last time I checked, you one hundred percent were *not*. Know your place and shut your mouth. At the very least, show some damn due respect to your colleagues."

Aiden's relief at finally admonishing Chris was matched only by Chris's rage at getting reprimanded at all. The humiliated agent opened his mouth, then clearly had second thoughts as he met Aiden's gaze. Without a word, he stomped toward the exit door, his rogue piece of hair still jetting out like a street sign.

Mia shook her head, misery and frustration competing for space in her expression. "I'm sorry, Autumn. My partner's being a complete ass. He's exhausted from Florida...and now this case."

"None of that was your fault," Autumn assured her.

Mia stacked her folders on top of Chris's before heading toward the door. "I'll go work on securing that warrant."

Left alone with Autumn, Aiden knew the best course of action would be to brush off the tiff. "We need to focus on this case, but Dr. Trent, should you continue to have issues with Agent Parker, I would appreciate being informed."

Autumn raised a haughty eyebrow. "I can take care of myself."

He nodded, having predicted her response and ready to drop the subject. "Let's talk about Dr. Baldwin. What's your opinion on the man?"

Autumn's face was flushed from the argument, but she'd composed herself by the time she picked up her nearly empty coffee cup. "I'm not sure. I need more time with him if I'm going to establish a good baseline of his behavior. Gut instinct...he's hiding something, and we need to take a closer peek at Baldwin, the great and powerful."

"He does seem to possibly be shrouded behind a curtain or two," Aiden agreed as he pushed the vacated chairs in around the table.

He was pleased that Autumn had assessed the situation without jumping to conclusions or putting on any blinders concerning Philip Baldwin. Autumn possessed an amazing intuition as well as a deep curiosity and empathy. Aiden hoped a little time at Quantico could remedy any limits she experienced from lack of training. He needed to get her into Quantico as soon as possible, for her own protection even.

And as an added bonus, Parker would then have less to bitch about.

"Any updates on the Justin Black case?"

Her shoulders relaxed a little at the change of subject. "I'm meeting with him tomorrow. He had contact with Evelyn that last day, so interviewing him won't hurt. But I'd also like to just sit with him for a while and let him discuss whatever he wants." Autumn grabbed the empty coffee cups from the table and tossed them in the trash can.

Irritation sawed through Aiden, ripping at his already frayed nerves. "Did you know that Winter visited Justin yesterday after…speaking to us and Noah?"

Autumn whipped her head toward Aiden. "No. Do you know what they talked about?"

"No. But I plan to connect with her and get an idea of where her mind is right now." Aiden already knew that Winter's mind was knee-deep in her little brother's bullshit.

"Wait on that please." Autumn stretched a hand toward his arm but seemed to reconsider touching him and clasped her hands together instead. "I'm worried about Winter. She's…I think she's very vulnerable to Justin's manipulations right now. He's her brother. Who could blame her?"

Aiden placed a tired hand over his face. "He's a murderer, Autumn. He's a psychopath and he's dangerous. She knows that, but she can't accept the truth when she thinks of him."

"She'll get there, Aiden. Give her time." Autumn clicked off the light to the conference room, and they walked silently down the hallway.

Aiden understood Autumn's sentiment. But how much time did anyone really have when dealing with a serial killer?

13

Winter paced the floor of her apartment, struggling to focus on the case she'd been recently assigned by Special Agent in Charge Max Osbourne.

The case was interesting enough. Of course, the Richmond Violent Crimes division rarely encountered a "boring" investigation. A woman suspected of murdering her husband and burning down the house to cover up her crime had disappeared. Just like that.

On a normal day, Winter would be all over the details, determined to hunt the suspect down. But today she was distracted. And bitter.

Right now, her boyfriend was working the case that she'd held close to her heart since she was thirteen years old.

Justin...

Meanwhile, she was here. Removed from the hospital investigation and fuming at the unfairness. Pacing like a damn wild cat in a cage.

Days like this tempted her to type up a resignation letter for the Bureau and become a private investigator. There would be so much less hand-tying red tape to deal with as a P.I.

Focus, Agent Black!

Winter scowled, disgusted that she'd allowed herself to become so distracted.

Again.

She sat back down at her computer and willed herself to concentrate on her new assignment.

The couple had been married for less than a month at the time of the husband's death. What could have possibly happened in that short amount of time to make the newlywed woman snap so severely?

Winter glanced around her apartment and frowned at the coffee mug sitting on the counter. Was Noah physically unable to place the mug inside of the sink? How about the dishwasher? The options were *right there*.

Worse, she knew if she entered the bathroom right now, Noah's boxer briefs would be laying two inches away from the hamper. Or hanging on the curtain rod after he'd attempted to make a three pointer from the toilet while taking a dump.

And did he ever use the air freshener sitting right beside the godforsaken toilet paper roll? Of course not. He could endure Quantico but pressing a spray button was too challenging.

"Okay, Mrs. Camilla," she muttered, focusing in on the case details. "Maybe I understand why you snapped. Maybe I understand *too well*."

The couple had dated for six weeks...wed in Las Vegas... and she just happened to have a million-dollar life insurance policy on the idiot.

"What did that asshole expect? *Moron*." Winter inhaled a deep breath through her nose and let out a slow, controlled exhale.

You're getting bitter again. Grow up and do your job.

Ten minutes later, she was so utterly engrossed in the case that she jumped straight out of her chair when a knock came at her door. She hurried to answer the interruption, embarrassed by her startled reaction, and peeked through the peephole.

Autumn smiled tentatively and raised her peace offerings —a tray of lattes and a large bag of what Winter instantly hoped was pastry related food. Preferably chocolate.

"If there isn't chocolate in there, I'll never forgive you," she threatened, yanking the door open wide and allowing Autumn entry.

Her redheaded friend gave a bright smile, handing over the bag.

Winter inspected the sack. Two chocolate-covered donuts, two chocolate croissants, and two sour cream chocolate cupcakes. She grabbed a cupcake and shoved half the treat in her mouth.

Heaven.

"You're forgiven." Winter narrowed her eyes, giving Autumn her best stink eye. "This time."

Autumn set the tray of coffees down on the kitchen counter and pulled her friend into an embrace. Winter hugged her back...still chewing...and squeezed her eyes shut.

I will not cry. I will not cry. I will not cry.

"Why did we both have to come from such screwed-up families?" she eventually murmured into Autumn's shoulder.

Autumn pulled away, her bright green eyes haunted and worn. "Cause we're..." she tapped her skull, "special."

Winter snorted and finished her cupcake. She pulled a donut out and grabbed a latte.

"Is Justin—"

"Did Justin—"

The women made the same inquiry simultaneously.

Autumn emitted a nervous laugh, and Winter waved a hand, encouraging her friend to speak first.

"I just wanted to give you an overview of the hospital case. I haven't met with Justin yet, so I'm not sure if he's fully aware of the situation. That was my question since you've been able to...visit him." Autumn reached for a croissant.

Winter gulped her latte and nodded. "He knows. He was really upset about the murder. Now, he doesn't believe he's safe...*anywhere*." She realized how ridiculous the words were. The big bad serial killer was scared. Boo-hoo.

But she hadn't found a way yet to separate from the sisterly concern overwhelming her every single day and night.

"He's safer in the hospital than prison. Given his situation, that's about the best he can hope for right now." Autumn walked to the couch, kicked off her shoes, and slumped down into the soft cushions. "But I really don't think he's in danger."

Winter followed Autumn, bringing the bag of pastries with her. "So, update me."

Her friend gave a heavy sigh. "We don't know much. Mia, Chris, and I interviewed a portion of Evelyn's patients. Aiden spoke with the nurses, orderlies, guards..."

"Nothing?" Winter was shocked. Someone in that damn building had to know something.

"We've gathered that Evelyn was well liked by her co-workers and patients. And that the medical director, Dr. Philip Baldwin, deeply disapproved of Evelyn's methods *and* chewed her out the same day she was murdered." Autumn curled her legs beneath her body.

"Baldwin is an ass. Everyone knows that. The team thinks he's capable of murder?" Winter pictured the pompous man. The disdain Philip garnered was apparent, but she couldn't imagine him carrying out an actual murder in his own hospital.

You don't shit where you eat.

"One of the patients I interviewed—*a nearly mute* patient —called Baldwin a bad man. When Aiden and I visited the doctor in his office, he got super pissed about surveillance questions. Refused to hand the audio over without a warrant." Autumn frowned in frustration. "Our original warrant only specified files and charts. Loophole 101."

Winter perked a bit at the information. "Okay, now that does make him seem way more suspicious. But he's a doctor...and a control freak. He probably can't fathom being made to hand over information that's supposed to be private."

"Private goes out the window about the same time dead nurses show up in your elevator shaft," Autumn reasoned, closing her eyes.

Winter studied Autumn's pale, drawn face. "Are you okay? After...the elevator? I'm sure you had the joy of being told terribly disturbing stories with the interviews."

"I'm fine. I need about four million hours of sleep, but I'm fine. We're going to dig a little deeper on Baldwin. Cuddle up a bit closer. Which he'll absolutely loathe." Autumn wrinkled her nose in disgust.

"Let me guess. He despised you the most for being a female doctor with the authority to invade his control bubble." Winter rolled her eyes. She'd experienced the same type of discriminatory treatment numerous times by dozens of highly positioned men.

"I think he hates all of us, actually. But yeah, he definitely doesn't appreciate my presence. Or my degrees. Or my lack of a Y chromosome." Autumn grinned. "Now ask me if I care."

They collapsed into fits of laughter, which struck Winter

as amazing after all the negativity she'd been harboring and obsessing over.

Still smiling, Winter pulled a blanket over her legs, and she didn't miss how quickly Autumn sobered at the change of subject. "I just...I know I haven't shown enough effort to be there for him, and I told him that I was sorry for not visiting him more often."

Autumn grabbed Winter's hand and squeezed. "You've been a little busy. And I'm sorry, but the best of us would fail at knowing how to 'be there' for a sibling locked up for the reasons that Justin is."

"We hugged, and in the moment, I had a lot of hope for us...for him." Winter raised her gaze to meet her friend's. "Every hour that's passed since the visit, I'm increasingly convinced that he was playing me."

Do not cry. Do not cry. Do not cry.

"Your connection to Justin is complicated. Anyone would struggle to trust their intuition when their little brother was involved. You're too hard on yourself." Autumn wriggled her feet underneath Winter's blanket.

Winter burrowed deeper into the cushions, wishing she could hide in them. "I get why Max won't put me on the case. I really do have no perspective when Justin is involved. And even the clarity I manage to gain is wishy-washy at best."

"I think that's called loving your brother. You aren't weak for that, Winter. You're strong as hell to love him through all of this." Autumn's eyes welled with emotion.

Winter swallowed the giant lump in her throat. "I think the hardest part is being scared of finding out that he doesn't love me back at all. That nothing is there on his end."

A tear slipped down Autumn's cheek. "I understand. You *know* I understand."

Winter looked up at the ceiling, willing her own tears away. She'd been selfishly hogging the sibling drama limelight for far too long. "I do. Have you considered any more about Sarah? What your next move is?"

"Well, I'm sure whatever I do won't be as fantastic as Angel Devine's dance on Noah." Autumn shot Winter a wide smile.

"One can only hope to achieve such greatness," Winter replied, her expression solemn.

They cracked up again, taking a momentary reprieve from the tension and sadness.

"I wish my name was more creative. How can you compete with Violet Star?" Autumn threw her hands up in mock frustration.

"Violet struck me differently than the other…employees." Winter's brow furrowed as she recalled the "waitress."

"Different?" Autumn cocked her head.

"She was pretty calm around us, in comparison to the others. She knew we were cops in about two seconds flat. Her hair was obviously a wig and she was wearing colored contacts. Maybe she was undercover." The idea hadn't occurred to Winter before, but now as they discussed the woman out loud…

"You think Violet Star was a cop? A Fed? What?" Autumn laughed at the idea.

"I dunno. Wouldn't be a surprise after everything else we've ran into. Anyway, you can't avoid the question. What are you thinking about the Sarah issue? Are you going to keep searching for her?" Winter refocused on the painful topic.

"I don't know. After witnessing just how bad the situation is and the mess that her life has become…ugh." Autumn smacked a hand to her forehead. "I'm just not sure I have the time or the heart to try and drag Sarah into a better life. I'm an asshole, aren't I?"

"You're a human, Autumn." Winter straightened back up

on the couch. "And that isn't your responsibility. You aren't required to try and save her."

"I know, but I want to anyway. I'm just worried that… well, what if 'rescuing' Sarah from her current life doesn't…" Autumn stopped short, and Winter understood why.

"What if your rescue attempts don't work? Like mine haven't with Justin?" Winter offered the words that Autumn hadn't wanted to speak.

"I'm sorry, Winter. I shouldn't have said that." Autumn shook her head in frantic apology. "There is *always* still hope. Always."

Winter studied her friend's face. No matter what Autumn said, she could detect the doubt clouding her expression.

Autumn doesn't think he's able to be saved.

"Honestly, miss doctor friend of mine, I just want to *know*. If Justin *is* a hopeless case, and I knew that, then I could get off this damn emotional fence and come to grips with the truth. The not knowing is just *killing* me." She swiped a hand across her eyes.

Autumn opened her mouth to respond—Winter guessed her doctor friend was going to attempt to reassure her yet again—when her phone rang loudly. She grabbed the cell. "Sorry. This is Mia. Have to answer."

Winter watched and waited while Autumn took her call. Maybe there had been some sort of breakthrough with—

Piercing pain spread like lightning through Winter's head and warmth trickled onto her upper lip.

Before she could even cry out…she was somewhere else.

Justin was on a gurney, being wheeled down the hallway by a nurse whose features she couldn't make out. She tried to focus in, but there was only a thick, hideous blur where the face should be.

14

Paula Wingfield scowled at her housekeeping cart. She hated the damn thing, just like she hated her godforsaken second job as a nightshift housekeeper for the administrative wing of Virginia State Hospital.

But she didn't hate anyone as much as Peter. Her estranged husband ran off with the next-door neighbor seven months ago. When Paula pictured the anorexic divorcee bitch "Lexi" with her blonde extensions and false eyelashes, she believed herself to be capable of murder.

Two, to be exact. A double homicide.

I felt sorry for you, you unbelievable whore. I cooked you casseroles! Homemade hot meals straight from my kitchen! Straight from my heart!

Lexi was only twenty-four. She'd moved into the Wingfield's neighborhood after an "ugly divorce" from her "crazy ex."

Paula was positive now that if Lexi's ex really was crazy, the little hooker had been the sole cause.

Peter, her dumb bastard husband, was forty years old, as was she. Paula hadn't thought for two seconds about the possibility of him being attracted to Lexi. Lexi was practically a child.

Paula had instantly been overtaken by maternal instincts upon meeting the girl. Faithfully tending to her own three children, working full-time as a grocery store checker, and taking Lexi under her wing had kept her busy.

But meanwhile, Lexi had kept Peter busy in a much different way. And apparently, whatever she did with him, for him, and *to* him was worth more than eighteen years of marriage to a loyal woman and three growing children who worshipped their father.

They certainly had experienced a major change of heart on that count.

Paula continued her full-time day job, but that hadn't been enough. Since Peter had just run off like a worthless coward, she couldn't even garner any child support from him. She was the sole provider, and because of her married status, Paula didn't qualify for any type of state assistance.

So, she took a second job. The only positions she could find that she actually qualified for were waitressing...*no*...or housekeeping vacancies, and those openings filled in fast. The second her dull, brown eyes—mud, her mother had always said her eyes were the color of mud—spotted the "help wanted" ad for Virginia State Hospital, she pounced on the job.

There'd been a little competition, but Paula's eagerness mixed with her pathetic life story had somehow pushed her to the front of the line. She'd gotten lucky.

Yes. Lucky enough to spend forty hours a week in this looney bin shitpot, cleaning up after a doctor whose car is worth more than my damn house.

Now, she had the privilege of functioning on four hours of sleep per day to work two full-time jobs that still didn't bring in quite enough money for her to properly take care of her children, whom she never spent time with anymore anyway.

They're basically raising themselves at this point.

Paula emitted a heavy sigh and pushed her cart to the next office of the never-ending hallway. Dr. Philip Baldwin's.

She'd worked in the crazy house long enough to know that knocking before entering Dr. Baldwin's office was of extreme importance. The man didn't like surprises. Or intrusions. Or, as far as she could tell, other human beings.

In her experience, if Baldwin was still behind his desk, he'd simply tell her to come back later…or not at all. He often worked late, she'd learned. And just because her watch read after eleven in the evening, there was no guarantee that the doctor was gone.

She gave a solid yet polite double knock. No answer. She knocked again just to be safe.

Still no answer.

Paula gave the door a gentle push and confirmed that she was alone. Relieved that she'd missed the sour man and his disapproving glances, she started cleaning.

Cleaning *fast*.

For all she knew, Dr. Baldwin was simply taking a piss and would be back any second. She picked up her duster and kicked herself into overdrive. Cabinets. Shelves. Books. Frames.

And that tape recorder. She'd often wondered what exactly the doctor used that little machine for. Did he record *everything* that happened here?

The thought made her nervous.

But audio wasn't video, and she never spoke while cleaning. Not like his patients and nurses did. Was he recording them?

And did they know they were being recorded?

Paula pushed the ideas away and continued her duties.

Probably could dust this room blindfolded. So sick of cleaning the same offices every mother effing night. I'm killing myself working both these jobs, and they're not even—

A stack of folders went flying off a filing cabinet as her back end caught the corner of the metal beast. Instead of falling in a neat little stack, they fanned out under the doctor's desk.

She'd overestimated her ability to speed clean without incident. And possibly underestimated just how much emotional eating she'd done in the last seven months.

Paula dropped to the industrial carpeted floor and gathered the renegade charts together. The pile she stacked appeared neat enough, but she knew everything would be out of order, which would mean a reprimand and possibly worse.

She prepared to stand and caught glimpse of a tape recorder on the lowest shelf of Dr. Baldwin's bookcase. Between constantly chewing out his staff and speaking with nutjobs all day, the doctor had to have gathered several pretty interesting conversations on that nifty little thing.

Intriguing.

Paula knew she was taking a wild and unnecessary risk, but she hit the play button regardless. Life was awful. A little entertainment wouldn't hurt anybody.

The audio may have proved amusing if she hadn't immediately recognized Evelyn Walker's voice.

"They're still human beings...not science experiments. They deserve a chance at getting better." That was definitely Evelyn.

"Those human beings are not going to magically get better by being buddies with Evelyn Walker. You are a nurse. You are not their friend. I want you to do your job, make your rounds, and absolutely nothing more. Understood?" And there was Dr. Baldwin, being a complete prick as per usual.

"I understand what you are saying, yes."

"You understand and you will follow my protocol, Evelyn."

Paula pressed the stop button. She had never heard Dr. Baldwin quite that rageful. He seemed to truly despise Evelyn Walker.

And Evelyn Walker was now dead. She'd been *murdered*.

Paula grabbed the tape from the recorder. This could be evidence. This needed to go straight to the authorities.

Although…

She turned the tape over and over in her hands as her mind worked out a different course of action.

Philip Baldwin was a horrible man. He even reprimanded her once because she hadn't placed his freaking stupid trash can back in its freaking stupid exact spot.

Paula had cried when her shift ended that day. She'd sobbed in her car and cursed the world and Peter and Dr. Baldwin and Lexi and trash cans…

"Screw that pompous asshole." Paula stuck the tape in her pocket. "Maybe this is my turn to finally get ahead in life. Seize the day and make him pay."

Perhaps Baldwin might agree to send her on her way with a generous severance package in light of the fact that she now had possession of a tape he couldn't possibly want law enforcement to get ahold of.

She'd never blackmailed anyone before…the method wasn't her style, and generally, she preferred to keep her integrity intact. But being a single mom with three kids wasn't her style either, and somewhere right now Lexi was probably keeping Peter's aging nether regions intact.

Integrity is overrated.

Paula had barely stepped back into the hallway when she stopped cold.

The administrative hall lights were off, leaving only the much dimmer night lights burning. Just enough light for her to make out someone standing right there in the middle of the hallway, less than three feet away.

"What are you doing?" Angry. The gruff voice of her surprise visitor was very angry.

"Oh. Just finishing up the office. Should be good and clean." She tried to be nonchalant, but her voice squeaked with fear.

The man held out his hand. "I saw you take the tape."

Her hand instinctively went to her pocket. Fear and dread mixed together into a toxic combination that made her heart pulse in her throat. "I'm sorry. I'm so sorry. I know you probably think I was snooping, but I promise I wasn't. This...this is just an accident. A silly accident."

He took a step toward her. "I. Saw. You."

She held up both hands, pressing her palms together in a gesture that was universally understood as begging. "Please don't tell. I don't want to get into any trouble. I *need* this job. You don't have any idea how badly I need this job."

She backed away, one step, two steps. As she backed up a third, she was no longer afraid of losing her job. She was simply afraid.

You are in danger. Run. Now.

With a burst of adrenaline fueling her body, she turned on her heel, but before she could take a single step, a hand clamped down on her shoulder, sufficiently holding her in place. Terror seized her heart, and she opened her mouth to scream.

"Hel—"

The rest of the word was cut off as fingers wrapped around her throat.

Squeezing and squeezing...

She kicked and struggled as the hands pressed harder. His hot breath streamed across her face, into her hair. She jerked to the side, and her arm knocked into something solid.

That mop...is covered...in bleach. Turn it. Hit his face. Burn his skin off...

Paula flailed before managing to grasp the handle of the mop standing tall in the cart beside her. Her fingers wrapped around the wood, and she pulled with all the strength she could muster. Though she tried, her hands could no longer obey orders.

The hallway was dimming darker...darker...

Please don't! My kids! What will happen to my children?

One last rush of adrenaline kicked in, and Paula heaved the mop with every ounce of strength her body still possessed.

To no avail.

The wooden handle rattled against the floor. A few minutes later, the mop was joined by an incredibly dead Paula Wingfield.

WHY? Why couldn't people just mind their own damn business? What was so difficult about not interfering in other humans' affairs?

I dragged Paula Wingfield's substantial body to the nearest linen closet in the wing and propped her up against the back wall. Taking her farther away would have been ideal, but the woman had obviously been spending a lot of time in Twinkieville and Ding-Dong City.

The living never cared for their precious gift of life the way they should. A person had to die before loved ones admitted the fact that a jog or two around the block might have prolonged the deceased's inconsequential lifespan.

I experienced a momentary sense of guilt over the loss. I had taken her from her children. I knew this...*everyone* knew about her forsaken children...because the woman hadn't been shy about using her sad story of marital abandonment and single motherhood to secure her job.

But the children would do fine without her. She wasn't a very good example for them to follow anyway. Not much of a lady.

Paula was a schemer. I'd never taken her for one. She always appeared to be interested only in doing her job and going home.

"You were going to use Evelyn's murder to your advantage. What kind of a person does that? What's wrong with you, Paula?" I stared down at her surprised face.

Her lids were still open, which I preferred. Staring into her eyes assured me that she was attentive to my reprimand.

And paying attention was certainly the respectful thing to do when you were receiving a stern talking to.

If only she had been this respectful in life…she might not be dead.

Paula could have survived this night just like any other had she not gotten greedy and taken that tape.

I pulled the recording from her pocket and stared at the peevish thing, planning my next step. Whatever I did, I needed to take swift action.

Time was of the essence.

The hospital was quiet in this moment, but that wasn't a guarantee of privacy. Someone was listening, no doubt.

Someone was *always* listening.

Wasn't this tape proof that everything done in secret would come to light? That nothing hidden would not be revealed?

The universe maintained a very fine balance between good and evil.

Sometimes, human beings were the instruments used to unveil other human beings' wrongs.

I was such an instrument. And apparently, so was Paula

Wingfield. Together, we would tell a story that brought due diligence to an otherwise hidden monster.

Everyone would take heed then. Everyone would witness.

Just as someone was most assuredly witnessing me right now.

I lifted my eyes, letting my sight pass through the ceilings and floors of brick and mortar until I could witness heaven.

Ah. Yes. There.

Someone was watching, indeed.

Always watching. Waiting.

I needed to get busy.

I glanced back down at Paula. She was still staring at me dutifully, which was appreciated, but no longer necessary.

I'd said my piece to this woman, and she had fulfilled her purpose.

Paula Wingfield could rest now.

We were done here.

I stripped off my gloves, shoved them deep into my left pocket and pulled out a fresh pair from my right.

Time to do what must be done.

15

Noah cleared Virginia State Hospital's stairwell steps two at a time, his dark hair still damp from the rapid-fire shower he'd taken immediately after his phone rang a half hour ago.

Another murder at the hospital.

Two hours of sleep hadn't exactly refreshed him for a brand-new day or a brand-new homicide, but when had exhaustion ever stopped him before?

The past two nights had been hell. The first one, he and Winter had barely spoken, even as they lay in the same bed.

Torture. Those hours of silence had tortured him. But Winter wasn't a woman you pushed into forgiving you or making peace. She'd come around when she decided to.

When she was ready.

With no other choice, they'd both set off yesterday morning for their separate workdays on their separate cases. He'd hoped the demand of his job would at the very least block out the fact that his girlfriend wasn't speaking to him.

But no respite had come.

Noah had spent the day unable to fully concentrate on his

career or his relationship. By the time he'd returned home, life seemed like one conglomerate blur of puzzles that he would never be able to solve.

When he first arrived home around nine in the evening, Winter was sitting on the couch, covered in two thick blankets. A pile of bloody tissues was on the floor, and two half eaten chocolate pastries sat abandoned on the coffee table.

Her eyes slid to him in a gradual, hesitant turn. She'd been crying. And he didn't have to ask about the bloody tissues. He knew what those meant.

Noah wasn't sure how shaky their ground was right then, but locking eyes with her in the darkened living room, he knew she understood the situation he was in and had forgiven him. More so, that she desperately needed him.

He went straight to her and sat at the edge of the couch. "Another one?"

She nodded, blue eyes instantly filling with tears that didn't come easily or often for her.

"Headache too?" Noah took her hand in his own.

"Yes," she whispered. "But Autumn was here. She tried to make me comfortable...after. She had to leave, though."

"How long have you been sitting here by yourself?" He wasn't sure he wanted to know.

"An hour or two. I'm fine." She offered him a smile that barely tipped up the corners of her lips.

Noah shook his head and placed his hand on her cheek. "You're not. You wanna talk about it?"

"Tomorrow. Can we just go to bed?" Winter's eyes pleaded with him to let the subject go.

"Whatever you want."

They went to bed, but an hour of tossing and turning later confirmed the fact that Winter wouldn't be able to sleep so easily.

He cajoled her a bit until she finally relayed her latest

vision to him. Justin, the gurney, the faceless nurse. The premonition that something awful was going to happen and her baby brother was involved.

But she also expressed a conviction she'd never had about one of her visions before.

"This one doesn't feel right."

She insisted, repeatedly, that something was different this time.

Noah's opinion was that she didn't *want* the vision to be accurate. Who would be pleased to picture their brother on a gurney?

The headache, the nosebleed...her symptoms had occurred like normal. Well, as normal as a recurring brain trauma induced and seemingly impossible phenomenon *could* happen.

Winter was convinced, though. This vision was off.

He hadn't argued with her. She was smart as hell, and he would trust her instincts no matter where they led her...or him.

After sharing her nightmare, she'd been able to calm down a little. She put her head on his chest, black hair splayed out around him, and sighed with deep-seated sorrow. "I'm cursed. These visions are a curse, and they'll *never* leave me alone."

Noah tightened his arms around her, aware that he couldn't free her from the "gift" she'd been given. "You're not cursed. You're special. And I love you."

He didn't sleep until Winter's breathing became smooth and peaceful. When he was sure she was out, he'd allowed himself to fall into a much-needed slumber.

Not long after, "the murder call" came through. He'd tried his damnedest to sneak out of bed without disturbing her. But the phone had also woken Winter, and she was alert in an instant, irreversible second.

Alert and worried.

She'd begged in desperation to know what was happening, but he couldn't tell her. They both were aware of that. They both knew why.

And he really didn't have very much information right then to tell.

"I'll let you know if Justin is okay the absolute second that I'm able to." He held her face in his hands for a quick moment, wishing he could allay the distress in her sapphire blue eyes. "I promise you."

She'd been slightly mollified by the promise, but *only* slightly. He planted a kiss on her forehead and prepared to leave with reluctance, knowing he was leaving his girlfriend alone with her apprehension.

Walking away from Winter Black under any circumstance, let alone a nerve-racking situation such as this, was by far the most challenging task in his life.

Noah'd eyed her climbing back into bed with her laptop before he left the apartment. She was most certainly going to attempt to bury herself with work from her new case.

Good. Keep that mind occupied, Darlin'.

The amount of stress that Justin Black caused his sister on a daily basis was criminal, both in the literal and figurative sense.

Winter was smart, kind, funny, and incredibly good at her job. She had a healthy relationship, good friends. Goals. Dreams.

Justin effed all of that up just by existing.

Noah would have been sympathetic toward the kid if he wasn't convinced that Justin was a full-blown psychopath who had absolutely no intention of "getting better."

Justin used his sister's love for him as a tool. He'd sucked Winter into his manipulative little world with ease simply because she was capable of still loving him despite his crimes. He'd snagged her by the heart.

Knowing this infuriated Noah, but he couldn't change the state of affairs for Winter. She had to fight this battle alone.

Noah waited, patient and hopeful, for the day when she could look at Justin and perceive the truth that every single person who *actually* cared about her had identified.

Justin was gone. Justin was a deranged, dangerous serial killer, and he *liked* the person he'd become.

Right now, she still envisioned her six-year-old little brother. Noah compared that image of Justin to a ghost. The little boy was dead…and kept alive only by the memories inside of Winter's heart.

Shake it off, Agent Dalton. You have an actual dead body to worry about.

He busted through the stairwell door onto the third floor and charged down the hallway, around the corner to the administrative wing. Crime scene techs and the medical examiner had already arrived on-site.

The hallway was swarming with law enforcement.

He spotted Adrienne Lewton and went straight to her. "Chief Lewton. Nice to see you again, although the circumstances could be better."

She turned fatigued gray-blue eyes toward him and pointed at an open closet door. A small perimeter had been taped off surrounding the entrance. "The victim is in there. Paula Wingfield. You can't gather much from the hallway, but I suppose you need to take a peek regardless."

Noah nodded respectfully and donned the appropriate crime scene gear before approaching the site. Chief Lewton was correct. He was able to view very little from the hallway, but he made out the head of the dead woman resting against the back wall. She'd been propped up and faced straight toward the doorway.

Her eyes were still open. He hated that.

Noah tensed and stared at the murky brown irises and their surrounding whites, now broken with a multitude of red fault lines. If a victim's eyes were closed, he was almost able to imagine the person was sleeping.

The tactic helped tremendously when coming into contact with cadavers.

But Paula's horror was frozen on her face in an eternal grimace. The purple marks around her neck brightly contrasted with her pale skin. Her last sight had been the face of a madman mercilessly choking the life out of her body, and the barbarity of her final conscious seconds on earth lay in her fixed gaze.

Paula Wingfield had met a terrible death.

Noah turned back toward Chief Lewton, who had followed him in silence to the closet. He shook his head. "That's a rough way to go."

Adrienne glanced toward the open doorway. "How? How could this happen with all the eyes we've had on this godforsaken facility?"

"The killer is clearly several steps ahead of us. He knows the ins and outs of the building. He knows the schedules." Noah scuffed his bootie-covered shoe against the tiled floor.

"You're assuming the killer is male," Adrienne commented, her calm judgment straightforward.

He considered the observation. "Strangling someone to death is physically demanding. So is transporting a body to an elevator shaft or a linen closet."

"There are women who are perfectly capable of handling that type of physical demand." Adrienne placed her hands on her hips, challenging Noah to debate.

Noah snorted. He knew several women who could do all that and more. "Chief Lewton, I would never argue that point. There are also a lot of men who *couldn't* handle the job. Whoever did this, he *or* she is strong. That's all I'm saying."

Adrienne gave him an approving glance before turning her attention to the Bureau's newest arrival. Autumn was speed walking straight toward them. Noah noted the dark circles beneath her eyes.

"I can't believe this is happening again in less than four days." Frustration warred with the weariness in her words. Her bright red hair was pulled back in a low ponytail. Noah assumed she was operating on pure fumes just like he was.

"Absolutely insane." He immediately wanted to shove a foot in his mouth. "Poor choice of words. I meant, the chaos is nuts…shit. That's not good either."

"We get the point." Adrienne rolled her eyes at him while Autumn emitted a giant yawn.

Noah started to guide Autumn toward the crime scene when Dr. Baldwin came bustling down the hallway, extreme rage twisting his face into an angry, cartoonish façade.

"Here we go," Autumn muttered and crossed her arms, seeming to be arming herself for battle.

"Do you *all* really have to be in this hallway at the same time? There's no monetary reward for squeezing in as many damn law enforcement clowns as possible! Or were you all hoping for a world record instead?" Philip appeared to have made a trip to hell and back.

His dark hair wasn't completely styled into submission. His fury-filled green eyes were surrounded not just by dark circles, but giant, sleep-swollen bags. Even his tie was crooked.

Chief Lewton walked toward him, her vexation immediate. "I'm sure you're already aware, Dr. Baldwin, but we're handling a crime scene here. Another *murder.*"

Dr. Baldwin glared down at the policewoman. "You do understand that dead people *stay dead* no matter how many 'officials' swarm around them, don't you? This crowd is ridiculous."

Noah spied Adrienne's hands turning into fists at her sides.

"I'm sorry if we've upset you, Doctor. We would never purposely inconvenience such an *important* man as yourself for something so trivial."

Baldwin narrowed his eyes in response to Chief Lewton's sarcasm. He raised an arm, indicating everyone gathered in the administrative wing. "There's a parking lot *in the back*. Did any of you consider that before you clogged up the front entry?"

No one replied, but they all stared in silent awe.

"Oh, the hell with it!" Dr. Baldwin turned on his heel and retreated to his office, slamming the door hard enough to make the decorative pictures on the hall walls shake violently.

Noah met eyes with Chief Lewton, then Autumn. "Does he even care that he has another dead employee?"

His hospital is rapidly turning into a damn morgue.

"I'm not sure he cares about *anything*." Chief Lewton shook her head in disbelief.

But Noah knew that much wasn't true. Philip Baldwin most definitely cared about one thing in his human existence. His job. And even it wouldn't be safe with a murdering madman on the loose in his halls.

16

Aiden Parrish marched down the hallway straight toward his team. Autumn, Noah, Mia, and Chris had all arrived. The four of them appeared worn...but ready.

Excellent.

Adrienne Lewton intercepted him when he was barely five feet from his agents.

"Chief Lewton." He gave a courteous nod.

"Agent Parrish. Right this way." She gestured toward an open closet door farther down the hall. Law enforcement had practically gated the immediate area off with yellow tape.

Aiden slipped protective booties over his shoes before walking toward the crime scene. Viewing the victims' bodies exactly as they'd been left after succumbing to murder was the most disturbing part of his job. But occasionally, the raw image of fatality created a motivation that pictures alone couldn't inspire.

And as a free addition, a few impending nightmares were automatically thrown into the deal.

Paula Wingfield stared at him while he studied the scene. Purple strangle marks boasted their color from her neck.

Whoever did this didn't even try to cover up the crime. Didn't pull her collar up. Didn't shut her eyes.

"Why would he 'hide' her somewhere so frequently used as a linen closet?" Aiden mumbled this to himself, but Adrienne Lewton had stayed close enough to pick up the question.

"Where should he have hidden her, Agent Parrish?" The chief cocked her head in curiosity, eager to pick the SSA's brain.

"Dropping Evelyn's body into an elevator shaft...he knew it would eventually be found. And Paula here," Aiden waved a hand toward the corpse, "was the same. Guaranteed to be found. Even faster this time."

Adrienne scratched the tip of her nose. "Wouldn't know why someone so strangle-happy would want to be discovered. But psychopaths do seem to enjoy having their work admired, in my experience."

"What I don't know, Chief Lewton," Aiden forced his eyes away from the body, "is how this happened at all. You told my agent that you had this handled. This was *'your case.'* But your stationed officers sure as hell missed something rather important."

Adrienne bristled at his observation. "The criminal has to be hiding in plain sight. And if that's true, then it's by no fault of my people that they remained vigilant for someone who goes in and out of this building on a regular basis."

Aiden didn't fully agree, but he decided to let the matter alone. He imagined that Chief Lewton didn't hate anything so much as the FBI crowding around her territory, except for failing right before the Bureau's eyes.

She'll punish herself enough internally with sheer regret and embarrassment.

Mia joined them. "A guard that *won't* miss anything… audio surveillance. The judge signed just a few minutes ago." She waved the paper in the air like a peace flag.

"Why wasn't I informed of this?" Adrienne glared from Aiden to Mia.

Aiden smiled at her. "You just were." He grabbed the warrant from Mia and nodded at Adrienne. "Let's go, Chief."

They turned toward Dr. Baldwin's office door and began to walk. Aiden pointed at Autumn as they passed, and she joined them in immediate response.

He handed Adrienne the paper, as she clearly desired to take the lead. His innumerable experiences working with local law enforcement had taught him to step back when necessary. He didn't have to be in charge.

He just needed to nail this killer.

Adrienne gave the office door three solid pounds. "Dr. Philip Baldwin, this is Police Chief Adrienne Lewton. I have a search warrant. Open the door."

Aiden wondered if Baldwin would be difficult and refuse, but the doctor swung his door open with the wrath of Satan. Adrienne was immediately before him, yet his hateful eyes homed in on Autumn.

"You did this, didn't you, *Doctor* Trent? You disapprove of the way I run *my* hospital! My methods! Just because I don't provide adequate group hug time for the criminally insane, you're trying to get me fired!" Philip pointed a finger at Autumn as he screamed.

Autumn stared back at the raving physician but remained silent. Aiden was unsure if her quietude was due to shock, anger, or sleep deprivation.

Probably all three.

"If *any* of you think you're just going to come in here, and I'm going to leave while you go ripping through personal files and information that you have no right to, you've lost your damn minds!" A vein throbbed in Dr. Baldwin's forehead.

"We *do* have a right, Doctor. This warrant *gives* us the right." Adrienne held up the paper in front of Philip's face.

"So patient confidentiality is no longer of importance? Just like that? I want the hospital's lawyer on-site and present before the commencement of any search!" Dr. Baldwin directed his gaze at Aiden, who offered a mere shake of his head.

This guy is completely losing his shit. What are you so worried about, Philip?

"Agent Parrish!" Chris Parker's voice carried down the hallway. "You'll want to see this!" The agent ran to meet them.

Aiden met Philip Baldwin's gaze for a brief moment before turning his attention to Parker.

"I've been going through Paula Wingfield's locker, and I found this." Chris held up an evidence bag. Inside was an audio tape marked in black ink with the date of Evelyn Walker's murder.

Aiden raised his eyebrows and turned toward Dr. Baldwin. The man appeared stunned and snatched the tape from Chris's hand, a terrified expression flooding his face.

"How was this taken from my office? How!" Baldwin circled his gaze to Autumn once again. "You! You would stoop this low? Because you think you can run a maximum-security hospital for the most dangerous criminals in the state of Virginia better than I can? How dare you!"

Autumn came to life at that, scowling and stepping closer to the doctor. Aiden predicted an imminent screaming match, which was entirely unnecessary.

They had the warrant. Dr. Baldwin's tantrum didn't matter.

He stepped between the two, forcing Baldwin to back

away merely to regain personal space. "Take note, Doctor. You don't have a choice about this search. We followed protocol. We're coming in."

Baldwin glowered at Aiden. The medical director of the hospital had apparently run out of objections.

"Now, what you *do* have a choice about, is whether we listen to this tape in the privacy of your office or down at the police station. I'm fine with either." Aiden smiled while Philip trembled with indignation.

After a five second stare down, Dr. Baldwin crossed his arms and held up his chin. "*No one* is doing *anything* until my lawyer gets here."

Aiden laughed and walked past Philip into the office. He pulled open the top drawer of the first filing cabinet. "I'm afraid that's not how things work, Dr. Baldwin."

"D r. Baldwin could have a flourishing side-business as an organizational consultant...if he wanted." Autumn thumbed through the meticulously ordered pages of a patient file. The fact that the man even kept paper records of his entire hospital's information was impressive.

"He's not gonna have any business at all when he's serving a life sentence for multiple murders," Chris grumbled from his spot on the floor. He had immediately gone for the lower drawers of the filing cabinets.

Autumn guessed he wanted to make her struggle to reach the top ones, since she was shorter and he detested her. But a simple chair had solved that issue.

In contrast, nothing would help Agent Parker achieve any level of comfort in his giant man-body pretzel position on the carpet.

Increased video surveillance would be worth the trouble just to have footage of Chris tangled up like an overgrown preschooler at circle time.

"Don't be too sure, Parker," Noah cautioned from his comfortable position in the doctor's luxury desk chair. "For one thing, we only have two murders. Not exactly multiple. For another, we have no proof, which is kind of important in these types of situations."

"We have no proof *yet.*" Chris winced as he stretched out his long legs. "We'll find what we need. I guarantee you that tape could wrap all of this up pretty quickly if Parrish would just play the damn thing."

Adrienne held up her phone, reading straight from the screen. "Multiple. Having or involving several parts, elements, or members. Agent Dalton has you on this one, Agent Parker."

"For Christ's sake." Chris scowled at Chief Lewton. "Okay. I misspoke. Two. We have two murders, and that tape is going to prove the obvious damn fact that Baldwin committed them."

Noah shot Autumn a small grin, and she lifted both shoulders in return.

Aiden had decided to wait to play the recording until Philip's lawyer appeared. Yes, they had the search warrant, but the SSA warned that reviewing the audio without Dr. Baldwin's attorney was walking a fine line between a suspect interview and a legal search.

Autumn understood how vital following proper procedure was in this investigation. Anything they uncovered needed to withstand all possible questioning in court by the defense. Aiden was practicing patience and wisdom.

Both were qualities heavily lacking in Chris Parker's character.

"Aiden is doing the right thing, the *smart* thing, by holding off." Autumn shared her opinion over her shoulder, her attention still on the files.

"Oh, as if you'd ever say anything different about your *special* agent friend. Give me a break." Chris robotically rotated the ankle of his left leg.

Autumn was instantly triggered, and she forced herself to take a deep breath before responding.

"Parker, you might wanna shut your mouth," Noah warned, shooting Chris a wide smile. "Dr. Trent here is a trained Krav Maga expert."

"What in the hell is Krav Maga?" Chris muttered. He'd progressed to smacking his foot.

"Ninja stuff, but cooler." Noah's response sent Autumn into a short fit of laughter.

Leave it to Noah Dalton, class clown, to diffuse the damn situation with humor.

His method worked nearly every time, evidenced by his nine out of ten success rate.

Mia was keeping the doctor under supervision in the hallway. Philip Baldwin had yelled consistently about patient privacy, HIPAA, Joint Commission... "and *I'm going to sue you all*! I will sue you as individuals. I will sue the police department. I will sue the entire damn FBI!"

Aiden is one-hundred-percent correct about waiting for that lawyer. Dr. Baldwin will be out for blood after this. He will use anything he possibly can...

Agent Parrish stepped into the office with urgent determination. "The attorney has arrived. Tape time."

Autumn, Chris, Noah, and Adrienne all stopped their search to gather around the desk. Adrenaline rushed through Autumn's veins.

This could be exactly what we need...or not.

Chris stamped his left foot wildly against the floor, and she assumed he'd lost feeling in the limb altogether.

They all ignored him. They had more important business to attend to at the moment.

Mia appeared at the doorway first, followed by a fuming Philip Baldwin and an aging man in a sharp six-thousand-dollar suit. *Give or take a couple thousand.* The hospital's lawyer, Stanley Bradshaw, was perspiring profusely. His forehead was glistening with sweat.

Aiden closed the door with a firm slam behind him. "Chief Lewton, please read Dr. Baldwin his Miranda rights. Precautionary, of course." He smiled at Philip.

The doctor's cheeks blazed red as he flushed with anger up to the very tips of his ears. His counsel whispered heatedly to him, and Autumn imagined that Dr. Baldwin was being instructed to keep his temper in check and his mouth shut.

His lawyer possibly doesn't understand exactly how hard of a time Philip will have following that advice.

"You have the right to remain silent. Anything you say can and will be used against you in a court of law. You have the right to an attorney. If you cannot afford an attorney..." Adrienne performed her dutiful recitation while Noah prepared the tape player.

The police chief finished her official notification, even going so far as to have the doctor sign the Miranda statement. When it was official, Aiden gave Noah the nod to press play.

The first clip was a patient interview from the morning hours.

"And then I think about how pretty she was before I took her face off..."

Noah fast-forwarded the tape only to land on a monotone Dr. Baldwin reviewing a different patient visit.

"Patient presents with hostility...no remorse..."

More advancement brought yet another doctor and patient discussion.

"I just want you to understand what I done saw, Doc. If I hadn't seen that damn hooker..."

But finally, Evelyn Walker's voice filled the office.

Autumn stopped herself from shuddering. She could still

recall the vivid image of Evelyn's top half hanging a foot in front of her face...still smell the feces...

The memory was even more disturbing now that she understood just how well-loved Evelyn Walker had been. The woman deserved to live out her years in peace. She should have reached retirement and found repose in a rocker on her front porch, drinking tea, and reading Thoreau.

Instead, she'd had the life squeezed out of her by a probable psychopath and messed herself in an elevator shaft. If ghosts were real, Evelyn's had every reason to be pissed off.

And now they were purposely giving life to the woman's ghost.

Autumn had experienced physical contact with exactly one...mostly...dead person. Hearing Evelyn speak wasn't quite the same experience, but Autumn's blood ran cold regardless.

"The troubled minds we deal with here, Evelyn, require a much more formal code of conduct than you persist to display. Your 'Susie Sunshine' act is going to stop. I will tolerate it no longer." Baldwin's recorded words displayed his obvious hateful demeanor, but that didn't exactly differ from how he interacted with humans on a normal day.

"I don't find anything wrong with bringing a cheerful attitude into the hospital's environment. This place is depressing enough as it is. The people in those rooms are thinking, feeling individuals. Not just specimens for us to observe and study."

Autumn silently applauded Evelyn's moral stance as well as her willingness to stand up to the likes of Philip Baldwin. The nurse's bravery matched his disdain, and the good doctor couldn't possibly have experienced that level of bold defiance often in his career.

Philip quite visibly had different opinions about the dead nurse's regurgitated words. He appeared to be angry with her all over again.

If he didn't kill her, he sure as hell doesn't miss her either.

The discussion ended, and Aiden instructed Noah to rewind so the team could focus in a second time.

He doesn't want to miss anything...but there's not much to miss. No proof, anyway.

The second playthrough ended and all eyes turned to Dr. Baldwin. He was smug as hell. Autumn wondered if any of her co-workers felt the same abhorrence for him that she did.

"You understand now, I was just offering training advice to an insubordinate employee." Philip sneered at each of them in turn.

The doctor obviously considered himself venerated by the audio. He didn't seem to understand that probable cause was a very real and impending issue for him, based solely on that tape.

Autumn pointed at the tape player. "But Nurse Walker clearly sounds upset with your orders. How did you feel when she argued with you? She was rather insistent. I mean, based on *that* conversation I'd say that she didn't intend to obey your orders *at all*."

Philip's eyes narrowed and he opened his mouth to respond, but Stanley held up a hand to silence him. "Dr. Baldwin's feelings aren't at play here."

"If those feelings led to the action of murder, then they are *definitely* at play here," Autumn fired back at the wrinkle-faced lawyer.

She hoped to ignite Baldwin's temper, and the doctor didn't disappoint. He turned on her, fury aflame in his wild green eyes. "I did not kill anyone! That tape was *on my desk* last night! How the cursed thing traveled to Mrs. Wingfield's locker, *I do not know*."

Autumn silently cheered, ready to enjoy every moment of what was coming after she shared her next comment.

"Too bad there isn't any video surveillance to prove that, huh?"

But Philip didn't explode this time. Instead, he sank down into a chair, completely losing his bluster. "Fine, Agents. If I was the killer, *if* that were the case, why in god's name would I not demand the tape before Paula's death?"

Autumn met eyes with Aiden. The point was valid.

"Why leave evidence in her locker that points a finger in my own direction?" Philip continued in weak obstinance. "Or better yet, why wouldn't I delete the audio in the first place?"

The questions were reasonable. Rational. In fact, Autumn had already been mulling over those exact issues. What idiot would leave a bread crumb trail that evident?

Not even crumbs. The killer left a freaking loaf trail...and the path led straight to Baldwin.

There was, however, the other possibility. No one in their right mind would have set themselves up so exactly. *Unless* that setup was the exact compelling argument they planned to use as corroboration for their "obvious" innocence.

Chief Lewton held her chin while she concentrated. "Maybe Paula came across the tape when she cleaned the office, and once Baldwin spotted that the audio was gone, he searched her body. But he came up empty-handed because Paula had already stashed the steal in her locker for safe-keeping."

Chris looked pleased. He was apparently happy to support a valid series of events that pointed to the doctor as the murderer. "That's completely plausible. Baldwin could have pulled that off."

"I'm right here, you idiots." Philip shot malicious glares toward Chris and Adrienne. "Surmise all you'd like, but that is not what happened. I. Didn't. Kill. Anyone."

Chief Lewton bent slightly until she was eye to eye with

Baldwin. "Well, of course you're not going to tell us if that's exactly what you did. But if my theory is correct, that audio evidence does not bode well for you, buddy."

Philip closed his eyes. He appeared ready to combust. "I didn't kill Paula. I didn't kill Evelyn. And you have no actual proof that I did because *there isn't any.*"

From the corner of her eye, Autumn glimpsed Aiden staring intently at his phone, his eyes somewhat widened. He placed his phone down, sat on the edge of Philip's desktop, and cocked his head, locking eyes with the doctor. "Okay, Philip. Let's say you're right. You didn't kill Paula or Evelyn. What about Colleen Hester?"

Autumn studied Philip Baldwin's expression, mesmerized as every hint of color drained from his face.

18

Noah stood at the hospital entrance. He'd just walked the medical examiner out of Virginia State Hospital and was aware that Dr. Baldwin would soon be following, accompanied by his lawyer and the rest of the team.

Parrish had decided to take the "interview" to the station.

Noon was still two hours away, and Noah's energy reserves were draining in rapid plunges.

Relationships and the FBI don't seem to go together very well.

He desperately wanted his bed…and Winter.

The disgraced Dr. Baldwin passed through the doors, an officer on each side. He wasn't handcuffed. Those weren't deemed necessary. Yet.

Aiden and the chief followed closely behind while Mia and Chris trailed the pair in silence. Autumn stepped outside and leaned against the ancient brick of the building.

"I don't know about you, but I need a few thousand hours of sleep." She closed her eyes and fake snored for emphasis.

Noah grunted his commiseration. "This has been a rough run. And I don't think we're anywhere near the finish line yet."

Autumn groaned. "We *so* aren't. Not even close."

He watched the hospital guards close the doors and get back to the duties of securing the building. "Just another day in the life, right?"

She ran a hand through the rope of hair hanging over her shoulder and asked the question Noah knew was coming. "How's Winter? I felt like such an ass, leaving her there right after she'd had…a headache."

"She's better. We talked about the…headache…for quite a while last night. She was having a hard time sleeping, and me getting called out so early definitely didn't help."

Autumn studied his face, seeming to read all the way through to his mind. "Is she *actually* better?"

Noah threw his hands in the air. "Yes? No? I don't know. She's being pulled in so many different directions right now. I think she's having trouble finding a center, you know?"

Autumn nodded with fervent sympathy. "I do."

His phone beeped. One glance at the screen was enough to set his heart racing.

Speak of the devil.

The text from Winter made him groan. *I'm sorry. I just needed to see him again.*

He certainly didn't have rocket science credentials, but he didn't need them to know who the "him" she was referring to was.

"Shit." Noah smacked a hand to his forehead.

"What?" Autumn walked toward him with instantaneous concern, and he held up his phone for her to read. "Oh no."

They stared at each other for a brief moment.

"She just can't stop. She *loves* him." How could you love someone so much and want to throttle them at the same time?

Autumn chewed her bottom lip as she gazed back and

forth from the hospital to the parking lot. "I'm supposed to leave with Adrienne. She's already in her car. But Winter…"

Noah felt the frustration and indecision flowing from his friend. He gave her the brightest smile he could muster. "Winter is your best friend, and she's currently upstairs with her mentally unstable brother. I understand the dilemma, but you should go." Noah gestured toward Adrienne's vehicle. "I'll check in on them."

"You're sure?" Autumn was obviously not sure at all.

He leaned down so she could fully see the seriousness on his face. "Go take that asshole down or make absolutely damn sure that he's innocent…*fully* innocent of these murders. I want this case to be *over* so the woman I love can find some semblance of *peace* again."

She seemed frozen with indecision before her shoulders slumped. "Yes. Okay. You go too. Don't leave her alone with Justin. That's not safe anymore. In my honest opinion, that was probably never safe." Autumn met Noah's gaze one more time before the two dispersed in opposite directions.

"Don't have to tell me twice," Noah muttered. He entered the godforsaken stairwell yet again and ascended even faster than he had a few hours ago, despite his mounting fatigue.

When Noah reached the patient wing, he slowed his pace to avoid garnering attention. Walking in silence down the hall, he glimpsed that Justin's door was open, an officer standing at the entrance to the room.

Noah halted once he had a clear line of vision to Winter and Justin's interactions. He tuned in, striving to pick up the conversation.

Justin was using his little boy voice again. "…and one day, maybe I'll be free again. I know that's far away, but I would be so happy if I could make up the past to you."

Winter stared into Justin's bright blue eyes in what Noah

could only describe as a trance. "We've lost so much time as brother and sister. I would love…someday…for you to be free and live a real life outside these walls with me."

What in the hell is she talking about?

Justin would never be free. Justin should never be free. She was completely forgetting the truth of who her brother had become.

"I know my bad decisions hurt you, Sissy. I was so confused by all the things he taught me. I didn't know how to be good…but I do now." Justin had managed to work up a few tears, and Winter leaned in, pulling him into a tight hug.

Noah's heart broke for her—for the amalgamation of emotions that she must be experiencing. Winter wanted her little brother back and hadn't, as of yet, been able to accept that *he didn't exist* anymore. She was being sucked deeper and deeper into Justin's manipulations every damn time her brother opened his lying mouth.

Noah was convinced that every word Justin said was a complete lie, and he was done witnessing this bullshit.

Before he could fully think through his actions, he charged into the room, straight past the guard, focused only on Justin. Winter seemed stunned by his interruption, her piercing blues focused solely on him.

Noah ignored her for the moment and gave Justin a single, straight-faced nod of acknowledgement.

In less than two full seconds, Justin's features mutated from a sensitive lost soul into a demented, depraved demon raised straight from the bowels of Hell. He stepped forward, his stance aggressive and wild, closing the gap between them.

Noah wasn't the only one to monitor the instant alteration. The guard immediately stepped farther into the room but stopped when Noah held up a hand. He would handle this himself.

"So, *you're* my big sissy's fuck toy, aren't you? Mr. Big Ass FBI." Justin pounded his chest and let out a wail that would rival Tarzan.

"That's me." Noah's voice was low…deadly. He tightened his hands into fists so he wouldn't punch the evil shit-stain.

"Mr. Noah Dalton. Special Agent for the Efff Beee Eyyye." Justin smiled until nearly all his teeth showed and began skipping in circles around the room. "Thirty-two-years of age, born July twenty-third. Originally from Texas and *proud of it.*"

"Good job. You know who you're dealing with." Noah's entire body tensed, ready to act in a heartbeat. Justin's skipping was one of the most disturbing atrocities he'd had the honor of viewing.

"Yesss, I dooo! An outgoing, fun-loving jock type. Doesn't like to be alone. Has social media accounts but doesn't use them." Justin giggled with glee as his words struck their target.

Noah's eyes narrowed in anger and confusion. "What in the fu—"

"Former Marine who served *two duties* in the Middle East. Get this man a cookie! Worked on the Dallas PD like a true cowboy. Yee-haw!" Justin smacked his own rear and the skips turned to gallops.

Noah glanced at Winter. Her jaw had dropped, and she appeared frozen in a mixture of horror and sadness.

"Likes cats cause he's a pussy licker. Likes poker but sucks shit at it. Family oriented but hasn't managed to have his own yet. Has a truck named Beulah! Fucking Beulah!" Justin laughed again, his gallops slowing down as he ran out of air.

"How in the hell do you know all that? I know Winter hasn't told you shit about me or her *real* life. You know, the one you will *never* be in because you're a twisted psychopath!" Noah instantly knew he'd gone too far, but that couldn't be helped now.

Justin came to a standstill, smiling through his heavy breaths. "You going to be my big bro-in-law? You gonna let me come to your wedding? Be your best man?"

Winter pushed to her feet and reached for Justin's hand. Instead of taking the offering, he grabbed her by the arm and pulled her close to his chest. In a flash, the little brother was whispering in his big sister's ear.

Winter's expression grew pained...sickened...and tears welled in her eyes. Noah hadn't caught Justin's comment, but he didn't have to.

Whatever that little fucker said had been vile.

She tried to pull away from Justin's grip, but he refused to let go. Noah took two steps and grabbed Justin's hand, crushing the boy's much smaller bones inside of his own giant fist, and forcing him to let Winter loose.

He stared all his hatred at the gleeful little bastard. "Apologize." Noah spoke calmly but continued to tighten his grip around finger bones that were beginning to compress together.

Justin sneered back. The psycho didn't even flinch. It was like he couldn't sense a bit of the pain.

Maybe he can't.

"You want me to apologize to your whore girlfriend because I told the truth? Because you're not man enough to make my big sis an honest woman?" Justin's free hand shot out and grabbed Noah's dick. "Well, well, Agent Dalton." Justin licked his lips. "Impressive! Now I know why she's so willing to slut herself out to you!"

Noah pushed him away in disgust, and Justin fell sideways into the concrete block wall. Hard. Blood began to flow down his face from a cut on his forehead. Winter screamed and attempted to rush to her brother, but Noah grabbed her around the waist and refused to let go.

Justin laughed maniacal elation as crimson streams meandered across his features. He stuck out his tongue and licked some of the blood from his cheek. "Mmmm...tastes like chicken." The laughter continued, growing to a fever pitch of hysteria.

"Get backup and a nurse!" Noah barked at the door guard, unable to take his eyes off Justin and unwilling to loosen his grip on Winter. "Now!"

She'd gone as solid as a two-by-four in his arms. Stiff. Still. Noah couldn't examine her face...not yet. He knew what was waiting for him.

Giant sapphire eyes filled with hate. Hate for *him*.

Two orderlies and a nurse rushed past them, and Winter yanked away from Noah's grip. His stomach tightened as she turned toward him with slow, deliberate steps.

Her eyes full of loathing, Winter uttered one simple word. "Leave."

Noah's chest filled with ache, and he attempted to protest. But the words didn't come.

If you argue with her now, she'll only grow more hostile.

He'd revealed the creep's true face. He pulled off the mask, and he couldn't take that back. Not ever. How Winter handled it now wasn't his call.

Winter didn't blink or move as Noah processed the dismissal.

"Okay." He didn't know what else to say.

He'd already said and done too much.

She knows you love her. That will have to be enough for now.

Justin's laughter faded gradually as the sedation set in. Noah refused to even glance at the sick bastard before turning to leave.

In the hallway, he grabbed one of Adrienne's officers by the arm. "You go in that room, and you *stay in that room* until Winter Black leaves. No breaks, no exceptions. Understood?"

He received an alarmed but dutiful nod from the officer and released his arm. Winter's safety was assured, even if he'd lost her love forever.

Noah strode down the hallway. His exhaustion seemed to have heightened several times over during the short visit to Justin Black's room.

Winter would never forgive him for this. Even if she still loved him and wanted him, their relationship would be transformed indelibly by this day.

Justin was a monster, and Noah had broken through the foggy haze of manipulation that laced itself around Winter's heart and mind, revealing the beast.

He'd single-handedly confirmed that there *wasn't* hope for Justin. There was no future where the two siblings would spend happy hours together in the outside world. No pot of gold at the end of the rainbow.

The rainbow wasn't real.

Justin didn't love Winter. Justin wasn't *capable* of loving her or anyone else.

The full, illusion-shattering realization had screamed from her miserable eyes. She knew the truth. Noah was sure of that.

All efforts to bring her brother back were futile.

Winter didn't have a brother. She had a savage fiend who shared her DNA.

And Noah would forever be the man who had presented the raw, ugly truth to her without permission or warning, stealing away all hope.

He tried to shake off the emotion. The others would be expecting him at the police department, where Philip Baldwin's interrogation would shortly commence. He couldn't bring his heart to work, and he wouldn't.

Special Agent Noah Dalton drove away from Virginia State Hospital with the stark understanding that his image had been permanently altered in Winter Black's beautiful blue eyes.

19

Aiden glanced at the one-way glass of the interrogation room window. Dr. Trent and Agent Logan were stationed directly on the other side. Agent Parker and Agent Dalton would be joining them soon.

Adrienne and Aiden would be conducting the interrogation, but occasionally, a switch-out with another agent helped to throw the suspect off-kilter and accelerate the process.

Philip Baldwin sat in a scuffed metal folding chair, his hands clasped together on the small table before him. Stanley Bradshaw stood directly to the doctor's right, alert and, Aiden assumed, entirely aware that Dr. Baldwin's temperament could cause the man to bury himself in a split-second.

The attorney's sweat gleamed in the low-watt light of the hanging overhead bulb.

Philip appeared calm for the moment. Being escorted from "his" hospital by law enforcement and transported to the police station had doused a large portion of his fiery demeanor.

Aiden suspected that he'd regain a bit of his vim and vigor

as soon as the accusations resumed. He was counting on this, actually. Worked up suspects generally gave away far more information than they intended to.

"Dr. Baldwin, I assume you know why you're sitting in that chair?" Chief Lewton began, sitting directly across the table from the medical director.

"If my memory serves me correctly, you barbarians forced me to come here and demanded I sit," Philip sniped back at her.

Adrienne smiled and let out an amused chuckle. "Many would say that strangling two women to death was rather barbarous as well."

Philip's cheeks began to flush. Aiden sensed that the doctor was regaining his animation.

"I didn't strangle anyone. But yes, the acts *are* rather brutal. You and your dimwit colleagues might want to go find the person who actually committed the crimes before another strangled body shows up in my hospital."

Philip's attorney whispered with frantic urgency in his ear.

"Are you saying there will be more strangulations? Are you planning another murder, Dr. Baldwin?" Adrienne tilted her head with interest.

"I. Didn't. Murder. Anyone." The doctor's breathing accelerated, and his sneer returned.

There. There's Philip Baldwin. Now we can ask the real questions.

Aiden casually slid into the folding chair next to Chief Lewton's. "No need to get angry, Doctor. We're just talking here."

Philip turned his glare on Aiden. "Right. Talking. In a locked room with a two-way mirror and my legal counsel at my side. Do you think I'm blind to what's happening right now, Agent Parrish?"

"Tell me what you think is happening right now, Dr. Baldwin," Aiden returned, placid as he leaned back and crossed his arms against his chest.

The doctor emitted a low growl. "I'm a shrink. I *know* this is just one big mind game. You and your cohorts believe you can bully and upset me into admitting to a crime I didn't commit."

Aiden held up a hand in protest. "Let me assure you. I would never want nor ask for that. I'm only here to discuss the *truth*. I do have a few inquiries for you, though."

Philip's eyes narrowed as he hunched over the table. "Of course you do."

"We've obviously discussed, in great detail, the reprimand you believed was necessary to give to Evelyn Walker on the day of her murder. Insubordinate, I believe that's how you described her behavior." Aiden spoke in a calm and deliberate tone, giving plenty of time between his statements for Philip's rage to recharge.

"Defiant. Stubborn. Troublesome. Rebellious." Bitterness and anger wove themselves through Baldwin's words.

"Right," Aiden confirmed. "That's how you perceived Ms. Walker's actions. Now, tell me how you perceived her as a person?"

Philip squirmed in his seat. "Excuse me?"

"Was Evelyn a good person? You two weren't eye to eye on hospital policy...I get the picture. Outside of that. What did you think of Ms. Walker overall?" Aiden tapped a pencil on the table.

"I didn't know anything about her outside of her role as a nurse under my supervision," Philip declared, his upper lip curled up in what appeared to be revulsion.

"Do you think she was a good person?" Aiden repeated, leaning forward and placing his elbows on the table.

Philip's nostrils flared. "Probably? I don't know. I sure as hell wouldn't want to live with her. Entirely too headstrong."

Chief Lewton grinned. "Remind you of anyone?"

The doctor shot her a dagger-filled glare.

Aiden turned Philip's answer over in his mind. Strangulation was an incredibly deliberate, intimate form of murder. The victim and the killer, eye to eye, while one exacted their plan through fatal means.

Whoever had killed Evelyn and Paula had some type of vendetta or mission. Two women in the same hospital. Both strangled. Both left to be found...but not immediately.

The killer in this case cared about matters far darker than hospital policies and insubordinations. Philip either had a very personal hidden issue with Evelyn *and* Paula or a message he deemed as massively important to share.

The problem with this was that Aiden couldn't detect, outside of his obvious desire to mandate hospital policy, that Dr. Philip Baldwin thought of or cared about Evelyn Walker at all. The medical director didn't seem to think of or care about *anything* aside from running the state hospital.

And Aiden hadn't abandoned the other possibility. Maybe the doctor simply hadn't killed the women.

"My methods as the Medical Director of Virginia State Hospital are not now, nor were they ever, up for debate amongst the nursing staff. Outside of work, Evelyn could have been a saint. Inside my hospital, she was a pain in my ass. She defied me on several occasions and threatened the respect of my title." Philip was rambling now, his rage building.

"You needed *complete* control." Adrienne crossed her legs with casual indifference.

"Yes!" Philip barked. Bradshaw leaned in again. Aiden assumed the attorney was attempting to get the prick to shut his damn mouth.

He wasn't helping his case at all. But at the same time, he was so very obviously *hurting* his own position of innocence with his commentary that, to Aiden, the man seemed less and less capable of being their unsub.

"How far would you go to maintain that control, Dr. Baldwin?" Chief Lewton stood and began pacing.

Philip appeared confused. They were talking in circles, purposely trying to wring out any detail the doctor might let slip. And now Adrienne had something new to throw into the merry-go-round.

"Colleen Hester." She let the name hang in the air and stared at him.

Aiden studied the doctor's face. No one had mentioned Colleen since the office, but they certainly hadn't forgotten about her.

The decision had been made to bring Baldwin to the station for further questioning, and Colleen Hester was a card in their pocket they intended to play.

Just waiting for the right time...

"Or how about Mildred Harbison? Should we start with her instead? Mildred was your former assistant when you were in private practice. Yes?" Adrienne shared the information with smooth tenacity.

"Yes. That has absolutely nothing to do with—"

"And she died under suspicious circumstances several months before you came to work at Virginia State Hospital." Adrienne's voice echoed off the walls. "Correct?"

"No." Dr. Baldwin held up a finger and wagged it at his interrogators. "You will not put that on me. I was cleared of any connection to Mildred's passing. She was a sixty-two-year-old woman with diabetes and multiple heart problems. She mixed up her own medications and died in her sleep."

"So you claim," Adrienne needled the already distressed man.

"Her death was declared accidental!" Philip shouted, pounding a fist on the table. "Why would I want to kill an old woman?"

"Mildred's death was preceded *only a month* by the suicide of Colleen Hester, who, according to the records, was a patient of yours. Someone under *your* care who took her own life." All indifference in Adrienne's voice had been replaced with severe insinuation.

Philip crossed his arms and slammed against the back of his chair. Defensiveness flooded his face. "Yes. And what of it? She was a very disturbed young woman. I can't be expected to help *everyone*. And Colleen had no connection to Mildred!"

Aiden found the change in behavior intriguing. Philip clearly cared very little about Evelyn or Paula—dead or alive. But the man definitely had internal conflicts about Colleen.

"*You* are the connection, Dr. Baldwin. Your patient. Your assistant. Assistants are often privy to very personal information. Is there any possibility that Mildred defied you in an unforgiveable way just like Evelyn? Or perhaps she knew something you couldn't risk being shared? Is this your pattern, Dr. Baldwin? Do you handle your problems by silencing them forever?"

Philip stood, slamming his hands on the table. Before he could get a word out, his lawyer intervened. "We're done here. Unless you intend to arrest Dr. Baldwin, he has absolutely nothing more to say."

Aiden noted Philip's troubled expression. There was something in the Colleen Hester matter. But they couldn't force him to speak about Colleen any more than they could arrest him.

They didn't have enough evidence to legally accuse Dr. Baldwin of anything.

Other than being an arrogant asshole.

"Agent Parrish, if you wouldn't mind, I'd like to have a word with you in private." Adrienne gestured toward the door.

Stalling was preferrable at this point, and Aiden wanted to convene with his team regardless. Combine their insights.

Assuming they have any.

He stood and gave a polite smile to Dr. Baldwin and his attorney. "Excuse us, gentlemen. This could be awhile."

There was a certain gratification in leaving the doctor hanging.

Adrienne opened the door, and Aiden followed her into the hall where they were met by his team exiting the viewing room.

Autumn appeared deep in reflection, while Mia displayed more of an exasperated face.

Noah had arrived during the interrogation, and the man looked grim. Worse than grim. Aiden wasn't particularly fond of Agent Dalton, but they'd been through many troubling cases together.

Traumatic situations bonded two people, like it or not. And Aiden leaned toward the latter.

What in the hell happened to you, Dalton? You look like absolute hell.

Noah usually only wore that expression when there was something the matter with Winter. A pang of anxiety pulsed in Aiden's stomach, but there wasn't time to worry about anything other than this case right now. They had close to nothing. Not enough evidence to arrest Baldwin, whom he personally no longer believed was prime-suspect worthy. And no other leads whatsoever.

They'd hit a brick wall.

The only thing Aiden was certain that his team did have was two dead women at the morgue.

But there were two more deceased females, one whose

passing had severely rattled Philip Baldwin. Perhaps the doctor truly hadn't murdered Evelyn or Paula.

He may not have even killed Mildred.

But the mention of Colleen's suicide had struck a deep chord with the doctor, and Aiden intended to make him sing.

20

Adrienne led the team to one of the Richmond Police Precinct's conference rooms. A giant white board covered the north-facing wall, and a long rectangular table stretched across the room's expanse.

Autumn sat and waited in patient contemplation while her colleagues settled. Her mind spun, weaving the new information on Mildred Harbison and Colleen Hester through the web of knowledge already in place concerning Dr. Philip Baldwin.

Aiden deferred to sit and instead stood at the head of the table beside a visibly frustrated Chief Lewton. Though his expression was neutral, Autumn speculated that the SSA was every bit as exasperated as Adrienne.

Noah tapped his finger on the table in a rapid, discomposed beat beside her. Autumn longed to know how much of his agitation was case related versus the amount caused by whatever had taken place in Justin Black's hospital room.

She considered putting a comforting hand to his shoulder, knowing the nature of his worries could be revealed to her in an instant, but opted to wait. That was cheating. They would speak later.

The possibility was great that any insight she gleaned about Winter could be a significant distraction from the case before them. Focus was paramount.

One train wreck at a time, Dr. Trent.

Aiden crossed his arms and surveyed the team. "Agents, you all were privy to the questioning that just took place. Now is the time to share any insights you may have gathered. The clock is ticking, and the reality of this situation is that we may be alerted to a new victim at any given moment."

"Philip's former assistant died under questionable circumstances." Autumn voiced the most striking news revealed during the interrogation. "That certainly muddied the waters a bit more for Baldwin. *Three* dead employees on his watch."

Mia rested her elbows on the table. "Agreed. I didn't predict that one. His shady levels just rose about ten thousand percent."

"I think Baldwin's creep factor was already off the charts." Chris stretched his arms above his head. "Mildred Harbison's death just further cements what we've previously figured out about this jackass. He kills his problems. Evelyn threatened his control of running the facility the way he saw fit, and he axed her out of the picture."

Autumn waved her pen in protest. "Philip Baldwin is a smart man. Any connection he had to Colleen and Mildred was somehow kept completely under wraps for months. There's no logic in killing a nurse inside of his own hospital. He would have found a way to kill Evelyn offsite and destroyed that tape immediately."

"And Paula?" Chris stared at Autumn with pronounced skepticism.

"He never would have been so obvious with her murder

or the disposal of her body. Or more accurately, the *lack* of disposal of her body. The pieces just don't fit together." Autumn frowned in concentration.

The team had developed tunnel vision, determined to prove Dr. Baldwin's guilt. That focus had kept them busy enough to temporarily place other possibilities on the back burner. But the longer they hunted in Baldwin's direction, the less likely he appeared to be responsible for Evelyn or Paula's murders.

Autumn didn't harbor fond feelings toward the doctor, and she was highly aware that he abhorred her. Neither of those facts meant that pinning the crimes on Philip Baldwin based *only* on circumstantial evidence was the right course to take.

Fundamentally disagreeing with Dr. Baldwin didn't make the man a murderer.

Then again, death did tend to follow Philip around like a shadow. The odds of one doctor being somehow tethered to four dead women all within a single year of his life...

How could that be coincidental?

Adrienne paced just as she had in the interrogation room. "We don't know that we've even gathered all of the pieces just yet. If Baldwin is *that* intelligent, he could have orchestrated this entire dog and pony show. His sheer intent could be to force our eyes on him so that we doubt ourselves and search elsewhere. I'm not ready to write him off yet as our prime suspect."

"Prime? As if we have a ten-page list of suspects competing for that title?" Noah spoke for the first time since the meeting began. All heads whipped toward him. "I'm just saying. We've got crap."

Autumn studied his face for a moment, convinced by his edgy tone and the tight set of his jaw that what had transpired with the Black siblings was worse than she'd anticipated.

Aiden cleared his throat. "I think what Agent Dalton was so eloquently attempting to relay is that we have *no* physical evidence linking Dr. Baldwin to Evelyn nor Paula. And we have no better leads. Unless someone has a gem of information I don't?" His cool blue eyes scanned the group.

Silence.

Adrienne emitted an exhausted huff. "We have to release him."

"Precisely," Aiden concurred as he walked toward the door.

"That's it?" Chris called after him. "You're just going to let our *only* suspect go?"

Aiden spun on his heel to face the perturbed agent. "I am. Meeting adjourned." He returned to perpetrate his legal obligation, Adrienne following behind.

Innocent until proven guilty.

"This is such bullshit," Chris muttered, rising from his chair and shoving it into place under the table.

"Tantrums are bullshit too, Parker," Noah sniped back with uncharacteristic testiness. "You can't hammer a nail you haven't found."

"We. Have. Found. Him." Chris waved his hand toward the door. "He's right down the hall in a secured room. Surrounded by law enforcement. About to be set free by a federal agent and a police chief."

"Yes." Noah took a step toward the other man. "Two trained and dedicated professionals. All the more reason for you to shut your mouth and do your job."

Chris hesitated, his hand on the doorknob. "I don't answer to you, Dalton. And whatever crawled up your damn ass today isn't my problem." He retreated into the hallway, slamming the door behind him.

Mia rose and trailed after Chris, shaking her head. She said nothing, and Autumn empathized with the agent. Alongside the daily exhaustion their careers doled out, Mia Logan had the additional burden of dealing with the continual consequence of her partner's discontent.

Though, to be fair, Noah wasn't exactly in Mr. Rogers mode today.

Autumn turned toward Noah. "Things went bad, huh?"

The muscles in his face gave away his agitation. "That kid...is evil."

Autumn envisioned Justin with his jet-black hair and penetrating blue eyes so very much like Winter's. "He's a human, Noah."

He shook his head. "The two aren't mutually exclusive."

She eyed his tall form as he left the conference room, not uttering another word.

Noah Dalton was known for operating beneath a thick layer of good humor and friendliness. Justin had somehow managed to eradicate that pleasantry altogether.

And it was apparent that Noah wasn't quite ready to talk about the visit.

Autumn stood, walked toward the door, and attempted to refocus. Keeping personal and professional lives separate was Basic Job Skills 101. But when the two overlapped...

How were they to partition situations so intrinsically loomed together?

Autumn stopped short in the doorway, realizing she'd left her bag in the viewing room. She sighed, knowing that no matter how hard she fought against the distraction of Winter and Justin, the toll on her psyche was evident and unavoidable.

Aiden's booming voice traveled down the hall as he opened the interrogation room door and stood aside. "You're free to go, Doctor, but don't get any ideas about leaving town. We'll be in touch." Stanley Bradshaw guided his aggra-vated client out of the interrogation room, the sounds of their retreating footsteps echoing down the hallway.

The SSA stepped back inside the space, allowing the door to close. Autumn seized the moment to scurry down the hallway and reenter the viewing room to retrieve her bag. She froze as Chief Lewton and Aiden's voices blared on the other side of the two-way mirror.

"That went nowhere. A giant circle of word vomit." Adri-enne's vexation was clear. Autumn watched as the chief threw her pen aimlessly across the room.

"Maybe there's nowhere to go." Aiden leaned against the wall farthest from his pen-throwing colleague.

"You don't think he killed the women? Not a single one?" Adrienne exaggerated each syllable. "Simple as that?"

"Nothing about this case is simple, Chief Lewton. But I do have my doubts as to Dr. Baldwin being our killer. Puzzle pieces fit together, even when some are missing, because *they fit together*. You don't have to force them." Aiden glanced at the glass, and Autumn tensed.

Does he know I'm in here?

Adrienne gazed at him with troubled gray-blue eyes. "What about Colleen Hester?"

"What about her?" Aiden returned, impassive as always.

"Do you think he had anything to do with *her* death? She's the only one who wasn't an employee, and he appeared immensely affected by the mention of details regarding her passing."

Autumn took a few steps toward the door. She should leave now, but she wanted to hear Aiden's response. The SSA was hesitating, and she knew he generally didn't share his hunches with anyone...especially non-Bureau officials...until the team had gathered some foolproof evidence to place his theories on solid ground.

"I think he had something to do with *her*. And possibly her death. But we won't know that for sure until we gather enough evidence to arrest him and question him more about Colleen's suicide along with the rest of the facts." Aiden shoved his hands into his pockets and sauntered toward the door, giving the impression that he was done with the conversation.

Time to get the heck out of here.

In the hallway, Autumn attempted to appear as nonchalant as possible. Her inadvertent eavesdropping on Aiden and the chief's closing synopsis left her with a slight sensation of guilt.

But she'd have to shake that off too. With any luck, she could catch up to Dr. Baldwin before he left the building.

She intended to have a conversation of her own.

PHILIP PARTED with Stanley just as Autumn gained sight of the two men. Stanley entered the elevator while the doctor opened the precinct's stairwell exit door.

Breaking into a jog, Autumn caught up with Dr. Baldwin within seconds.

He started as she cornered him on the first landing. "What in the hell else could you possibly want from me? They said I could go. *I'm going.*"

Philip turned from her and put a foot on the first step of the next flight.

"You wouldn't have killed Evelyn at the hospital," Autumn blurted, desperate to gain the doctor's full attention. "You would have killed her off grounds. You would have made her disappear. And you sure as hell would have made the tape disappear."

None of the evidence made sense. She'd worked through

the details over and over, attempting to find any logic in Baldwin having taken the route their killer had chosen. He couldn't have done this, and she needed him to know she was on his side.

Philip froze.

Autumn's heartbeat accelerated as Dr. Baldwin turned back toward her. She was so getting fired for this, but her goal was discovering the truth.

She lowered her voice. "You certainly wouldn't have murdered your own wing's custodian and then put her in a linen closet *in your wing* for every other employee to discover."

Yes. Listen to me. Please.

"What are you attempting to do right now?" Baldwin looked around, almost like he was waiting for a camera to appear and some handsome celebrity to declare that he'd stumbled onto a *Candid Camera* episode. "You can't fool me into a confession, Dr. Trent. I don't have one. And frankly, this game is growing tiresome."

Autumn raised her hands, waving her proverbial white flag. "I don't believe you committed these murders, Dr Baldwin."

Relief flooded Philip's face, and his hard-set features softened for an infinitesimal second. But the dark cloud that shadowed the doctor since she first met him returned, bringing along a shower of fury.

"How nice it would have been if you had only come to this conclusion sooner, Doctor." He narrowed his eyes, practically snarling the words. "A valiant attempt, but I'm afraid I will not be set up so easily. Was your next move to rub up against me with your tits and whore out an admission of guilt?"

Autumn just stared at him, unable to believe what had come out of the psychiatrist's mouth. But could she blame him? If she were in his shoes, would she readily trust someone who had been looking at her like she was a murderer for days?

"I realize you have no reason to trust me. That doesn't mean you shouldn't. I might be able to help you."

"You've 'helped' make me the prime suspect in two murder investigations." Philip hurled the words like daggers and began a prompt jog down the next flight of stairs. "I think it's time for you to go assist someone else while I figure out how to deal with the ruination of my career."

Autumn refused to give up. She *had* played a hand in the facilitation of Philip's crucifixion and was now prepared to devote just as much energy to proving the man's innocence.

Following right on his heels, she closed in on him as they both reached the next landing. Before another word could be said, the overhead lightbulb flickered and went dark. The blackout lasted several seconds before the bulb glowed back to life, revealing a trembling Philip Baldwin huddled against the painted white cement wall.

"Dr. Baldwin? Are you all right?" Autumn grabbed his hand out of instinct, the instant fervent charge of emotion informing her that Philip was nowhere near "all right."

He's utterly terrified of confined spaces. But more...he's afraid because he's being set up for these crimes and has no way to prove his innocence.

Autumn, inundated with compassion, wished to offer a comforting sentiment, but Dr. Baldwin yanked his hand away and stormed down the stairwell.

She listened to the echoes of his footsteps and the eventual slam of the exit doorway.

Regardless of the doctor's rejection of her aid, she was more convinced than ever that the team had been targeting the wrong suspect.

Autumn resumed her descent, a new determination rising in her chest. She was going back to the BAU.

Dr. Philip Baldwin had been served to them on a silver platter...saving...and *preventing* them from the deep digging usually required to even begin narrowing down to a prime suspect. They'd focused solely on Dr. Baldwin by default, hand-fed the clues like hungry, well-trained zoo animals.

She burst through the exit door into the frigid January air. "Well-trained...yes. But not stupid. I'm on to you, asshole. Whoever the hell you are."

21

Winter drove away from Virginia State Hospital shaken and torn.

Justin's rabid laughter echoed through her mind. But his image was worse. Her bloody-faced little brother, lost in a dark hysteria of lunacy...possibly forever.

And Noah?

Of course he'd only been trying to protect her. But how far was too far?

He hadn't unmasked Justin. Winter knew what her brother was. But Noah had stolen a moment in time...and there were ever so few...when she'd felt hope. Tangible, palpable hope.

None of her friends and colleagues seemed capable of understanding that she *was* able to concede the monster Justin had become and *still* love him with a painful, enduring, innate resistance.

She didn't need her eyes opened, and closing her heart was an impossibility.

There was a tightrope walk she hadn't yet mastered that was the only feasible path where her brother was concerned.

On one side was the murderous beast, covered in the gory remains of his victims, and on the other, a silky haired six-year-old boy in SpongeBob pajamas.

Her challenge was to conquer the balancing act of pacing that thin, gilded string...suspended at a death-defying level of soaring peril. Forever.

"I should just run away and join the circus. I've got to be qualified by now. Winter Black, aerialist extraordinaire," she muttered as the FBI's Richmond Field Office came into view.

Then again, this job is a sideshow in and of itself. No clowns required.

Autumn. She needed to find her friend and snap out of this godforsaken muddled haze.

Entering the BAU office, Winter sought out the redheaded doctor. Sure enough, Autumn was at her desk, body bent in a posture of intense concentration. Winter's approach went undetected until she was close enough to tap Autumn's shoulder.

"Busy?" Winter grinned as Autumn jumped, whirling sideways in her rolling chair to view her accoster.

Autumn blushed and gave her computer screen a light tap. "Research. Diving deep into the world of one Doctor Philip Baldwin."

Winter had guessed as much. She leaned over Autumn's head and took in the webpage contents. A much younger Philip stood amongst a group of teens, all of them holding their graduation caps and preparing for the traditional toss.

His mouth was open in a wide, carefree smile, and another boy, who Winter assumed to be a high school buddy, had an arm slung around the young doctor-to-be's shoulders. The fact that this was the same sour, hateful man now being investigated for murder struck Winter with absurdity.

But stranger than that...why was Autumn wasting her time digging into this part of Philip's life? Curiosity?

Winter doubted that her highly educated friend would waste the Bureau's time indulging in personal inquisitive pursuits.

"Um. Am I missing something? Did Baldwin take out his biology teacher? Principal went missing after slapping the doc with a lengthy detention?" Winter let out a stiff laugh.

Autumn gave her a small grin and closed the laptop with an awkward, rapid movement. "I thought the team might benefit from a deeper search into Dr. Baldwin's history."

Winter cocked her head. "The historical timeline of Philip's trip through puberty? I don't get it."

"A more encompassing view of his life. Who was he? Has anything happened that could have pushed him over such an extreme edge? Did he show any tell-tale signs of psychopathy as a young man?" Autumn's tone was edged with conviction.

Winter's legs felt weak, and she leaned against the desk. "Okay. And has that proven helpful? Found anything that supports the blatant murders sitting in his lap?"

Autumn straightened in her chair and crossed her arms. "No. Nothing. And that's what's bothering me. Present or past, I think we're focused on the wrong man."

"The *wrong man?*" Winter guffawed, slapping her thigh for added emphasis. "I get that I'm not on the case, but Autumn, come on. He practically has neon arrows hanging over his head. And they're pointing...flashing...screaming... at his head."

Occasionally, Winter forgot how new to this job Autumn truly was. Her friend's skillset was amazing and beyond beneficial to the BAU, but her actual federal training was sparse. Autumn's giant brain couldn't be expected to always point her in the right direction, regardless of her rare and impressive insight.

"Doesn't that seem overly convenient to you?" Autumn

wrapped a strand of red hair around her index finger. A self-soothing gesture. A sign that she was growing more agitated.

"Evidence is always convenient, Autumn. Those clues literally solve the case, give us the advantage we need." Winter tried to keep her rising irritation at bay. "We're lucky this time. There's a lot of 'convenience,' and god knows this job would be easier if that were always the situation."

"I understand that the circumstantial evidence points to Baldwin. I'm only saying that if we focus just on one single person, we could miss the actual criminal." Autumn's frustration was apparent, but Winter couldn't deny her own.

"So, in layman's terms, you're trying to exonerate the man who, most likely, is the killer." Winter regretted the bite in her words but stood by the sentiment.

Autumn blew out a hard breath and laid her head against the back of her chair. "I'm just attempting to unearth the truth."

Winter was wont to argue the matter further but considered the exhaustion her friend must be experiencing. This job took a toll. That was a well-known fact. Autumn had to be a bit overwhelmed, and a lecture from her best friend wouldn't help matters.

If she feels better checking all the nooks and crannies, let her. She'll learn, and no real harm will be done.

"Well, good luck with your searching. I guess this isn't really my case to worry about, anyway." Sarcasm sharpened the words as the still-present bitterness of not being an actual part of the investigation reared its ugly, obnoxious head.

"I'm sorry." Autumn's expression held genuine sympathy. "I know that must be frustrating."

Somehow, her friend's condolence only served to irk Winter's silent vexation. "Not a big deal. I've got other things on my mind. I suppose you know Noah made a surprise appearance during my visit with Justin?"

Autumn's quick nod reeked of guilt.

Of course she knows. Autumn has all the deets nowadays. She's got the lowdown on cases I'm not even allowed to touch.

Winter knew, deep down, that her resentment wasn't fair. Autumn had intel on the case she'd been assigned, just as Winter had committed to memory the grand story of Mrs. Camilla and the Vegas wedding murder plot.

But logic wasn't comforting her in the current moment.

"He just barged in, like some roided-up pit bull on a mission. The dumbest part being that the visit was going fine...going *well*...until he got there. Noah set Justin off just by walking into the room. Made him go somewhere completely dark and awful in a split-second." Winter placed a hand to her temple, desperate to forget her brother's instant mutation into whatever he'd become in those minutes.

"Noah *made* Justin go somewhere dark?" Autumn was none too delicate with her implication.

Ouch, Dr. Trent.

"He *triggered* him, and the entire intrusion wasn't necessary. Justin and I have really...connected in the wake of all this chaos." She lifted her chin, not caring that her intentions were edged in defiance. "I plan to be there for him through his recovery. My presence isn't going to be a question anymore."

Emerald green eyes full of concern locked with Winter's rebellious blues. "That might not be the best idea...increasing your time with Justin right now. He's improving a bit, but he's far from stable. An upsurge of visits from his biological sister could exacerbate that instability."

"What?" Winter's shock mingled with anger. Surely Autumn hadn't meant that. At least not in the way she'd said it.

"We have to get to the bottom of all the crimes he's committed. We need the truth. We need to know how many people he's actually killed, where the bodies are, and even what other horrifying crimes The Preacher may have committed that Justin was witness to. I know you wouldn't want to interfere with that." Autumn studied her, clearly not knowing what Winter wanted at all.

"*Interfere?*" Winter hadn't meant to raise her voice, but he was her brother for Christ's sake. "With my own brother's recovery? I'm the *only* one here who knows the person he was…the person he still is somewhere underneath all of that jacked up mental damage. He was an innocent little boy, Autumn, and not that long ago. I'm the best person to help him find his way back from this madness!"

Autumn winced as though she'd been slapped. "Do you not trust me with your brother? Or are you just questioning my skills as a Doctor of Psychology in general? I'm *trained* to work with patients like Justin. You *know* that."

"No offense, but if you're spending all of your time trying to exonerate the current case's most *obvious* suspect, maybe your 'skills' *should* be called into question." Winter stood tall, slapping a hand to her hip.

Autumn remained outwardly calm, but Winter knew from the bond the two women shared that she had struck her friend deep. She hated herself for doing it, but she couldn't seem to stop herself either.

"I'm trying to view *all* sides of the situation." Autumn's rage bubbled just beneath the surface of her calm façade. "That's an important method that you might want to remember when you visit with Justin. You're *purposely* forgetting how unbalanced he is and all of the *horrible* things he did before he was finally caught because he's your brother and it hurts to see what he's become."

Winter shook her head so hard her hair flew into her eyes. "That's not true."

"He's dangerous, Winter. Didn't you witness how unstable he is just a few hours ago? You're not being honest with yourself." Autumn wasn't giving. Not even a little bit.

The words Justin had whispered into her ear flew through Winter's mind. How much worse would this conversation be if Autumn knew about that little commentary?

No one will ever know about that because I will never tell *anyone what he said. He wasn't himself. He wasn't Justin. He didn't mean it.*

"*Was*. Shouldn't you say 'how unstable' he *was*? He's made strides toward getting better. Triggers are going to happen while he recovers, but he is recovering." Winter straightened, beginning to walk away as her temper piqued.

Autumn threw her hands up in frustration. "Why are we even having this conversation? We both know I can't break doctor/patient confidentiality and discussing Justin like this is inappropriate. On top of that, I've only met with him a handful of times. He could require years of treatment to even begin clearing the brainwashing Douglas Kilroy instilled in him."

Winter halted, her fury morphing into disbelief. Discussing her baby brother with her close friend was inappropriate? Of course she was aware of the FBI's red tape, tight-lipped policies on open cases. And she would never expect Autumn to break her ethical oath, either.

But who exactly *could* she turn to with her Justin-related turmoil?

Noah?

Hilarious. Noah hated her little brother. He would never say the words out loud, in part from loving her too much to inflict such a grave injury, but also because he had to know that she could never forgive him if he did.

No one. She had no one to lean on where Justin was involved...except for Justin. And even she knew that going to a serial killer for advice or comfort *regarding a serial killer* was ludicrous.

The irony was that he had no one either, aside from her, to lean on for anything in this whole entire world.

I won't let him be abandoned. Not again.

Autumn reached a hand toward her, but Winter took two steps back and refused to grab it. Autumn dropped the signature of kindness and leaned forward, her elbows on her knees. Their eyes met, but her crimson-haired friend seemed a million miles away.

"Winter, I know this is incredibly difficult to hear. Even more heartbreaking than me finding out that Sarah is now a stripper...and a prostitute. But you have to give Justin's situation time. I'm devoted to working with him, to getting a handle on his crimes, and creating his profile for the BAU's files. The sessions are both medically privileged and the BAU's business. Discussing them with you would be wrong."

Winter's stomach ached for a short moment before steeling over.

Justin was a BAU file in process. Autumn was a contractor with the BAU. And she...was Agent Black. Nothing more, nothing less.

She had her own case to work on, her own assignment for the Violent Crimes Division.

Go sit at your desk and do your damn job. You should have checked your emotions at the field office's front doors. Handle that shit on your own time. Alone...

Tired to her core, she tried to give Autumn a neutral nod before walking away but knew her sensitive friend sensed the bitterness and resentment emanating from every fiber of her being.

Autumn was right.

Justin's "case" wasn't Winter's business. His heart, his soul, his fate...*those* were her concerns as his big sister. And they didn't have a place inside this building, regardless of the space they consumed in her mind.

As Winter turned her back on Autumn, she vowed to focus on nothing aside from bringing her own criminal case to justice. Let Dr. Trent throw away hours finding an escape route for the murderous medical director of Virginia State Hospital. Let her do whatever she needed to do for the BAU with her brother.

While Autumn was doing her job, Winter would do hers.

Winter nailed the bad guys.

And as there wasn't a shortage of criminals in this dark and dreadful existence, she didn't have time to waste consorting with her naïve friend.

A FEW HOURS alone at her desk distracted Winter from her troubles. But the uneasy feeling in the pit of her stomach never fully went away.

When Noah came striding toward her, she fought the urge to stand and embrace him. She hadn't known how the sight of him would affect her, but now that he was here, her desire was simplistic. Childlike. She just wanted all the bad things to be good again.

He pulled a chair next to hers and took her hand in his own. His brooding green eyes reflected the distress she'd been drowning in. "I'm sorry. I hate that you're going through so much right now. I hate seeing you in pain."

She squeezed his palm and swallowed the emotions

threatening to swamp her. "Nothing that's happening right now is your fault."

"I can't stand anything coming between us like this." He laced his long fingers with hers. "I start losing my mind."

"Neither can I, and we're not going to let that happen. You and I are solid. I promise you, we'll *stay* solid." She bit her tongue, fighting back tears she refused to let fall.

Noah cupped her chin in his hand. "I love you. Good things. I want the best things for us."

"Agreed. I love you too." Winter pulled her head back with a gentle tug. They were still at work. Opening the door to her emotions too wide could backfire in a very unprofessional breakdown.

"Can I ask you...you seemed so upset when..." Noah tilted his head, relentless concern appearing to embolden him. "What did Justin whisper to you?"

She'd known the question was coming. She'd also known she wouldn't give a truthful answer.

Winter waved a hand, trying for indifference though her insides stiffened. "Just some mumbled nonsense. I was mostly just disturbed by how incoherent he became."

She doubted that Noah believed this, but he made the wise choice to let the inquiry pass.

I will never tell anyone. Never. Not even you, the man I love.

Her mind shifted to Autumn, and she was glad to segue to something...*anything*...that did not directly involve her brother. "I had a conversation with Autumn a few hours ago that didn't go well at all."

Noah studied her face, his beautiful eyes seeming to examine all the verbal wounds still lingering inside her. "A conversation? Or an argument?"

Winter figured FBI credentials weren't necessary to divine the nature of their "chat." The disturbance must have been evident in her expression. "She's hellbent on finding favorable evidence or proof of some sort that Baldwin is innocent."

"Innocent? Baldwin?" Noah slumped back in the chair he'd dragged over, throwing his feet onto Winter's desk. "That guy is a complete ass. Arrogant as hell and a total control freak. Why would she even *want* to help him?"

Winter shoved Noah's giant shoes off her workspace. "I wondered the same, but she's not budging on this hunt. I'm beginning to think she sees a bit of herself in Philip. Maybe more than she cares to admit."

"Autumn and Baldwin hate each other," Noah countered, putting a playful foot on Winter's lap.

She shot him an even stare and smacked his leg away with a dramatic stroke. "I'm aware. They can't stand each other. Because they both think they're right about everything."

Noah shook his head, his expression full of disbelief. "Oh, come on. That doesn't sound like Autumn."

He was wrong.

Winter recalled her friend telling her with a calm, straight face that Justin was the BAU's business.

"Right now, *Autumn* doesn't sound like Autumn."

22

I tapped the browser icon three consecutive times, opening one window for each major local network. Their online news streams were easy to access by the swift typing of my fingertips, bringing the websites alive one by one.

But listening to the local yokels wasn't enough. I needed the nationwide broadcasts. My fingers flew across the keyboard, pulling up CNN and MSNBC. Hell, even FOX would work at this point. News, fake news, who cared? I wanted declaration of the doc's savage crimes running rampant, regardless of the station.

Truth could take a vacation while justice was served.

He *technically* hadn't killed Evelyn nor Paula, but he deserved this hailstorm of retribution.

What wasn't fake at all was the footage of the great, almighty Dr. Philip Baldwin being led to a detective's car. Reporters speculated that he was a person of interest in the recent rash of crimes afflicting Virginia State Hospital.

Delightful.

I clicked through the windows, stopping on my favorite

thus far. A closeup of Philip's aging, distraught face as he stared out the back window. His dark hair was ridiculously mussed, and his eyes...

A small laugh escaped me. The man was *terrified*.

Absolutely heartwarming.

Disgrace. Dishonor. Despair.

The doctor was ruined, and rightfully so. The evil son of a bitch had led himself to this point. His disgusting black heart and cold-blooded soul were his own undoing.

I'd long ago stopped believing that I could ever be at peace again, but the high of taking down Philip Baldwin was close.

His wealthy, sophisticated ass was going to flip a lot of heads in federal prison. And then he'd get turned inside-out on the daily. They might as well just send him in with a skirt on.

The most enjoyable part, aside from the still frame of his utter demise, was the flood of stories coming through about the unsafe environment of the state's only maximum-security hospital.

I adjusted the windows' sizes so I could view all of them at once. The cable networks had gone straight for the nitty-gritty details, interviewing former staff, and better yet, *current* staff. The disgruntled employees were more than happy to spill the dirt on the gargantuan brick edifice. Some of their comments were true, many were exaggerated, and a few were outright lies.

CNN, for instance, currently featured a former nurse, Lydia Jackson. Lydia's face was red with anger as she spoke her hateful piece into the camera. *"...I worked in that bleeeep-ing hellhole for three years. There wasn't a single day where I didn't fear for my bleeeep-ing life. Do you think the bleeeep-ing administration gave two bleeeep-ing bleeeeps about my welfare? I coulda been shanked, strangled, raped, and they'd just replace me like a disposable bleeeep-ing napkin!"*

Not true.

Truth be told, security was handled with extreme serious-ness at the hospital. A veritable army of guards and orderlies were kept in constant rotation twenty-four hours a day. And even though the camera footage was lacking altogether, the audio surveillance was massive.

I knew that little gem with certainty.

But there was some accuracy to the statement in that every employee *was* easy enough to replace. I'd found the job ad listing for Evelyn's replacement in the paper just this morning.

Had they even scoured all her fecal matter from that elevator yet?

I turned my attention to MSNBC. *"...and no one is actually working with those psychos. They're prisoners. Sick, rotting nutjobs pumped up with drugs and left to die."*

Interesting. This informant was listed as a current employee. No name was given, the face was blurred, and the voice disguised. The fuzzy, indistinct form appeared to be that of a man, but it was impossible to tell for certain.

I wasn't sure of my opinion about that particular senti-ment. Some of the patients seemed to improve from my observations, but those were few and far between. And while there *was* a plethora of sedatives pumping through the veins of the building's tenants, the medications were given for damn good reasons.

Those people were *crazy*. Crazy as could be.

There were days when the toxic mix of mental illnesses even got to *me*, and I had a pretty thick skin compared to the average human being. I was more stable than anyone else I knew.

I knew I'd want my loved ones to medicate the hell out of

me if I ever went over the deep end the way these poor bastards had.

Besides, anyone who died in that building, aside from the two women I had killed, more than likely never had a chance of making their way back into society anyway.

Lifers.

And come to think of it, I'd probably done Evelyn and Paula both a favor by relieving them of their duties. Evelyn would have eventually been killed by one of her murderous best friends. I had no doubt about that.

Such a silly woman, that one.

And Paula led a miserable life, both at work and home. She hated everything in this world, and the world seemed to hate her right back.

Life shouldn't be wasted on the ungrateful.

Two casualties of war that weren't worth two seconds of regret. Not really.

Reports claiming to be based on actual prisoner/patient squealers were now leaking across the feeds.

All was well, and my plan was working out with beautiful synchronicity.

While no one else would understand how access was gained to these dangerous minds and their batshit crazy two cents, I was perfectly aware.

Contraband phones, delivered in numerous methods of stealth, connected the nuts to the news. And not a single patient would have anything negative to say about *me*, because *I* was the man they turned to when they needed something the hospital denied them.

I knew how to get things. Important things. And I never failed to deliver.

I made as much in a single month off of those "special deliveries" as I did on my paycheck. And the biggest perk of all…I made friends in low places.

My Lone Ranger black-market distribution service gave me access to the patients' trust...to their *loyalty*. That was a priceless gift that allowed me free reign of the entire building.

I could access anything, and I could access anyone.

Everyone liked me, just like Red from *The Shawshank Redemption*.

The local NBC12 featured an anchorwoman reading quotes from anonymous male patients, her tone grave. *"...'and if you don't need to go to the bathroom, they beat you with batons until you piss yourself and then beat you again for getting the floor dirty.'"* The woman's hair didn't even move as she shook her head. *"This horrendous accusation comes from an actual prisoner at Virginia State Hospital."*

I smiled as I eyed the other feeds. The claim was complete bull, but it sure did make for good news reporting. Philip's face was getting so smeared with shit that the man would forget how to *spell* freedom before he ever experienced it again.

An article on FOX's homepage shared the highly detailed story of one patient who avowed that his nurses made constant sexual advances on him, using his dick like a twenty-four-seven merry-go-round.

You wish, buddy.

My attention turned back to channel twelve's live feed, where another quote was being shared. *"...the doctor puts on red high heels and makes me watch while he screws the orderlies. He makes them call him Nancy Drew, and they're his Hardy Boys..."*

The declarations of atrocious misconduct were far exceeding my expectations.

Even better than Christmas. This day was a celebration both for me and the precious soul watching from above.

I was mid-paragraph, taking in an account of forced starvation and water rationing from another loose-lipped wacko, when a flashing red banner spouting "Breaking News" stole my attention. I clicked and read the latest update in the Dr. Philip Baldwin scandal.

Baldwin was being asked to step down from his position at the hospital. The board expressed they had several frustrations over the internal rules of the hospital that Philip had allegedly broken.

They had to be referencing the audio surveillance. Not a single soul had given Baldwin permission to use his preferred method of watch-dogging the facility. Any idiot with half a brain could have surmised that there had only been a matter of time before he got busted for that illegal fuckery.

But what about the murders? And why such a soft sell?

He was being "asked" to step down over "internal frustrations."

That's what they were reporting after I'd hand-delivered a dead nurse *and* a dead housekeeper?

And that housekeeper bitch was heavy. I bulged a damn disc dragging that heifer down the hallway.

But not a single mention of Evelyn's murder. Nor Paula's.

And certainly not Colleen's.

Hadn't these federal bastards had enough time to dig into the villainous doctor's past and realize he was a horrendous, stone-cold, murdering monster who would only keep killing if he wasn't locked away immediately?

"How many bodies do you need? How many mutilated bodies do you need, you assholes!"

I punched a hole in the cheap, paneled-wood wall next to my desk.

Unbelievable! Law enforcement was mocking...*wasting...* those women's sacrificial deaths with every minute they hadn't gathered together enough brain cells to connect the homicides to Dr. Baldwin.

To connect them to *Colleen.*

But why was I so shocked? They'd been incompetent when Colleen died. Of course they would continue with their incompetence now.

I laid a hand over the rough-edged hole in the paneling. I hadn't meant to abuse my home.

"I'm sorry. You didn't deserve that. I was just upset, you know? I lost my temper. But you didn't deserve that. Forgive me?"

I leaned my forehead against the cool brown board. Instinctively, I knew I'd been forgiven.

But Philip Baldwin was not. He would *never* be forgiven.

And if I continued to leave this up to the authorities, he'd never be punished, either.

I pulled up the zoomed in picture of the doctor's face.

So smug. So evil. So hated.

"Oh, Philip. This isn't over. I'm a man who doesn't give up. You *will* pay for your sins."

Everything done in secret will come to light. All that is hidden will be revealed.

With a hope-filled heart, I ogled the replayed video feed of Baldwin being led by the detectives away from his facility. His fallen kingdom. And there, in the background, was the redheaded psychologist standing at the hospital doors.

An involuntary growl came from my throat.

She'd started this mess. My original plan had been much smoother, and every last step could have gone off without a hitch.

But she'd interfered. She'd found Evelyn Walker's body before anyone was supposed to.

Sometimes, human beings were the instruments used to test one's devotion to a path of righteousness.

That doctor. She was such an instrument. She was an obstacle purposely set before me to assess my dedication... my allegiance to justice.

I would leave no uncertainty behind for the ever-present eyes staring down from the heavens.

My commitment was unshakeable.

The flash of red walked down the sidewalk, confident and composed.

She *challenged my faithfulness*, and just like Philip, she would have to pay.

23

Autumn was beginning to accept the fact that "a good night's sleep" might permanently be a piece of the past. The previous night hadn't even come close to providing adequate shuteye.

She could blame Toad's rampant snoring or Peach's affinity for shoving her furry butt right in her face. But the accusations would be inaccurate.

Her sweet pets weren't the problem.

She'd laid in this bed for a solid eight hours, and most of that time had been spent ruminating over an endless list of woes.

This case of the strangled hospital employees wore on her psyche. On top of the initial surprise of Evelyn Walker's dead body dropping into her elevator car being forever emblazoned upon her memory, Autumn was unceasingly tormented by her conviction that Philip Baldwin was innocent.

Although there was no existent physical proof of his involvement in the murders that they knew of, clearing the cloud of suspicion that now hung over the doctor's head was a monstrous undertaking. Her colleagues, *his* colleagues, local law enforcement, and the "always eager to judge" general public had all but declared the man guilty.

And her argument with Winter. That conversation had gotten completely out of hand, regarding both Baldwin *and* Justin.

Autumn hadn't meant to be dismissive or severe...only firm. But she was aware that her words had hurt Winter, and her regret for the offense was enormous.

Likewise, her friend's biting commentary had struck deep into Autumn's own heart.

The predicament appeared insurmountable. Her job required discreetness concerning Justin's case. But in what world could she possibly expect Winter to sit by in happy silence while her brother was being evaluated by her best friend?

Winter loved him. Autumn understood. She understood all too well.

But she also understood the necessary lines drawn between work and friendship. Crossing them could cost her the career she'd spent so much time and money obtaining.

And as harsh as those limits seemed to both of the women, Autumn believed that, for this situation in particular, they were for the best.

She'd witnessed Winter fall deeper and deeper down the rabbit hole, trying to find the little boy Justin once was. Autumn desired more than anything to find him as well.

Giving Winter back some semblance of her brother would be a beautiful gift. She wanted more than anything to glimpse peace in her friend's sapphire eyes.

But the constant question of whether or not Justin Black...the real Justin Black...was gone forever had consistently been leaning in one direction, toward one answer.

He was most likely damaged beyond repair.

Still, Autumn hadn't given up, and she wouldn't. Her determination wouldn't allow her to throw in the towel, and her love for Winter would keep her trying even if she ever did reach some point of no return.

In the meantime, keeping an acceptable balance between the Black siblings was a challenge she didn't fully know how to conquer. The perplexity of this undertaking ate away at Autumn's essence every single day.

The burden was relentless.

And, of course, there was still the matter of Sarah. Her sister wasn't a box on a to-do list she could simply check off. "Finding her" in Florida and learning who she'd become hadn't resolved the matter.

She worried and wondered about Sarah with intense consistency. A voice forever ingrained into her mind whispered her sister's name with incessant disregard for her attempts to focus elsewhere.

What had happened to the girl she once knew so well? How had she come to make such negative choices for her life?

Could Sarah be saved, or was she another case of irreversible injury?

Autumn couldn't answer that question, but she *was* certain that she would never forgive herself for not trying...again.

"Get up. Go run. Pull yourself together," Autumn commanded herself. Peach opened a wary eye, and she gave the feline a reassuring pat. "Not you. You can stay in bed."

The run helped. Autumn focused on the steady pat-pat-pat of her shoes hitting the pavement. The rhythmic beat had a considerable calming effect, and by the time she was back at her apartment, any leftover angst that survived the bout of exercise melted away in the steam of a much-needed hot shower.

Autumn emerged from her home in a crisp black pantsuit, feeling competent and professional and yet again ready to take on the madness brewing inside of Virginia State Hospital's foreboding brick walls.

Justin was her prime focus today. She'd missed her promised meeting with him due to the sudden outbreak of murder at the hospital, and she was aware that Justin took her cancellations personally.

In fact, her absence might have been one of the factors of his breakdown with Noah and Winter. Justin was often triggered by any action resembling abandonment.

Awesome. You're doing a superb job with this one, Dr. Trent.

Autumn squared her shoulders and strolled into the building. She reminded herself that being in two places at once was impossible, and she had been giving one billion percent of herself to the job.

"Slacking" had ceased to be a word in her vocabulary quite some time ago.

As she passed through the administrative wing, she spotted Philip Baldwin in his office. The doctor was gathering his belongings into a few cardboard boxes. One of Chief Lewton's officers stood guard at the doorway, keeping the disgraced physician under strict watch.

Autumn stepped toward the policeman and flashed her temporary credentials. "I can take it from here, Officer. I'll keep an eye on Dr. Baldwin and ensure he is escorted from the building when he's ready."

The officer gave a nod of approval and immediately abandoned his post.

He was probably bored out of his mind. No action to be seen here, folks.

She knew she was the only one, aside from Dr. Baldwin, who held the opinion that the man didn't pose a threat of any sort. But it was possible she could help change the doctor's image by proving his innocence.

Philip was less than pleased to catch sight of her entering his former office. He pressed his lips together and began tossing items into the boxes with rampant carelessness. The man didn't even flinch when a framed document landed with a brutal crash against the previously chucked items.

Autumn closed the door with a discreet nudge of her elbow. "I've been digging into your background."

Dr. Baldwin shot her a sneer and proceeded with his haphazard packing. "How nice for you. Go away."

Lord knew it was tempting, but she leaned a shoulder against the wall, settling herself in for a long fight. "I can't. I'm your babysitter now. But you should listen to me because I want to help you."

Philip said nothing, and like a child, refused to even glance in her direction.

"I've uncovered some things regarding your past. I know you had a successful private practice. You were doing quite well for yourself in that line of work until you allegedly became too involved with your patients."

He turned his back to her and proceeded to grab books from the shelves, dropping each of them with unnerving thumps into a fresh box.

Autumn analyzed his physical response as she continued to say what she needed to. "There's a particular case that threatened your career long before these murders."

Philip still said nothing, but he hadn't been able to prevent his body from stiffening. His book hurling displayed a considerable slowdown.

"That case is the reason you took the medical director position here. And I'd be willing to bet quite a few chips that coming so close to having your license revoked has *a lot* to do with your strict patient/caregiver policies as well."

Autumn crossed her arms and waited, letting silence be her friend.

It didn't take long.

Philip whirled around and stacked his boxes together, lifting the pile with ease. "We are not having this conversation, Dr. Trent. I'm ready to go now." Even with the boxes in his arms, he managed to open the door and stride down the hall.

Shit.

The man's legs were considerably longer than her own. She had to jog to keep up with him as he ramrodded his way through the building, down the stairwell, and straight into the ground floor level of the parking garage.

"Dr. Baldwin. Philip! I believe I can help clear this up for you. My co-worker, Agent Ming, is still digging, and she's a brilliant..."

A dark figure emerged from the shadows of the garage, striking Philip on the back of the head with an object Autumn couldn't see well enough to identify. Before she could say or do anything, Philip crumbled to the ground, boxes landing around him.

Autumn began to backpedal, frantically looking for a place to hide.

The attacker turned toward her. She froze as the gun he'd just used as a hammer on Dr. Baldwin was aimed her way, barrel now facing forward.

Shit.

Even as shock vibrated through her system, Autumn recognized the man. His shaved head was unmistakable. He'd helped pull her from the elevator she'd been trapped in with Evelyn Walker's body hanging through its ceiling.

What had his name tag read? Autumn strained to recall the tiny detail from her memories of that day.

Albert. Albert Rice.

"What do you want? Why are you doing this?" She had to get him talking. Stalling and distraction were her only available weapons.

But their assailant did not answer. He shifted his aim to Philip as the doctor began to stir on the cold concrete. "Give me your keys. Now."

Autumn intuited that the demand was not made in jest. Albert would shoot either of them without remorse at any given moment, should he see fit to do so.

She handed him the keys. He pushed the lock button, spotting the responsive flashing lights of her car only a few spots away.

"Get up on your feet," he commanded Philip, who was now aware enough to follow the order. "Now!"

When the doctor appeared ready to fall, Autumn propped one of his arms over her shoulder, supporting him as the duo was directed toward her car by Albert and his firearm. The doctor's terror flowed from his body, compounding upon her own, as he struggled to stay upright. He leaned heavily against her much smaller frame, and she began to perceive that his foggy waves of fear were multifaceted.

Albert followed behind them, his gun no doubt fixed hard on his captives as they stumbled toward her vehicle.

We cannot get in that car. Never get in the car. Statistically, you will more than likely never return.

As her Camry loomed closer, Autumn's mind raced for possible modes of escape. "If you'll only tell me what you want, I'm sure I can help you. I know you probably believe violence is the only answer to your problem at this point, but there are *always* other ways. I work with the FBI. Dr. Autumn Trent. I can make sure that any issue you may have with Dr. Baldwin is settled in a legal and fair manner."

A firm prod of the steel barrel at her back was the only

response she received, and the car was now a mere ten feet away.

"Albert, I remember you," Autumn continued. "You helped me out of that elevator. I know you're not a bad person. Just tell me what you need." She'd given up hope of garnering an actual response, but if she could slow this process in any way...

"Run." Philip's sharp whisper broke the silence. "Get help."

The gun pressed hard against her kidney, and Albert's large hand gripped the arm that wasn't supporting the psychiatrist.

Autumn wasn't going anywhere unless Albert said so.

He popped the trunk open with a single button press of her keychain.

Was he an orderly or a guard or maybe...a custodian? He'd *saved* her. Why rescue a person only to take them hostage?

"Get in, Dr. Baldwin." Albert's gruff voice echoed off the concrete columns like a macabre pinball machine.

Autumn braced against the heightened current of panic emitting from Philip as he hesitated. His deep-seated fear of confined spaces screamed from his body, which froze in statue-like stillness.

Just like his reaction in the stairwell when the lights went out...

Autumn was more convinced than ever that Philip never could have committed Virginia State Hospital's murders. He wouldn't have gone to the top of the elevator car to conceal Evelyn's body. The shaft was too dark, the space too small.

And taking the time to position Paula against the wall of the linen closet, yet another ill-lit and cramped space, was also a highly doubtful proposition.

The team had been focused on the wrong man all along, just as she had suspected.

"Albert, if your plan is for me to drive you both somewhere, wouldn't the best option be for you to sit with Dr. Baldwin in the back seat?" Autumn suggested, dizzy from the unrelenting surges of horror shooting through Philip's body. "That way you'd never lose sight of either of us."

The bald man observed her with a blank, emotionless gaze for a moment before repeating himself to Dr. Baldwin. "Get. In. Now." The gun tapped against Philip's forehead as Albert spat each word.

With no other choice, Autumn assisted Philip as he eased into the trunk. "I'm so sorry," she whispered, their green eyes meeting with an unspoken agreement of doomed comrades.

Philip had to get into that trunk, or they were both going to die right then, right there. Mercy was not a part of this abductor's persona.

Albert slammed the trunk lid down with a hearty push. The stocky, well-muscled orderly continued to aim his gun at her with his other hand.

He was strong...physically fit to the point of daunting intimidation. Taking him down, even without the firearm to stop her, seemed nearly an impossible feat. If she took him off guard, perhaps. But she had a rather solid premonition that Albert wouldn't let his guard down for a second.

"Your phone. Now." Albert held out his free hand toward her.

Autumn had known this request was coming. She'd intended to somehow thwart Albert's plan before the moment arrived.

Fail.

She pulled her phone from her bag in a slow, cautious motion and placed it in the outstretched palm.

Albert powered the device off, nodding toward the car. "You're driving. Get in."

She obeyed, attempting to stay calm and make no sudden movements. That gun was too close.

And Albert was too far gone.

He knelt at the open driver's side doorway, continuing to face her, and reached under the dash just left of the steering wheel. Two seconds of tinkering later, he pulled out a tiny device that Autumn recognized as a fuse.

Her heart sank as he tossed the fuse over his shoulder. He'd disconnected the navigation system so that no one could track her car. With her phone off, that little gadget had been her last lifeline.

Though everyone had seen this man as a lowly orderly, he was highly intelligent and organized. Autumn sought to find a chink in his armor, but with the black hole of the barrel in her face, her heart was racing too frantically for her to think.

Fight or flight.

The problem was…neither of those were a current option.

Albert pulled a crumpled piece of copy paper from his pant pocket. "Directions. Follow them." Autumn smoothed out the page and identified that he had indeed printed out a route to…somewhere.

She sat in silence as he ducked into the back seat, lying low so as to stay concealed. He pulled the hatch partially down, allowing himself a view of the trunk and the quivering grown man inside.

"Go time. I've got my gun pointed straight at your back, and you should know that your seat cushion won't help you out with that one. And if you should get the urge to give the game away, think again. I will blow that piece of shit's brains out if you so much as swerve in the wrong direction. Don't doubt me. I'm not a liar."

Autumn inhaled, forcing herself to retain composure. A simple shift into drive, and then they were exiting the garage.

Was she doing the right thing? Taking off toward the

BAU or police station would at least ensure they didn't end up six feet underground in the dense Virginia forest.

But Philip would most definitely not survive the detour. She wouldn't either.

Albert wasn't blowing smoke. He was more than ready to shoot Dr. Baldwin if she deviated from the ordered path. Philip would be dead, and there was no guarantee that she would be able to get away from Albert before joining the doctor in the afterlife.

Granted, she was aware that Albert wasn't taking them on a leisurely day tour of the scenic countryside. Whatever awaited them...wherever they were going...his intentions were dark.

As she drove farther and farther away from the heart of the city, Autumn decided she was doing the only thing still within her power to do.

She was giving herself and Philip more time to stay alive.

24

A iden's phone buzzed on his desktop. He glanced at his screen, not recognizing the number. Cup two of his morning coffee wasn't drained quite yet, but when had that ever mattered? Mornings, afternoons, evenings, and often throughout the midnight hours...information was being shared to, relayed by, requested from him.

He figured he was due for a vacation in the near future, but what would he really do with the time off? He'd think about the job and fight restlessness right up until the minute he walked back into the Richmond Field Office.

A tap of the speaker button, and he gave his standard greeting, "Special Supervisory Agent Aiden Parrish."

A vaguely familiar voice boomed into the confines of his office space. "This is Victor Goren, Justin Black's public defender. With all due respect, I would like to know who's running this federal shitshow of yours. Dr. Autumn Trent was supposed to meet with my client at nine sharp this morning. Lo and behold, she was a no show. *Again*."

Aiden frowned. He hadn't known Autumn was meeting

with Justin today, and just the idea of that kid put him on edge.

But Autumn wasn't "his" employee, and when they weren't running a case-related task together, he didn't keep the doctor under lock and key. He wasn't her babysitter or technically even her boss.

"I apologize, Mr. Goren, but I can assure you that if Dr. Trent was unable to make the appointment, there is a good and valid reason." Aiden tapped his pen on a notepad.

Yes. The last time she was unable to visit that sadistic little bastard, she'd had a rather unexpected run-in with a very dead hospital nurse.

"I should hope so. I believe the fact that Justin Black is mentally ill has not escaped you nor the rest of the Bureau. These constant cancellations have a serious effect on my client's well-being. An unnecessary effect, in my opinion." Goren sounded as though he might be sporting his own mental break in the near future.

Anyone assigned to defend Winter's little brother is bound to lose their mind eventually.

Aiden closed his eyes, reminding himself that his interactions with Goren needed to be nothing less than civil. For Autumn's sake.

"I will check into the matter, Mr. Goren. I'm positive that Dr. Trent will be calling you herself as soon as she is able." Aiden heard the hint of annoyance in his own tone, but Victor Goren was obnoxious if he was anything. Fake polite was better than zero polite.

"Oh, I hope she does. I have quite a few things to say to her." Victor ended the call.

Aiden reached for his coffee once again, then stopped, his hand suspended in midair.

Autumn *would* call Goren as soon as she was able. She didn't skip out on clients nor responsibilities in general. And if Goren was calling *him*, then the attorney had obviously tried to call Dr. Trent beforehand. With no luck.

She hadn't shown up, and she hadn't called, *and* she hadn't answered?

That wasn't Autumn's usual modus operandi.

Aiden decided to call his redheaded colleague himself when his phone buzzed again. This time, he knew the number.

"Chief Lewton. How can I help you today?" Maybe a new lead in the hospital murders or something along those lines.

"Well, I have some troubling news," Adrienne began.

Aiden sat straighter in his chair. "Yes?"

"One of my officers made a bit of a bad call." Adrienne cleared her throat. "He was supposed to keep guard while Dr. Baldwin cleaned out his office, and then escort him from the building. Dr. Trent apparently showed up and relieved him of his duties. She stayed to supervise…alone…and now neither of them is anywhere to be found."

"They're missing?" Aiden stood, grabbed his iPad, and tossed the contraption in his briefcase.

"I'm not sure we can use that term yet but—"

"You can't find or reach either of them?" Aiden finished for Chief Lewton.

"Correct." Though this wasn't her direct fault, Adrienne's voice dripped with guilt. "He's been reprimanded—"

"I'd like his name and badge number emailed to me directly. My team and I will be arriving at the hospital in the next fifteen." Aiden ended the call and typed a rapid text to Chris and Mia while charging down the main hall of the BAU.

Drop what you're doing and meet me in the parking lot. We're going to the State Hospital. Baldwin is missing.

He hesitated, then finished the message.

So is Autumn.

❄

Adrienne met them at the hospital entrance. Her grave expression did nothing to mollify Aiden's apprehension.

"Still no sign?" He barked the question.

She shook her head. "We've searched the parking lot and the parking garage. Dr. Baldwin's car is still on-site, but my officers can't seem to find Dr. Trent's."

Aiden stiffened. "Your officers can't seem to do a lot of things, Chief."

Adrienne bristled at the comment, but Aiden ignored her reaction. This wasn't her fault, and he was aware of that. He still didn't have to pretend everything was coming up roses this morning.

"I sent teams to Dr. Trent's and Dr. Baldwin's Richmond apartments. Both were empty, and both were undisturbed. Well…except for an accident left behind by her little dog. My officer said the cat seemed pissed that her kibble bowl was empty." Chief Lewton's dismay was evident, and it only served to charge Aiden up even more.

We will find you.

"Agent Parker, recheck the parking lots, front and back, and scour the parking garage. Dim lighting could have hidden something important during a casual search by undertrained eyes." Aiden refrained from shooting Adrienne a glare. "Agent Logan, recheck Dr. Baldwin's office. Look for any signs of an argument or struggle, as well as any of Dr. Trent's belongings that may have been left behind."

Chris and Mia took off in separate directions, leaving Aiden and Adrienne alone.

"You cannot blame this solely on my police department, Agent Parrish. Dr. Trent walked into that room of her own free will. *Her* idea," Adrienne defended her team before he'd even begun an attack.

"I'm not going to play the blame game with you, Chief Lewton. We need to focus on finding Philip Baldwin. He is our only suspect thus far in a double homicide case, and he has a special abhorrence for Dr. Trent." Aiden pictured Autumn jumping from the helicopter in Florida not so long ago.

And Dr. Trent has a spectacular way of throwing herself into dangerous situations. Literally.

"You think he intends to harm her?" Adrienne posed.

Aiden pressed his lips together. "I certainly don't believe they went picnicking, Chief Lewton."

"There's the possibility that they're not together at all." Adrienne's voice was hopeful.

Aiden's gut was not.

Too many red flags. A red flag parade.

"I'd like for you to question any and all employees who worked in the administrative wing this morning. Nothing formal. Fast. Thorough." Aiden walked at a quick pace toward the all too familiar hospital stairwell door.

"And what are you going to do?" Adrienne called after him.

"I'm going to speak with Justin Black."

"I could bring him to a meeting room," the guard stationed on Justin's floor offered. "Shackle him up for you."

"That won't be necessary." Aiden put his hand to the doorknob of Justin's room, mentally preparing himself to deal with the little horror.

The guard leaned in conspiratorially. "He's been a bit, well, *extra* unstable as of late. I would advise the shackles."

Aiden glanced through the observation window. Justin

sat on his bed, thumb in mouth, staring at the floor. "Like I said, that won't be necessary. I won't be long."

I won't be long because Autumn may not have "long."

Justin's hand dropped to his mattress. Saliva hung from his chin. "I know you."

Aiden crossed his arms, not needing nor wanting to approach the boy. "Agent Parrish. And I know you as well. I'm going to ask you a few questions, and you are going to answer them in a clear and concise manner."

Justin burst into giggles that had the hair lifting on the back of Aiden's neck. "Clear and concise...he demands of the mental patient."

Aiden raised an eyebrow. "I demand it of an intelligent criminal who has single-handedly murdered an unknown number of victims yet avoided all prosecution thus far."

The giggling ceased. Justin's sharp blue eyes focused on Aiden. "You appear to be upset, Agent Parrish."

"Do I?" Aiden held his ground, knowing his expression was indifferent and that Justin Black would like nothing more than to make him lose his temper.

"You do. Something bad happen to one of your federal tough guys? I vote for Agent Dalton getting his throat slit. Or my sister getting gang raped. Both at the same time would be preferable." Justin gave him a pleasant smile.

Aiden's jaw clenched. The bastard was *perfectly* coherent. "I'm sorry to disappoint you. Agent Dalton and Agent Black are in splendid condition. They're probably together right now, having a romantic brunch."

Justin bared his teeth and released a low growl.

"I'm here about Dr. Trent. You were supposed to see her this morning, or maybe you *did* see her this morning?" Aiden wasted no time with the questions now that he had pushed Justin off-center.

Always the mind games with this kid. Simultaneous offense and defense.

Justin appeared confused for an instant before his expression shifted to angry. "She didn't show up. She *never* shows up. She said she'd try to help me, but she doesn't really care. She's just like the rest of them."

Aiden noted the genuine bitterness in Justin's voice. The younger Black sibling's instant vexation told Aiden the only piece of information he needed.

Justin hadn't seen Autumn. Justin wasn't responsible for her disappearance. Not this time.

"Thank you. That's all for today." Aiden turned to leave.

"That's *it*?" Justin screamed across the room. "You ask me about that bitch doctor and then you just *leave*? You're all the same! Abandon, abandon, abandon!"

Aiden faced the young man with a calm stare as he gave the door a firm double tap. The guard opened the door in immediate response, and he exited the room.

The latch clicked, along with the automatic lock, and Aiden peered through the observation window once more.

Justin was off his bed, repeatedly throwing himself against the concrete walls headfirst while shrieking, "*Abandon! Abandon! Abandon! Abandon!*"

Aiden stepped aside as a nurse and orderly rushed into the room, no doubt to administer a fast-acting sedative. He squared his shoulders and made straight for the stairwell.

There was a large sense of relief in knowing that Justin hadn't harmed Autumn. Aiden was positive that the insane young man hadn't even laid eyes on her that day.

But he wasn't a single step closer in knowing where else to look.

He cleared the first flight of stairs and halted at the landing, his phone buzzing in his suitcoat pocket. *Chris.* Aiden swiped with haste. "Parker?"

"I'm on the ground floor of the parking garage," Chris relayed through labored breath. "There are a few boxes of Baldwin's office crap down here. But no Baldwin. I rechecked the parking lots too. Her car isn't here, Agent Parrish."

"Call Mia. Have her meet you in the garage. I'm on my way as well." Aiden took the stairs two at a time, ending his call with Chris only to dial Sun.

"Yeah," came Sun's rude but expected greeting...especially for him.

"I want a trace on Dr. Trent's car navigational system *and* phone. Immediately." Another flight cleared. No pause on the landing.

"On it. She okay?" Sun's cold voice betrayed a hint of worry.

"I don't know. We can't find her." Aiden ended the call, slinging his phone back into his pocket and picking up speed.

Bursting through the ground floor door into the parking garage, his first observation was Mia's troubled countenance. The second was Chris's slumped posture, which communicated his bewilderment without a word.

They both turned toward him. Chris pointed to the trio of askew boxes. "Nothing of Autumn's. Just Baldwin's belongings."

Mia knelt down, scanning the contents. "She didn't leave anything behind in the doctor's office either. And no signs of a scuffle. Zilch."

Aiden turned the information, or lack thereof, over in his mind. The minutes were ticking by with expeditious efficiency.

"Dr. Baldwin wouldn't have just left his property here, right? He's a control freak. Even if he didn't want this stuff, he would have thrown away the contents or set them on fire or something." Mia's assessment was disturbingly astute.

Aiden turned in a circle, hoping some clue would jump out at him.

Where are you...where are you...where are you...

Aiden's phone vibrated against his side. He seized the device and hit the speakerphone as Sun's name lit up the screen. "Where is she?"

"I wish I could tell you. Both GPS systems have been disabled. No phone. No car." Sun shared the bad news with blunt flatness, but Aiden knew Agent Ming a bit too well. In the last five or so minutes, her worry had transformed into alarm.

Autumn could be labeled as "missing" now, at least unofficially. But her absence wasn't the issue so much as his growing conviction that she was in the presence of a humiliated and vindictive as well as equally vanished Dr. Philip Baldwin.

25

"You'll want to mind the speed limit, Raggedy Anne. Too fast, I shoot him. Too slow, I shoot him." I nudged the gun deeper into the back of the driver's seat.

The sweet little pistol had been waiting for this day. I'd purchased her within hours of learning that Colleen was gone.

Generally, I wasn't much of a gun man. I preferred to work with my hands. So far, they hadn't let me down. But I knew I'd need some assurance of cooperation when the right time came. Humans were wired to escape threatening situations. You could never let them forget who was in charge.

I was the alpha dog now. The reality of my success brought a smile to my face.

Sure, kidnapping two people at once was stressful. And no, this was not the original plan, or even the modified original plan.

But I could work with whatever I was given, and I had.

Philip Baldwin was originally supposed to…of his own accord, of course…travel to his countryside farmhouse outside of Richmond and "commit suicide." The poetic justice would have been beautiful, considering that he'd driven Colleen to do the same.

But hers had been real. She'd lost herself in a deep, black hole of misery and made the ultimate decision to end her own suffering. The piece of shit doctor shaking to hell in the trunk was to blame.

He was finally, *finally* going to pay.

"Albert..." the redhead started in again, "you can't possibly believe that you'll get away with this. You're smarter than that. The hospital is under intense scrutiny right now from law enforcement, the media, and even its own employees."

"I'm aware. And yet, here we are." My snarky reply was nearly a shout, and I hated raising my voice. My father had been a yeller. When he was around, anyway.

This Dr. Trent was an obstinate one. She liked to talk. She liked to talk *too much.*

"But they'll find us, Albert. You know they will. The FBI won't stop...certainly not now that you've taken one of their own." She lectured me as though I were a child.

That calm, slow bullshit might work great on all her wacko patients and three-year-olds, but I wasn't crazy. And no psychobabble, smooth-talk tactic was going to throw me off the path of vengeance.

An eye for an eye...

"Eyes on the road," I barked. "I'm *counting* on them finding you, Dr. Trent. You can be sure of that."

I didn't doubt that she gathered my meaning. She had a Ph.D. after all. Had to be a sharp one, this woman. Which was genuinely funny. Some might even say ironic. The beauty of the matter came down to this...all the brains in the world wouldn't save either of my highly educated traveling companions.

I snorted, enjoying how well my plan had worked. "For all

those damn badges, a pissant orderly like me was still able to get this far. Two dead women. Not a single glance my way. All eyes on that whimpering pussy back there."

I'd known Philip Baldwin was highly claustrophobic long ago. I knew a lot of things about that man. One of my first ideas had been to leave him to die in a box in the woods. Give him his worst nightmare experience, stretched out over four to five days of deadly dehydration.

But that wouldn't do, and I'd written off the scheme. I needed to behold Philip's suffering with my own eyes. And then I needed to *watch him die.*

I peeked through the hatch. If the doc didn't stop shaking soon, he might go into an actual convulsion of some sort.

That was fine. As long as it didn't kill him, what did I care? The good doctor could have a damn seizure extravaganza back there, and I'd just grab a bucket of popcorn and watch the show.

"In fact, good ole Phil made my job just about as easy as pie with his ridiculous decision to get rid of most of the cameras." I pounded a fist against the back seat. "I know *exactly* why you don't want anyone watching *you*, you sick son of a bitch."

The redhead glanced at me in the rearview mirror. Her eyes were green…*bright* green, and she was rather attractive in comparison to most of the females I worked with in that shithole hospital. Too attractive.

There were a lot of nutjobs packed into that building. A lot of sex-deprived lunatics, and most of them rapists. She would have been pounded by some crackpot's hungry ding-a-ling eventually, and I guessed, killed shortly after.

The same fate Evelyn Walker was headed toward…but for drastically different reasons.

Evelyn's face had resembled a waterlogged foot while the

little firecracker driving this car had one of the perkiest sets of tits I'd ever laid eyes on. I could almost guarantee she was on the unspoken "waiting to be jumped" list amongst the patients.

Some nutso would have gotten to her for sure. What a *waste*.

At least I was giving her life and death *meaning* before the crazies got their cocks into her and god knows what else.

She was lucking out, really.

"Why exactly does Dr. Baldwin hate video surveillance so much, Albert?" Was this woman unable to just shut the hell up?

I may have put the wrong person in the trunk.

"If you think I'm telling you anything, you're out of your damn mind. Spendin' too much time with the wackadoodles. That's what your problem is." I wasn't angry, and I still refused to yell. There was no call for bad manners, even now.

A lady was a lady.

She was quiet for a minute or two, but not nearly long enough. "Maybe you could at least tell me why you hate Philip so much? Did he do something to you in the past? I've heard he's hell to work for."

I resisted the urge to grab her hair and give that pretty little head a hard shake. I met her eyes in the rearview mirror, shooting her my fiercest stare. "I know what you're doing, and you'd be better off giving up now. Nothing you say, and nothing *I* say for that matter, will change the outcome for that asshole."

I didn't add "or for you." She was driving. I wanted her relaxed.

"He *is* an asshole, Albert." Those pretty greens reappeared in the rearview mirror. They seemed sincere. "I mean, everyone knew the rumors. But the very first conversation I had with him, if you could even call it a conversation, proved right away that the gossip was true. I can barely stand him either."

"Assholes are everywhere. You got one, and so do I. Doesn't mean we're bad people. But that guy…he's the *bad* type." Heat spread throughout my body as the rage kicked in. "Heartless. Sneaky."

"Don't worry. I'm not going to argue with that, Albert." She flashed me a small grin in the mirror, and I reminded myself that she was working me.

Even using my name over and over. Getting familiar. Creating a connection.

More psychobabble, in my humble opinion.

Refocused, I poked her seat hard with the pistol again. A sweet little reminder that we weren't friends. We were never going to be friends.

"Yet he's the rich guy. He's the successful one. He's the one still breathing in air through his damn lungs. That's how things work in this world, Dr. Trent. I've accepted that."

I was beginning to feel melancholy. Thoughts of Colleen were distracting.

"You've accepted what the world has done for him, but you can't accept what he did to you?" She posed a rather pertinent question.

"What he *took* from me, you mean…" I fought against the lump forming in my throat. Now wasn't the time for emotions, but how I missed my sweet Colleen. I could still imagine her happy, sparkly blue eyes and hear her high-pitched yet somehow never annoying laugh…

"Just try a sip, Al. Come on. Don't be a spoil sport." Colleen pushed her girlie, floofy-looking, whipped cream topped Frappu-whatever toward me.

"I don't even like coffee. You know that, Col. Why waste an

eighty-thousand-dollar beverage on your simpleton, backwoods brother?" I returned the drink back her way with a gentle nudge.

She found this hilarious, and her laugh carried through the entire outdoor seating area, attracting glances from a bunch of prissy college kids nursing their own too-fancy-to-spell lattes of choice.

I didn't know how she could stand being surrounded by all these arrogant, spoiled jerks...day in and day out...but she managed. Colleen was smart. So much smarter than the rest of our family.

She was special, and she was going places. She'd probably be laughing the whole time she spent getting to those destinations too. She'd always been so damn happy.

People just naturally flocked to her.

"Okay, okay." The blues turned serious, and she bit her lip. "So, I have to tell you something, but you promise me first that you won't say a word to Mom. Promise."

"Like I tell Mom anything, ever," I scoffed, making it clear that I was offended. "Gimme a break. I'm older, but I'm not that old. I promise. There. Now what?"

She grinned and leaned over the table a bit. "I'm dating someone."

I raised an eyebrow. Why would I give a crap? Colleen was always dating someone. Big whoop.

"And?" I waited, skeptical at best.

"He's one of my professors." She giggled and clapped a hand over her mouth.

I instantly didn't like the sound of this guy. I was almost positive that professors dating students was against some sort of oath or...whatever. And aside from the rule breaking, what kind of creep tried to date his students anyway?

"That sounds like a really bad idea." I didn't want to be too harsh. She was so damn giddy about the announcement. She must really like the dude.

"Well, duh," she returned, not offended in the slightest. "My best ideas are always bad ones. And he's only thirty-two, so stop worrying. He's not like grandpa old." Still with that giant smile.

I shook my head. "I would like to state, for the record, that I officially disapprove."

She laughed again. "I didn't exactly expect your applause, Al. I just wanted to tell you. It's exciting."

"He'll lose his job if the board finds out," I reminded her. I wasn't one-hundred-percent sure that this was true, but the notion sounded accurate.

"And then we'd be able to date openly. Win-win situation." She took a giant slurp of her Frappu-doo-dah-day and waved at some girls walking by.

I thought of our father...that giant piece of shit who'd left when we were tiny little kids. Colleen had been too little to truly understand that "Daddy" did that because most men were total and complete jerkwads.

They cared about their dicks and not much else. Dad left for another woman. He was okay with seeing his wife and children destroyed as long as his cock was happy.

This guy...this professor asshole. He probably wasn't much different.

I wanted to warn her and somehow convince her that she was being stupid. Make her realize the perv was taking advantage of her in a real creep-ass way, but I let the subject drop.

The worst that could happen to her was getting her heart broken, and that honestly might be the only way she'd ever learn to not do something this ridiculous again. Colleen had always let her feelings lead her around like a blind puppy.

At some point, she had to grow up.

But I was her big brother, not her parent and not her priest. She knew about tons of stupid stuff I'd done. Me giving a lecture would be laughable, if anything.

And besides...look at that smile. My sis was living her life and having some reckless, college-girl fun. As long as that smile stayed on her face, I was willing to look the other way.

"What did he take, Albert?" Dr. Trent's pleasant voice brought me back to the present.

I wasn't sure how long I'd been away with her...with my little sis.

The redhead doctor was still peering at me in the rearview, which I didn't appreciate. But she was also still driving on the ordered route and appeared cooperative and calm.

I probably had only been gone a second or so.

"He took—"

I attempted to speak, relieved as the fury began to cast its shadow over the sorrow. I'd allow myself time to mourn after. After I'd completed my task.

After I'd avenged my sister.

"He took...your job? Your money? What?" The lady doctor's voice wasn't soothing anymore. She was digging, digging, digging...

"He took *her!*" I hated myself instantly for yelling, but dear god. This woman wouldn't shut up.

I'd just begun to believe that maybe she'd finished pestering when she spoke again. "Colleen Hester."

My head whipped up. Had she just spoken my sister's name? Occasionally, I heard things that I later realized were only in my mind. Not often enough to think maybe there was something wrong in the ole noggin, but often enough to fog me up.

Surely, she hadn't said—

"Albert? Did you hear me? Does this have anything to do with Colleen Hester?"

She *did* know. These federal bastards had made the

connection, and they were *still* letting Philip Baldwin walk free.

I ground my teeth together, fighting the urge to grab Dr. Trent by the back of the neck. Instead, I leaned close enough that my breath moved the strands of her hair. "I think you mean Colleen *Rice* Hester…my sister."

26

P hilip tried desperately to slow his breathing.

Slow. Steady. In. Out.

As a physician, he knew he was experiencing a severe bout of claustrophobia, which he'd developed from classical conditioning. Or, more simply, childhood trauma.

As a human...as that traumatized child now living inside of a grown man's body, he only knew that breathing was becoming impossible. He was going to die in this trunk.

Trickles of sweat slid down his face in incessant rivulets. The jet-black was too much. The darkness swallowed him whole. Unforgiving. Never-ending.

Trunk. You're only in a trunk. Just a trunk.

But Philip wondered if this trunk would become his coffin. No one escaped coffins. They were sealed...buried... designed for the dead.

He wasn't coming back. He was going to die here.

Or maybe he'd passed over already. Maybe the trunk was long gone, and the afterlife was nothing but blackness and walls. Maybe not even death could free him from this suffocating, hellish nightmare.

"I'm going to be here forever..." he mumbled into the rough trunk carpet.

His perspiration now mingled with tears.

There were voices he recognized as Dr. Trent and the orderly who'd assaulted him. He was still in the land of the living, sporting an excruciating head wound. He may have a concussion, but that didn't matter while he was trapped in this vehicle with an obvious maniac.

And what were they saying? Trent was asking questions. God, how he hated that woman. But now she was his only companion, his only hope of getting away from the psychopath who'd nearly cracked his skull with his surprise attack.

A lightning bolt of pain shot through his temples. Had such a vicious strike been necessary? And why? He recognized the man as a hospital employee, an orderly. Albert.

And that was where his understanding stopped.

The panic tightened its savage grip. His head throbbed.

Did the dead have headaches? Would the pain be eternal as well as the darkness?

One of the trunk walls moved slightly, letting in a beam of beautiful light. Philip grasped at the blindingly bright opening with desperate madness, only to have his fingers slammed by a ruthless fist.

Albert...Albert...Albert wouldn't let him out of here.

Why?

"Al...bert! P-please! You have to let me..." The wall closed, cutting him off from the living once more. "*No*! Albert! *Let me out!*"

Neither of them was listening. Their muffled voices continued on, as though he wasn't even there. He wasn't real anymore.

I'm dead. I'm dead. I'm dead.

He couldn't remember how to breathe now. Out. All

oxygen was abandoning him, just going out and never returning.

The merciful light shone through a crack again, and he cried out with joy.

Not a coffin. This is not a coffin. You're in a trunk, Philip. The trunk of Dr. Trent's car.

"Why are you doing this to me?" The hysteria in his voice sounded foreign...wrong. Surely this was all happening to someone else.

"Why don't *you* think back a bit, Doc?" Albert barked through the crevice. "Think about your days in private practice, *long and hard*. See what you come up with."

Philip's head pulsed in agony, and the world went blurry for a moment.

Albert the orderly was angry...so angry. Because he'd done something...wrong...in private practice...?

Philip struggled to picture his old office. Light gray walls. Large windows. Plants. His patients liked the plants. They found them calming.

What did you do, Philip? What did you do to earn yourself this punishment?

"Tell me what I've done!" he shrieked at the hateful man. "*Tell me*! I'm sorry! *I'm sorry!*"

Someone was crying. Sobbing. Someone was in this trunk with him, wailing endlessly. He had to make them stop... hush...so he could think.

But the weeping emanated from *him*. And he'd done something bad.

What did you do to earn yourself this punishment, Philip?

"Wow. It's really that hard for you to remember, isn't it? Try a little longer, Phil. Think about everyone you've ever let down in your lifetime. Might take you awhile, considering the kind of man you are, but who's at the top of that list?" Albert slammed the hatch shut again.

Blackness. Back into the abyss...except the trunk had changed...morphed into a closet...

Coats crowded over his head, reminding him of crawling spiders and slithering snakes. He ran panicked hands through his hair to rid himself of the attacking creatures.

The closet smelled of sweaty shoes and soiled jackets. Just like a trash can. The closet was just like a trash can.

Daddy put you in the trash again.

"Let me out!" he screamed, hearing his father's imperious, raspy breathing on the other side of the door. "Please! I'm sorry!" Surely Daddy wouldn't leave him in here as long as last time. That had been the most terrifying twenty-four hours of his entire ten years of life.

"You should be sorry! And you're gonna be sorrier! You sit in there and think, boy! What did you do to earn yourself this punishment? What did you do, Philip?"

"I'm sooorrry! I'm sorry! Let me out! Let me out! Let me out!" His small fists pounded against the wood.

A much larger fist pounded back. "You settle down right now! You sit in there and think about what you did! What did you do to earn yourself this punishment?"

Philip stopped pounding, fearful of even worse repercussion. Instead, he wrapped his skinny arms around his knees and rocked.

This would be over soon. Daddy wouldn't keep him in here forever. He hadn't done anything that bad.

Had he?

He couldn't remember...couldn't think. He wanted out. He needed out.

What did you do to earn yourself this punishment, Philip...

The cool moisture slathered across his face brought him back to the present. How many times had he woken up in a cold sweat remembering his childhood episodes of discipline and penance?

But he wasn't in his bed. He was trapped inside this car.

And he was supposed to be remembering something from his days of private practice.

He'd had so many patients during that time. And right now…he couldn't think…needed air…

Philip's breathing escalated to hyperventilation. A panic attack was coming on like a tidal wave, drowning him in inky, murky waters and crushing his every cell.

"How much longer do I have to be in here? Let me out! You have to let me out!" His fists were numb from beating on the trunk so hard. "Aaaaahhhhh! *Aaaaaahhhhhh!*"

The slit of light unfurled once more, and Philip dove toward what might be his only escape from this hell of nothingness. He pushed his head into the opening, intending to crawl his way out regardless of Albert's orders.

He'd roll the dice on being shot.

The hard handle of the gun cracked against his skull, and pain forced him back into his hole. His vision blurred as he curled into a fetal position.

Dr. Trent screamed from the front seat. "Philip! Are you okay? Philip?" Her voice became a mumble as Albert closed the breach again.

But he had some company in the trunk now. The searing pain. He was going to blackout and not know what was happening, where they'd been taken, how this was all going to *end*.

And he was certain a terrible end was coming.

Think. Focus. Calm yourself.

Philip forced himself to concentrate on his time in private practice. So many faces and so much success…until the end.

That girl. The one who'd committed suicide. The one that prick Fed and the bitchy police chief had brought up just to throw him off-balance.

Hester.   Cally…no…Coreen…no…Colleen.   Colleen Hester.

Colleen had mentioned a devoted brother. She'd spoken of him often in sessions, in fact. They were very close.

Was this all about Colleen? Her suicide?

Philip froze, his trembling ceasing for the first time since he'd been stuffed into this cursed torture cell. Was this about her family? He knew some of her relatives had blamed him for her untimely passing. A few had been enraged when he was cleared of any involvement.

If that's what this was all about…some type of revenge plot or quest for retribution…chances were good that he was seriously, irreversibly screwed.

27

Autumn brought the Camry to a stop on the paved driveway of their final destination point. An isolated farmhouse sat erect before them. The house itself must have been very old, but judging from the fresh blue paint and the well-manicured lawn, great care had been taken to maintain the expensive home.

The lot of land was quite private and surrounded by dense forest. Autumn hadn't spotted a single neighboring house as they drove. The relief of the drive having ended flowed straight into the uncertainty of what lay ahead.

Okay, Albert. We're here. Now what?

She didn't have to wait long to find out. Albert opened the driver's side door, grabbed her arm, and yanked her from the vehicle. He popped the back open, giving Autumn full sight of Dr. Baldwin post trunk ride.

He looked a mess. Physically, but more so, emotionally. His hair was drenched in sweat, and Autumn suspected, tears. Green eyes surrounded by puffy, reddened skin stared up at her with horror and confusion.

Albert jerked Philip from the trunk with minimal effort and threw him down at her feet.

Her instant, instinctive move to try and help the doctor up was thwarted as Albert boomed, "Stay still or pay the price." Their abductor made a great show of stretching his legs, always with the gun trained on his pair of captives.

Autumn met Philip's eyes and mouthed, "Are you all right?" Baldwin closed his eyes and inhaled a series of deep breaths. He then managed to roll over and raise to his feet.

He opened his mouth to answer but clamped it shut as he started to look around. Wide eyes scanned the surrounding area for the first time. "This is *my* house!"

Autumn swung her head toward him in alarm. Albert had brought them to a house that Philip *owned*? While that explained the meticulous upkeep of the grounds, Autumn was at a loss as to what the purpose of coming here could be.

Philip's properties would be some of the first locations law enforcement checked. They weren't just *possibly* going to be found here. They *positively* would be discovered. And in the near future.

"I'm counting on them finding you, Dr. Trent."

But just what exactly would be left of them to find?

Albert snorted. "Recognize your own house and everything. Maybe you're not as dumb as I thought you were." He rammed the pistol into Philip's back and kicked the doctor's legs out from under him, laughing wickedly as the man fell into a pathetic heap. Again.

The orderly's strong hand clamped down on Autumn's shoulder. He gestured for her to walk toward the house. "Not you, Baldwin. You crawl on your hands and knees. Maybe I'll even let you make it past the doorstep."

Albert gave a kick to Philip's buttocks, garnering a yelp from the already battered doctor.

"Get going. You're leading the way." He pointed the pistol

at Autumn, guiding her forward with a death grip as they followed the full-grown doctor crawling like a baby toward his home.

Autumn pitied Philip, assuming his embarrassment, pain, and fear were most likely at all-time highs. Regardless of her personal feelings toward him, Dr. Philip Baldwin was a respected and accomplished man.

Or at least, he had been up until the murders at Virginia State Hospital.

She couldn't imagine that he'd ever been more humiliated in his lifetime.

But worse than the current degradation was the impending danger awaiting him. Awaiting both of them. Albert had a plan, the details of which remained unknown.

Autumn inspected the ground and the front porch ahead of them, searching for a weapon of some sort. A stick. A rock. A forgotten and conveniently placed snow shovel. Anything she could use to defend herself.

She didn't even have her purse with her. Albert had stowed the bag in the back seat with himself, along with her dead phone.

Her knowledge of Krav Maga could prove useful if Albert didn't have his heavy hand on her shoulder, fingers pinched down into her nerves, and a gun pointed directly her way. She'd never be able to strike him before he pulled the trigger.

Even on her best day, she wasn't faster than a bullet.

Staying calm was the only weapon she had left other than to keep Albert talking, as she'd attempted to do on the drive. But he was too preoccupied right now with his madman parade to hold an ongoing conversation.

He clearly had a terminus in mind for Philip and was going to see that he had the doctor in the exact place he wanted him.

Autumn assumed he'd already decided upon her fate as well.

Philip crawled up the porch steps of the farmhouse. Albert scrutinized the entire process before yanking Autumn up the stairs alongside himself. He pushed her against the house wall until her cheek and the front of her body were pressed against the wood, biting into her skin.

Had Albert formerly been in the military or a branch of law enforcement? The tactics he used to keep her under control were familiar. Her hopes sank lower as she realized the orderly might also be highly trained in some form of hand-to-hand combat.

Their chances of escaping were shrinking. Fast.

Stalling. She would have to stall this man as long as possible.

In all likelihood, the team had discovered they were missing by now. She'd been a no-show to her meeting with Justin without any warning or explanation, and her phone was off.

Her phone was *never* off. The career field she'd chosen to step into didn't allow for a moment of total peace. There was always a call coming, and she understood that.

If they attempted to track her car's GPS, they would know for certain something was amiss. And then what?

She attempted to view the situation from the other side. Philip was still the prime suspect for two murders. All the agents knew he had a special loathing for her.

The officer she'd relieved would have been forced to admit that he'd left the two of them alone in the administrative wing, and they would accurately assume that Dr. Baldwin and Dr. Trent had left the hospital together. Philip's boxes were in the parking garage, her car was gone while his would still be on the grounds somewhere.

They're going to think he did this. They'll believe that Baldwin has taken me hostage. Or worse.

The idea upset her at first, and then she played the situation out further. If they thought Philip had her, they would check his properties first. The team would take quick action.

Her colleagues…her friends…would be arriving at this farmhouse today.

Albert had made himself very clear that he *wanted* them to be found, though the condition in which they were to be discovered remained murky.

He wouldn't have kidnapped two individuals only for them to be found perfectly fine and undisturbed. The man wanted them to be found in a very specific way, and his devotion to this unknown yet detailed plan did not bode well for Philip nor herself.

Keys jingled as Albert reached around her to open the door. He swung the thick wood wide open with a small shove of his palm. She was next to be shoved, stumbling across the entryway floorboards.

"Sit," Albert ordered, pointing to the floor. Autumn obediently dropped. "Stay." This was delivered as a growling command, and she was tempted to bark in return.

Philip crawled in behind her, still in his stance of mortifying indignity. She began to examine him, wanting to ensure the man wasn't critically injured. He'd taken two blows to the head from the gun, and kicks to—

Albert booted Philip firmly in the gut. The doctor slammed backward onto the floor, moaning in agony as he rolled onto his side, struggling to breathe.

Autumn saw no blood on her fellow prisoner, but her fears were not allayed. His internal injuries could be extensive after so many vicious blows to his body. And she had a sad suspicion that Dr. Baldwin hadn't yet received his last beating.

They sat in an expansive foyer on beautifully maintained wood floors. White-washed shiplap walls showcased numerous framed scenes of the forest.

Autumn never would have guessed Philip to be an outdoorsman. Picturing him hiking through the woods in a bright puffer jacket softened the otherwise foreboding façade of the physician who was generally conjured up when Dr. Baldwin was mentioned.

"A man can be an asshole and still be a good person."

Aiden's comment came back to her, and she almost smiled, but couldn't. They'd shared that lunch only two days ago. There was a growing possibility that no more meals of any sort would be shared by her again.

Philip's broken gasps for air beside her were growing louder. He may very well have several broken ribs, and if even one of them punctured his lungs…

She had to get them out of here.

"Do you know how this man killed my sister, Dr. Trent?" Albert's voice was soft, almost like he'd done nothing more than ask about the weather. The voice didn't match his stormy expression, though. He stared at Philip, a mask of hatred and something else…sorrow maybe…freezing his features in a grimace.

She jerked her eyes away from Philip and met Albert's steady gaze. "No, I don't."

She didn't know if this was the "right" answer, but she'd spoken the truth.

Albert grinned at her. His eyes were mirthless and cold. *Haunted.* "Well, Pippi, you're about to find out."

28

Winter huffed and dropped her pen in defeat. She'd attempted to balance the damn thing on her stapler for at least the last twenty minutes.

She was barely cognizant of the fact that this was what she'd been "working" on. The universe was hazy right now. Muggy. Unsettling.

Yesterday had been an absolute shit show.

The visit with Justin had gone horribly wrong. And maybe she wasn't so upset by that as she was mad at herself for being *surprised* by the downturn of events. A visit to *anyone* in *any* maximum-security facility was bound to be a bumpy ride.

And she'd gone to see her serial killing, mentally ill little brother hoping for giggles and grins. Pathetic.

She wasn't as naïve as she'd been behaving. There was just that forever undying desire to somehow normalize and repair a situation that was completely beyond fixing. She couldn't just Pinterest some DIY method for making her brother not crazy.

There wasn't an app for that.

And Noah. He loved her and wanted to keep her safe. That was the bottom line.

Being around Justin wasn't safe for her or anyone else. Noah and Autumn had both attempted to tell and show her this.

Maybe she reacted so harshly to their sentiments because she already knew what they were saying was the truth.

The truth about Justin broke her heart.

Unless her Fairy Godmother dropped out of the actual sky, waved a sparkling wand, and bippity-boppity-booed her brother into a magically better person, Justin was likely never going to return from the world Douglas Kilroy had raised him in.

The outcome just wasn't possible. At least not now. Maybe not for many, many years.

Maybe never.

The truth was that "never" struck her as the actual answer. Deep down in that unyielding place where hope existed, she'd already suffered the pricks of that needle. Her dreams for Justin were bleeding out each and every day.

Hearing the words from Noah...from Autumn...from Aiden or *anyone* else, turned the needles to knives and the pricks to stab wounds.

And even when no one said anything, even when they let the matter go, their eyes continued to express the same conclusion.

Her brother was dangerous. Visiting him was dangerous. If she wanted to see him, talk to him, connect with him, he should really be shackled.

But she knew demanding the cuffing would erase any attempts her brother made to behave, to be pleasant, to not be the monster he actually was. Binding him was essentially acknowledging the beast he'd become.

He'd stop with the deception and manipulation because

he'd realize that she saw him. *Really saw him.* If she kept pretending that he could recover, he'd keep pretending to *be recovering.*

Lies upon lies...just to have a few false moments of softness and peace with her baby brother.

That was the game they'd been playing. Every last second of their "happy visits" together was an illusion.

But that illusion was all she had.

Unfair. Unfair!

Winter propped her elbows on her desktop and rested her head in her hands.

She pictured the cuddly little boy with a lisp. That little boy had been headed toward being a fine young man, and then an actual man, a husband, father, grandfather, great-grandfather...

He'd been just as intelligent then as he was now. He'd loved building things with Legos and blocks. He'd loved showing his sissy how to recreate what he had made even more. He might have become an architect. A teacher.

Maybe he would have coached his own kid's soccer team. He would have laughed and yelled and cheered at the sidelines. Maybe she would have been sitting in the bleachers with all the other families, rooting on her nephew...or niece...or both.

You're torturing yourself. You have to stop. You have to let go.

The thoughts made her clutch the precious illusion tighter.

She knew a day would come when she was no longer able to even conjure up the fantasies. In fact, she felt that day approaching much faster with every passing week.

Winter was too level-headed, too logical to keep the wishing well operating forever.

Kilroy had pointed his evil, demented finger in Justin's direction and forever changed the life of an innocent child.

He'd stripped away all the good and pure inside of Justin and filled the holes with hate and vengeance. Simply because that was what Douglas had decided to do.

If there was any magic to Justin's story at all, it was of the dark sort. Kilroy and his evil, spell-casting wand.

Even in death, the perverted, deranged old man remained victorious.

He still had Justin. He didn't even have to be alive anymore to own her brother.

Winter felt the old, familiar hatred, hot as fire, stirring in her stomach.

The wrong couldn't be righted. Justice would never prevail. Not for her, and certainly not for her brother.

Justin's malign voice rang in her ears. She'd tried to bury the words...the horrible words he'd whispered to her just yesterday. But they were alive and well. They were loud.

"Grandpa had a hard-on for you, big sister. I do too."

If she hadn't pulled away, or more accurately, been *released* by Noah, she knew the threat Justin would have added. Or, more aptly, the promise that would have passed his deranged lips.

Winter knew what her brother was.

All this morbid ruminating was making her nauseated. She'd go to the breakroom. Eat some crackers. Maybe even visit Sun's desk and let Agent Ming's snark snap her out of this heavy trance.

As she straightened at her desk and prepared to do just that, she caught sight of Noah from the corner of her eye. She was happy to see him. Happy to see anyone right now that—

Something was wrong. Noah's expression was grim. No. Worse than grim. He was upset. Distressed.

Without greeting her at all, he set his phone down on her

desk. "Repeat what you just told me for Winter," he ordered the person on the call.

He can't even look me in the eyes right now...

Aiden's voice boomed across the speakerphone. "Autumn went to the hospital to meet with Justin this morning, but she didn't show. She detoured to Dr. Baldwin's office and was left alone with him by one of Chief Lewton's officers."

Sheer panic froze Winter to her chair.

"Now they're both missing. Baldwin's car is still at the hospital, but Autumn's is gone. Her GPS is off...phone *and* car. They're not at their residences...his nor hers. No one can reach either of them." Aiden recited the details with flat flawlessness, but Winter knew he must be a total train wreck on the inside.

Autumn was one of their own. Autumn was more than that. She was their friend. And for Aiden...she was something not quite articulated as of yet.

"Do you believe this to be some type of plot to exact his revenge? Autumn said she clashed heads with Baldwin pretty severely." Winter poured over the memories of her last conversation with Autumn.

Was that *the* last conversation?

I was an asshole. I was such an asshole. Now, she's gone. Now, she might never come back.

Winter couldn't stand the thought. No more losing people. Screw that.

She stood and gathered a few belongings as Aiden continued to speak. "Traffic cameras caught a few glimpses of her Camry. They went northwest. I believe they may have left the city entirely."

This information made the situation even more dire. The countryside didn't have cameras, or even always have people who might have seen something. Anything.

"Head west on 1-95. We'll be meeting somewhere along

that route. I'll inform you as soon as I know more." Aiden ended the call.

Winter and Noah ran through the halls of the Richmond Field Office, heading straight for the exit. They were buckled in and speeding down the highway in less than five minutes.

"God, I hope he hasn't hurt her." Noah's knuckles were white from gripping the steering wheel.

Winter refused to follow that path of thought. She couldn't break down right now. She had to save her friend.

"I just want to be positive she's *safe*," Noah sputtered in frustration. "Dammit all to hell. That's all I want for you too."

Winter and Noah exchanged a swift glance.

She knew what he was hinting at, and she refused to go there, either. She patted his arm, attempting to share the reassurance she was in need of herself. "Keep driving, Dalton."

The truth was that none of them were ever one-hundred-percent safe. Working for the FBI came with the obvious side effect of being placed in near constant danger. The majority of times, the team barreled through cases unscathed.

But not every time.

29

The smooth hardwood floor of Dr. Baldwin's rural Virginia farmhouse foyer provided no cushion from the blows Albert seemed so eager to inflict. Autumn had gathered that the orderly, pacing before them and seething with contempt, desired some type of penance from the doctor.

But she wasn't convinced her co-captive had the where-withal in his current condition to comply.

Philip moved his lips but struggled to speak. Autumn feared the punishment he would incur if he didn't manage to articulate something. Anything.

Albert gave a sudden, vicious kick to Dr. Baldwin's shins. "You know what you did to her! Say it! Say what you did, you bastard!"

Autumn had to take some control of this situation before Philip was kicked to death. He'd curled into a shrimp-like position on the foyer floor, his breathing deteriorating into frantic, hiccuping gulps. With less than ten feet between them, she was a clear witness of Dr. Baldwin's worrisome condition.

"Tell me why you're so angry, Albert." She couldn't keep the begging from her tone. "What did he do to her?"

Albert flashed her a hateful glare. "You are here to listen. You are not here to analyze, Doctor. Do you understand?"

"I *do* understand, Albert. But I just have so many questions. I want to know what he did to you. What he *took* from you."

The sneering orderly considered her for a moment. "Okay. Why not?" He paced the floor, the gun ever ready in his tightened fist. "Once upon a time, there was a doctor named Philip. Philip was a giant piece of shit."

Autumn swallowed, knowing she had given them a temporary reprieve by hooking Albert in. The orderly wanted his story told, and his desperate need to share Dr. Baldwin's wrongdoings would buy them some time. Not much, but every second counted.

The team would be coming. She only had to keep them alive until then.

"I took the task upon myself to punish the doctor for his evils. Of course, one would hope that justice would prevail through the *mighty* arm of the law. But, Dr. Trent, I can assure you, the legal system failed in an atrocious manner." He stood still for a moment, pointing the gun straight at her.

I'm a part of the system he believes to have inadequately handled Colleen's suicide. He resents me for being "one of them."

"Dr. Baldwin's former assistant, Mildred Harbison, was my first attempt to start a *very obvious* breadcrumb trail toward this murderous bastard over here." Albert turned the pistol toward Philip.

Autumn thought their abductor might go through with shooting him just to increase the doctor's suffering as they awaited the final steps of Albert's plan. But he didn't. She speculated that he either wanted or needed Philip alive. The chance of a gunshot wound causing Baldwin to bleed out was apparently not a gamble Albert was willing to take.

"Now, I should admit that killing a sixty-two-year-old woman was not the most pleasant undertaking of my life. But if anyone knew what happened in that damn office, Mildred was the lady. Switching her medications around was child's play, and her sudden passing should have made the authorities check into the good doctor a bit deeper. *Should* have."

Albert knelt in front of Philip, who still lay on the hardwood floor emitting a terrible, consistent wheezing.

"How do you feel about that, Dr. Baldwin? How do you feel about being responsible for an old woman's death? Mildred was a sweet lady with a lot to live for. Retirement. Grandkids…I think she had *eleven*, but my research on the old bat is a bit fuzzy at this point." He tapped his temple with the gun.

Autumn needed to regain his attention.

"I suppose you have a lot to keep track of." She shared her observation with a cautious, judgment-free air. "You've been a very busy man."

She was aware that her words could cause him to snap and kill both of his captives in a hot second. But an ongoing dialogue was also capable of sending Albert into a state of confusion. In her professional experience, confused criminals lost the ability for deft operation.

"I wouldn't have to be so 'busy' if people like you were competent enough to do your damn jobs," Albert growled. "I've been 'busy' doing what everyone else *refused* to do. I'm *making* justice happen. *Forcing* you people to honor integrity."

"How was Evelyn Walker a part of that, Albert?" Autumn cocked her head as though she reveled in the details of this killer's "integrity honoring" actions. "What made you choose that particular nurse at the hospital?"

Albert looked pleased, almost agreeable and happy to elaborate upon his deeds. "Evelyn and Baldwin clashed. Damn near seemed to hate each other. Right, Phil?" He prodded Philip's leg with his boot. "Enemies aren't so bad until they drop dead and *everyone* points your way."

Philip moaned, and Albert let out a small chortle.

"And Paula Wingfield...?" Autumn led the orderly back to his story, hoping to spare Philip from another kick to the gut.

"Good ole Paula came across the audio of Baldwin's last 'chat' with Evelyn, and she stole that tape to use to her own advantage. That's a rather horribly selfish thing to do when an innocent woman's murder is under investigation. The authorities needed that tape, dammit. Very unladylike of her." Albert's face contorted with disgust.

Despite her current situation, Autumn was fascinated by how this man's mind worked. It would serve her well when she dealt with murderous revenge killers in the future.

If she had a future.

She shook away that thought and gazed up at the bald man with every ounce of sympathy she could muster. "So, Paula wasn't an original part of your plan, but she got in the way. She was really just a greedy woman, anyway. Am I following along well enough, Albert?"

"Getting in my way is a *big* mistake," he replied, pointing the gun toward Autumn with a menacing frown.

Oh shit.

Had she "interfered" with Albert's objective by being the unfortunate occupant of that elevator car when Evelyn fell through? Was she another human who had "wronged" him in an unforgiveable manner?

"I made Paula's little faux pas work for me. Planting that tape in her locker *had* to add some heat to Baldwin's 'guilty as shit' fire. I was sure of that. And I was right. Your people swarmed him like killer bees." Albert smiled, but the duration was brief. His eyes were rageful as he shouted at Autumn, "But that still wasn't good enough for you assholes!"

Autumn trembled but managed to maintain a cool demeanor.

Albert slapped a hand to his forehead. "I'm sorry. I didn't mean to raise my voice. I don't like yelling."

The sincerity of his apology struck Autumn's empathetic heart. Maybe Albert was an angry, revenge-seeking killing machine *now*, but at some point, Autumn guessed he'd been a young boy who was frequently the recipient of such brutally vocal attacks.

"No worries, Albert. We all get a little upset sometimes, and you have more than enough reason to be unhappy right now," Autumn assured him with light, soothing tones. "Were you not pleased that Philip lost his job? Or how about that walk of shame from the hospital to the cop car the news keeps replaying?"

Albert tapped the barrel of the gun against his temple. "That was great, but not enough. They *let him go*. Free as a damn bird. He deserves a *far* more brutal punishment for what he did."

Philip hadn't said so much as a word during Albert's soliloquy thus far. The doctor's intermittent groans and gasps were the sole reassurance that he was still alive at all.

"I roll with the punches, though. That's just the type of man I am, Dr. Trent. I finally understood the fact that *no one* would *ever* make Baldwin pay for his crimes." Albert stared at Philip with distant, disassociated fervor. "So, I decided to kill him…after making him suffer."

He stayed silent long enough for Autumn to speculate that he'd lost his train of thought and perhaps his grip on his surroundings.

Where did you go, Albert? What are you seeing right now?

"I *was* going to engineer the grand spectacle of Philip Baldwin's suicide. How perfect would that be? I mean, that ending is practically the textbook definition of poetic justice. But you," he focused in on Autumn again, "keep stepping into places you shouldn't. Have you always been such a pain in the ass, Dr. Trent?"

The comment would have been humorous under different circumstances, but in this moment, with Albert's straight-faced stare trained on her, not to mention the gun he held, Autumn failed to appreciate the satire.

"I suppose that depends on who you ask. I want you to know that I never meant to interfere with your plans. I'm sure you've invested a lot of time and energy into your quest for justice." She gathered from the orderly's stone-cold façade that he neither wanted nor cared about her contrition.

He began pacing again, though his gaze and gun remained trained on her. "I have a *new* plan now, and you're a big part of it, Dr. Trent. There wouldn't be any fairness in punishing Paula's meddling yet letting *you* off scot-free. I'd be just as useless as every last one of your colleagues if I let your crimes slide." He took a few steps her way. "I don't forget when someone crosses me…not ever."

Icy trepidation trickled through Autumn's veins as she determined that Albert had no intention of letting her leave this house alive.

"Of course you don't, Albert," Autumn declared, earnest conviction alive in each word. "And you shouldn't. I know why you want Philip to suffer. I know what he did to start this entire mess."

Albert's jaw clenched. His anger was escalating, which meant her time, as well as Philip's, was dwindling.

"I've been searching into Dr. Baldwin's past," she continued. "I know he worked with a young woman who was trying to come to terms with the ending of her relationship with her professor. The professor died in a car crash, and she was ruined. Heartbroken and destroyed. Philip was *supposed* to help her, but he failed."

Autumn held her breath, unsure of Albert's response to such a triggering conversation. The orderly's entire body tensed as his attention returned to the psychiatrist.

"Yes," he agreed, "he failed my sister. He failed Colleen. But what's worse, Dr. Trent, is that he took advantage of her while she was grief-stricken and weak."

This was news to Autumn. She knew Philip hadn't killed anyone. She also was all too familiar with the fact that treating suicidal patients was a tricky and sometimes devastating task. When an individual was to the point of being ready to take their own life, they'd usually gone over "the list of reasons not to" already.

The decision had been made in their mind, and their healthcare provider was left with the daunting task of breaking down brick walls with a butter knife. A crack had to be made in the foundation of their logic.

But one wrong move and the intended crack became a hungry ravine that swallowed the lost soul whole.

Had Philip been that ravine? Had he pushed Colleen toward her fate by somehow taking advantage of her fragile state?

"How do you know this, Albert? Did Colleen tell you she was involved with Dr. Baldwin?" Autumn wasn't just stalling now. She wanted to know the truth. Philip wasn't a murderer, but that didn't rule out the possibility that his deplorable nature had led him down a very improper path where a young impressionable woman was concerned.

"I've viewed the video footage. Phil used to have the cameras rolling all day long with his patients. But times have changed, huh, buddy?" Albert smiled down at Philip, his creepy calm demeanor disturbing. In his own way, *he* was suicidal.

He'd made up his mind to take actions that would destroy, if not end, his life. Autumn had no doubt that he'd meticulously browsed his "why I shouldn't do this" list long ago.

"What's so strange and convenient to a simple guy like me, is how that video of you and Colleen had no audio. *None*." Albert spat the words at Philip.

Autumn tried to sort through the slivers of information she'd been granted in the last two minutes. There was a video of Dr. Baldwin and Colleen that showed inappropriate interaction? Even without audio, the footage would have been enough for Baldwin to lose his license to practice had actual inappropriate actions been recorded.

Which meant Albert was misreading the situation somehow. Or, the possibility existed, that Colleen had misinterpreted some aspect of her time spent in Philip's office.

"The microphone was accidentally muted," Philip interjected for the first time, his voice like gravel coming from his throat. "And yes, it *was* an accident. I would give anything, *do anything*, to go back in time and unmute that mic. I never was inappropriate with Colleen. Not once!"

Albert seemed to grow taller and wider, his anger building him up in every direction. "Why would I believe you? There isn't one good reason! Do you know that my mother drank herself to death after Colleen died? She'd drink until she blacked out every single night and start drinking the *second* she woke up the next morning." Fury like she'd never witnessed seeped from Albert's every pore. "Except for the last morning when she didn't wake up at all!"

Autumn watched helplessly as Philip tried to prop himself up and speak in his defense. "Albert, I am sorry for your loss. Both of th—"

Their captor kicked Dr. Baldwin with such force that the already weakened man rolled over twice, crying out in pain as he flailed.

"I don't want your pity! I want you to pay! You're going to pay!" Albert stepped forward and gave yet another vicious kick to Philip's body. He raised a foot to strike again—

"Stop!" Autumn screamed. "Is this what your sister would want for you? Would Colleen want you to just throw your life away?"

The orderly's foot lowered, and he turned toward Autumn with a vacant sneer. "That's the funny thing, Doc." His face softened and his lip trembled for a split-second before returning to its glacier-like mask of hate. "I don't have a life without my sister and mother. They were everything. Everything that mattered."

Autumn pictured Albert smiling, walking down the street with his sister and mom. She thought of how scared he must have been when Colleen dove deep into her depression.

If one thing had gone differently...just one. Albert wouldn't be this monster so hellbent on revenge. He'd just be a normal guy who loved his family. Just. One. Thing.

Sarah's sweet little face resurfaced from the depths of her mind, as she often did. She had to help her sister. She had to find her. *Really* find her. Save her.

But the way things were going, she'd never get that chance. She was going to die here on the floor instead. Punished by a madman whose fury was fueled by the devoted love he held for his little sister.

Albert lost Colleen. But I'm not going to lose Sarah.

"You matter, Albert," she told him, swallowing hard. Genuine emotion burned through her sinuses and into her eyes.

Someone needed to tell this man that his life was important too. Maybe he would hear it. And maybe it would cause him to pause before he continued with the execution of his plan.

He closed his eyes and ground his teeth together. "No. I don't. I need to end this now so I can find peace. Justice for Colleen is all that matters." He pulled a plastic bag from his pocket and opened his eyes. Not a trace of softness remained.

He stepped toward her, and Autumn instinctively backed away on the floor. "Albert…" She tried to regain his attention but comprehended how futile the effort was. Albert was lost in his fogged-up haze of hateful determination.

He grinned. "I'm going to do better this time. I'll create a killing where there is *no* question or doubt as to whodunit."

Panic nearly closed her throat, but she managed a whispered, "Albert…"

"You're going to die here, Dr. Trent." He smoothed the plastic bag between his fingers. "Right in Baldwin's house."

A tear escaped as he grew closer…closer… "Please…"

"He won't be able to wiggle his way out of this one, slithery snake that he is. He'll be found guilty of murder, and justice will *finally* be served."

A iden wasn't often in the passenger seat, and this trip was reminding him why. When he had such limited information to act upon, driving was a somewhat adequate way to channel the adrenaline built up inside of him.

Somewhat.

But now, one of their own was missing. And not just a random agent at the Bureau.

Autumn.

The team was on a hot chase to nowhere thus far, following an approximate compass which provided little by way of guidance or insight. Dr. Trent's Camry had headed northwest, according to traffic cameras. They could follow the direction on the interstate, but the destination point would become necessary quite soon.

And the cherry on top of it all was that Chief Lewton was in the driver's seat, rendering him worthless. Or so he felt.

"You're worried," Adrienne observed, her eyes never leaving the road.

Aiden held in a sigh. "One of my colleagues is missing, as

is our prime suspect for the hospital murders. I suppose being worried goes with the territory."

"Of course." Adrienne went quiet.

Aiden assumed with mistaken relief that her observations were over.

"Dr. Trent is your friend as well as your colleague, correct?" Chief Lewton's tone said "nonchalant," but her question screamed "curious as hell."

Aiden hesitated. Adrienne was a police chief. Nosiness was a part of her job, and he assumed, a part of her nature as well. She more than likely meant no harm, but he wasn't about to divulge any deep, dark, or riveting information to a human he'd met less than a week ago.

"Yes, she's my friend as well," he offered with monotone indifference.

A side-glance at Adrienne caught her doing the same at him. He knew the chief wanted more, or believed herself to sense more, perhaps. But he suspected that she'd accepted there was nothing else coming.

Not from his lips, anyway.

"You know," Adrienne picked up the proverbial talking stick, "when I was in the police academy, I had on this *huge* pair of rose-colored glasses. Not real ones, you know, figurative. I was certain...no, *hellbent*...that I was going to have it all. The dream, you know?"

Aiden wasn't in the mood for story time, but anything that made the minutes pass faster couldn't be so bad. "I can't say that I do know, Chief. Lots of different versions of 'the dream' out there."

Adrienne grinned. "I get what you're saying, but I think you understand what I'm referring to as well. *The dream.* A career, a partner, kids, the white picket fence. Two cats, one dog...or something like that. Maybe a goldfish. And *brilliant* success in everything you do."

"And? How did that work out for you, Chief Lewton?" His necktie had grown uncomfortably tight and the air in the car was beyond warm.

"Ha. Didn't work out for me at all. Mostly because I paid attention. I saw what happened to my colleagues…their marriages. Law enforcement wasn't really made to coddle the family life, you know?"

He knew.

"So, you abandoned the dream?" Aiden despised small talk, but this conversation was of an even worse type. He could detect that Adrienne was getting to a specific point, and he had the underlying suspicion that whatever she said would not sit well with him.

Not that she would ever deduce exactly what his internal response was to anything. No one was ever quite sure what he was thinking, unless he spoke the words out loud. And even then, he seldom infused his statements with even a hint of emotion.

The only exception to that rule was an occasional slip when speaking to—

"I did abandon the dream. But not because I was scared of divorce or not giving my kids enough love or yada yada yada. I was pretty positive that I could control all that. Keep my ducks in a row. There was a different reason." Adrienne's grin had vanished, and Aiden regarded her with great caution from the passenger's seat.

"I guess you're wanting to tell me what that reason is," he conceded.

"I love that you say what you mean, Agent Parrish. You don't ask what the reason is, because you'd rather we weren't having this discussion to begin with. You 'allow' that I *want* to tell you. And somehow without a hint of condescension. Well done." She let out a short chortle.

Anywhere else. He'd rather be anywhere else right now.

"Okay, okay," Adrienne gave his arm a sympathetic pat. "I'll put you out of your misery. I was only going to tell you that within the first two years of being 'on the job,' two of my fellow officers were shot dead. Separate instances."

Quiet anger crawled up Aiden's spine. Why? Why did he need to be told this right now? Why had he let her prattle on in the first place?

"They both had kids. One of them even had the wife and the fence and whatnot…had *the dream*. At their funerals, I saw those little mini-me versions of their dead parents attempting to stand tall throughout the procession. Not a single one of them was even ten years old, but they were all trying *so hard* to behave honorably." Adrienne swallowed, more than likely seeing those young faces again.

"And thus, you decided you didn't want a family anymore?" If that was what this whole conversation had been about, Adrienne was a horrible storyteller.

Predictable.

"Nope. I do want a family. I'll always want a family. But I decided no kid deserved that. Or at least, that I didn't want to be the reason a six-year-old was standing in the cold rain saluting like a tiny little soldier while my dead body got carted by."

Aiden nodded, relieved to find her point had been so elemental. "Understandable. I think that's a common fear amongst professionals in our field."

"That's the problem, Aiden. Loss is a common fear amongst the entire human race. We think we're a different breed because we carry a gun and deal with criminals, but we're not. Cops and Feds are humans, and humans die all the time." Adrienne leaned back against the headrest, her fatigue betraying her.

The subject matter was morbid. Depressing. And quite frankly, talking about death in this moment when they were on the precipice of losing Autumn forever was too much. Adrienne must know better. Why would she bring up—

"No one escapes the betrayal of death, Agent Parrish. It's the ultimate 'Dear John' letter. That sucker is written and sealed the same day we're born…"

Adrienne trailed off for a moment, and Aiden wasn't sure how much more "small talk" he could digest. He was exhausted, and there had been no update, no breaking lead regarding Autumn. How long could they drive on this damn highway before admitting to having no idea as to where they were going?

"So, you're telling me I need to fall in love and have two point five children in the suburbs because I'm human?" Aiden wanted to lighten the conversation, although there was no real reason for doing so. They were just talking about life. Loss.

He was no stranger to loss.

"I'm telling you that if the thought of someone dying has the potential to bring you to your knees, it's okay. You can admit that you've allowed yourself to care, or rather, your humanity allowed the sentiment for you. And cop or Fed or accountant or bartender…doesn't matter. You're a human who is being the only thing he can be. A human."

"I exist therefore I am, eh Chief Lewton?" Aiden's jaw flexed as he stared at the passing countryside.

Adrienne adjusted her grip on the steering wheel. "Something like that."

"Well, as you can see, I'm not on my knees," Aiden quipped, his intended humor failing to release from his tight-set mouth.

Where are you? Where are you? Where are you?

Adrienne shook her head, a sad smile playing at her lips. "Yes, you are."

His iPad dinged, alerting him to an incoming email from

Sun, which he opened with unspeakable relief. The email contained a short video attachment with no audio. He pressed play.

"What is it?" Chief Lewton leaned his way, trying to get a glimpse of the footage while keeping an eye on the road.

"I'm not sure yet." Aiden studied the silent scene playing out before him and reran the feed again to make sure he had missed nothing.

Philip stood in the office of his former private practice and embraced an attractive young female patient in what appeared to be an innocent, straightforward hug. He quickly pushed the woman away, however, his expression stern and alarmed. Baldwin held up his hands, as if to deter all possible attempts at further physical contact, and she ran from his office in tears.

There was no way to know what had been said to cause the doctor's abrupt rebuff toward his patient. His actions, however, weren't criminal. Hugging a patient hadn't been a wise decision, given his field, but that seemed to be where the ill-advised conduct stopped.

Aiden grabbed his phone to call Sun. She answered after one ring.

"What's the story behind the footage?" He was relying on Sun right now, and despite their bumpy history, Agent Ming most always went into a mode of professional courteousness when the stakes were high.

"I've been helping Autumn dig into Baldwin's past. You just watched footage from a session—the *last* session that Philip had with Colleen Hester. No audio available, and she committed suicide not long after." Sun's rapid computer-key taps never ceased as she spoke.

"Okay." Aiden replayed the video for the third time. "What am I missing? We knew about Colleen. How does she connect to Evelyn and Paula?"

"Colleen Hester's full name is Colleen *Rice* Hester," Sun shared.

Aiden recognized the surname in an instant. Why was "Rice" so familiar...? His body tensed as the connection hit him. A man with a shaved head, muscular, appeared to be mid-thirties. "Rice. Wasn't that the last name of the orderly who helped Autumn out of the elevator she was trapped in with Evelyn Walker's body?"

"That is *exactly* the point. They're related. Albert Rice, employed by Virginia State Hospital, is the late Colleen Rice Hester's *brother*. There's your connection to Baldwin," Sun confirmed in triumph.

"Connection...and I'm assuming some bad blood as well. Pull up and text me any addresses linked to Philip Baldwin that correlate with the northwest direction of Autumn's Camry. He's a wealthy doctor. There's a good chance he has other properties aside from his city townhouse."

"I'm already on it. I'm also running everything I can find on Albert Rice or any of his relatives."

"Let me know what you find." Aiden ended the call and was preparing to relay the new information to a very eager Chief Lewton when he received Sun's text.

She'd already found the location of Baldwin's countryside farmhouse outside of Richmond.

Aiden entered the address into the car's GPS, his heart pounding.

"We may have found them. Hit the gas, Chief." He sank back against the headrest, relief and dread competing for his attention.

The team had needed this break. There was now at least a fighting chance of pulling Autumn out of harm's way before...

Aiden dug his fingers into the arm rest, not wanting to finish the thought.

But denying reality was ridiculous, and he'd never been good at doing so anyway.

There was a very existent possibility that when they discovered Autumn...*if* they discovered Autumn...she would be cold, still, and silent. Dead.

He shook his head, refusing to hold on to the image. Nothing was over yet. No final conclusion.

He was going to find Autumn Trent alive, and every other possibility could go to hell.

31

I'd been around enough doctors to know that having a second residence wasn't abnormal in the world where people hung fancy doctorate degrees on their walls. This fact had always been a bit obnoxious. Nobody needed two houses. That money could be put toward so many greater, unselfish causes.

But Baldwin having such a fine establishment on top of his expensive city townhome struck me as a direct, personal insult. Knowing he luxuriated in such wealth incited even more fury inside my every cell. It wasn't fair. In fact, it was both unfair and ridiculous the way life often played out.

My sweet sister was dead. She didn't even have her own existence anymore. But ole Phil had his health, a thriving career—up until a couple of days ago—*and* an extra house.

Sure. Why not.

Securing the gun in my shooting hand, I'd dragged a heavy, well-made dining room chair into the entryway and directed Dr. Trent to get up off the floor and sit. The grandeur of Baldwin's furnishings, what little I had seen of them, only fueled my dedication to exact justice for Colleen.

This. Man. Had. To. Suffer.

"All signs will point to Philip."

I smiled, patiently securing thick zip ties around the redhead's hands. I used two of them, knowing exactly how to bracelet them in a way that was near impossible to escape from, especially with her hands behind her back. "All roads will lead to him. I'd wager that even the great Dr. Baldwin, despite his remarkable skills of evasion, won't be able to talk his way out of the dead body strapped to a chair in his own house's foyer."

I'd practiced this method hundreds of times, one-handed. Just as I'd known the pistol would be necessary for cooperation purposes, I'd figured mastering the art of bondage could be just as vital.

Carrying a hand full of the plastic ties around in my coat pocket had been one of the easiest precautions I ever could have taken. And now, my foresight was paying off.

Dr. Trent wasn't going to fight or escape. Not with her hands stuck behind her back and my pistol aimed at her pretty red head. She would sit in that chair and behave like a good little girl. Good little girls didn't get shot.

However, I had no desire to actually shoot her—that wasn't how I meant for her to die. I prayed that she didn't force such an ending. My intentions were quite different.

There was a better way.

Her death needed to make a statement and remind the bastard psychiatrist of the hell he'd sunk my sister into. If he didn't already have nightmares about Colleen's last few moments of life, he was certain to experience some subconscious terrors after witnessing Dr. Trent die right in front of him.

I was used to death by now. Philip wasn't. He was only accustomed to lying.

He was about to witness a truth that would never leave him. Every hour he sat alone and ruined inside a prison cell, rotting away like the disgusting, disposable piece of shit that he was, he would be haunted by this day. Tortured by this murder.

And in doing so, he would remember Colleen.

I finished binding the lady doctor and decided to explain my method, so she could at least know what to expect. I was hopeful that she'd appreciate how her murder could be much worse and show gratitude for the fate soon to befall her.

"I'm sure, Dr. Trent," I said, kneeling in front of her, "that in your line of work, you're familiar with suicide bags."

Her emerald eyes focused on the plastic bag once again in my hand, her expression amazingly calm. "I am. They're marketed as a peaceful way to take one's own life. Generally, a large plastic bag with a drawstring, most often used in conjunction with a tank of helium connected to a gas valve. Does that sound about right?"

I turned the bag around in my hands, folding and flexing the smooth, cold plastic. "Flicks the lights off pretty quick, in most cases. I figured you'd know all about them."

"Of course." She licked her lips and frowned, but not out of fear. Her expression appeared to be complete sympathy. "Is that how Colleen died, Albert? She ordered a suicide bag?"

"I have to tell you something, but you promise me first that you won't say a word to Mom."

I should have said more than "a word" to our mother. I knew that then, but I knew it now in a way that hollowed out my insides and made me want to die. And in fact, maybe I would after Dr. Baldwin was locked away. My job would be done, and I didn't want to be here anymore. I didn't want to be *alone* anymore.

If I had told my mother about Colleen's fraternization with her professor, come hell or high water, she would have put an end to the situation. She would have pulled Colleen's tuition before she let something scandalous like that happen to her daughter.

The ill-fated pair would have broken up. Colleen would barely remember the professor by the time his fatal car accident happened. She may have retained a distant fondness for the man and experienced a bit of sadness. But her spiral would not have imploded in the extreme way that it had when everything played out in real time.

She still would have been Colleen.

There wouldn't have been any dark cloud surrounding her, consuming her, making her impossible to reach. Her smile wouldn't have disappeared. Her eyes would still sparkle.

None of us would have even known that she was *capable* of falling into that endless black void.

I should have said a lot of words to our mother.

But I hadn't, and there was only one way to make everything right now.

Justice.

I shook my head, forcing myself to answer the doctor. "She did. She ordered the damn thing right off the internet. But she didn't use gas."

The redhead's frown deepened. "Sedatives?"

Dr. Autumn Trent's deductive powers were strong, and for a moment, I thought I might puke. My stomach churned, and I turned just as a flicker of movement caught my eye.

It was her. Colleen. She was here. My precious sister was standing near the front doorway...crying.

Seeing her like that was comforting in its own way. It's one of the ways I most remembered her. My sister had always been crying toward the end. She didn't seem to know how to stop.

"Her toxicology report came back clean." A deep, broken voice said the words, but I wasn't certain that the voice was mine, even though I knew it was. "She didn't use anything. She wanted to suffer."

When I looked back at my captive, Dr. Trent appeared to have actual tears in her eyes. She was sad for me...for Colleen. She probably would have done a better job at keeping my sister alive than the smarmy dickhead still writhing on the floor, but none of that mattered now.

Dead. Colleen, my mother, and soon, the compassionate-faced woman tied up on an exquisite pinewood chair. It was the doctor's fault. My fault too. Not that the blame really mattered, I guessed. In our own separate ways, Philip and I were already dead.

I glanced at Colleen one last time. "I'm going to make you smile again," I called out to her. She couldn't understand me, but she would. She'd understand everything soon.

There was only one way to rid my sister of that abominable shadow forever, and the time had come to act.

Forcing the bag over Dr. Trent's head was easier than I'd predicted. Of course, she struggled, but with her hands tied behind her back, she could do little more than thrash like a doomed fish out of water. I was strong enough to hold her down, and without the use of her arms, she couldn't fight all that hard.

"*Stop!*" Philip Baldwin squalled like a newborn baby behind us. "You h-have to stop this, Albert. She's innocent. Me! *I'm* the one you hate. Kill me!"

He was watching, just as I had wanted him to. Excellent. I thought I might have to tape his eyelids open, but it seemed the doctor would be saving me the hassle.

I didn't relish ending human life, and in a perfect world, I wouldn't harm a hair on this woman's head. She'd done nothing wrong, aside from talking entirely too much and causing an unintentional interference with Evelyn Walker's body discovery. That had been a bitter annoyance, but I'd managed to work around the obstacle.

I always did.

Saving Dr. Trent from that elevator shaft only to have her end up as collateral damage now was a shame. But a very necessary shame.

Philip deserved worse than death. Killing him now would *end* his suffering. That wouldn't do. I intended for this day to be only the *beginning* of hell on earth for Dr. Philip Baldwin.

The FBI would show no mercy to him this time. Not after he'd murdered one of theirs. Everyone in the hospital knew how much Baldwin despised Dr. Trent. They wouldn't be asking if he would do such a thing…they'd be typing out an endless list of official reasons why he was, *unquestionably*, the killer.

The redhead gave a particularly violent jerk, attempting to topple the chair, but I held her steady. She was losing most of her air, and the panic was kicking in.

Oh, how the human body desired oxygen.

I trained my gaze on Dr. Trent's face, knowing we were entering the final stages of her impending death. My job would be completed soon. Over.

Her eyes had undergone considerable enlargement, giving her a somewhat cartoonish quality. Jet-black pupils dilated to a size that nearly overtook the bright green irises. A few blood vessels had already hemorrhaged, reminding me of Evelyn and Paula.

They'd taken on a similar semblance in their final moments. The difference being that Dr. Trent was much prettier. Smarter. Relatively innocent.

She was going places.

No…she *had been* going places.

Just as my sister had been.

Colleen.

So sweet and innocent and…

For a moment I was overcome by a manic fear that this wasn't Dr. Trent at all. Colleen…Colleen was on this chair, in this bag, and I was killing her.

"I have to tell you something, but you promise me first that you won't say a word to Mom."

I *had* been the one who killed my sister, hadn't I?

I could have stopped the train. Hit the brakes. Averted the situation altogether.

She would have hated me for a while, but she'd have forgiven me eventually. We were siblings. Close. We loved each other.

And even if she hadn't forgiven me…Colleen could have hated me for all eternity, and that would have been okay.

Because she'd be alive.

Not some ghost come back to haunt me with my failure.

Heart threatening to beat out of my chest, I glanced at the doorway of Baldwin's giant house, hoping she'd gone away. I couldn't bear to look at her knowing *I* was her murderer. *I* had ended her life by the mere act of not protecting my sister.

Instead of empty space, Colleen stared back at me, eyes sparkling blue the way they used to, but she was still crying. And worse, she'd figured out the truth.

She lifted one skinny arm, pointing a tiny finger toward me. Her downturned lips parted, and she mouthed a single word. "You."

"No!" An excruciating pain seized my body as the truth seared through my core. My bones seemed to shatter in a cascade of vile collapse.

I had killed her. I had killed my sister. She said so herself. She pointed at *me*.

"No!" I whirled toward Philip Baldwin, who was lying in a pathetic heap on the floor of his own house. "You! *You, you, you*! You did this!"

He had to pay. Turning back to Dr. Trent, I watched her struggle and fight with feral enthusiasm. She began to kick at me and flail in such a way that her chair threatened to turn over.

She sucked the bag into her mouth and chewed. *Chewed*. Like a dog.

A dog who was desperate to live.

"Was this how it went for you, Colleen?" I spoke to the form at the doorway but refused to peek at her. She'd only remind me that this was my fault. Her blood was on my hands.

And she was *wrong*.

That asshole moaning behind me, *he* was to blame. And this redheaded, meddling bitch—she was going to guarantee that Philip Baldwin paid his dues.

Finally.

"Did you regret your decision in the end, Colleen? Did you fight like this? Or did you let the darkness wash over you like a palliative wave? Did you *welcome* Death?"

I still declined to glance at my sister. Her ghost was confused. Confused and sad. But after this, all would be well. Clear.

Just a few more minutes.

One…

Two…

Dr. Trent was growing weaker. Her kicks and flounders were becoming less frequent. Pitiful, even.

"The desire to live is *so strong*, isn't it, Doctor? I wonder if it's the strongest instinct we humans have." I studied her once pretty features. "You probably know. Studied all that in college, didn't you? I bet you were the top of your class."

Her greens struggled to focus on my face. Even now as they bulged out like a stepped-on frog, I couldn't deny her beauty and the shame of wasting her promising life. Bright eyes, bright hair, bright future. But the woman was dying.

That was how things happened sometimes.

"Colleen was in college. She was going places. But I guess you know how that all resulted." I leaned in until our noses were millimeters apart. "We want to live so badly, but in the end, something as insignificant as a thin piece of plastic can take us out."

Her eyes began to close, then pop open, then close again. She was on her way, close to stepping through the last exit door. The door that answered that forever burning question burdening the hearts of all mankind.

What comes next?

No one knew, because the living couldn't see past death, and the dead couldn't speak to the living.

They could just stand and point.

My fault.

My fault.

My fault.

Philip groaned for the millionth time behind me, pulling me from the trance of responsibility. That bastard. Just look at what he'd done. He'd taken all these innocent lives.

"Tell Colleen I love her, and I *fixed* things, if you run into her. I don't really know how it all goes after this, Pippi. You might not even end up in the same place as my sister, but—"

Another grunt from Baldwin had me slamming my hands on my ears, not wanting a distraction. The timing of that man. He could wait. I'd deal with him, but not now.

I wanted to witness Dr. Trent's last breath, witness her

eyes glaze over. I needed to behold the crossover from suffering to peace. To wherever Colleen was.

More sounds from Baldwin. My irritation momentarily overtook my attention, and I began to turn toward the evil, cursed son of a bitch. I'd shut that asshole up with a good punch to the—

Philip's body crashed into me with the violent force of Hades.

32

Oxygen didn't receive nearly the amount of appreciation it deserved. Parties, parades, a national freaking holiday…

In this moment of truth, tied to a chair in Philip Baldwin's countryside home and unable to inhale even a puff of the precious commodity, Autumn understood how petty everything else in the world was.

Air. Breathing air. That was all that mattered. That was a miracle worth celebrating.

The problem being, of course, that she'd been deprived of the invisible element altogether. The plastic bag had leached itself onto her features like a mask.

This is your new face, Dr. Trent. This is how they will find you…beneath an unforgiving sheen of plastic hell.

Albert hovered over her, focused with apt attention. His fascination was evident, and she could tell through the blur of the plastic that he didn't want to miss a second of her struggle.

She'd watched death, studied death, *faced* death numerous times. But not once had she pictured leaving this world in such a way. And despite knowing the cycle of life made exceptions for no one, she felt this ending to be dreadful and unfair.

No warning, no prep time.

She had things *to do*.

Who would care for Peach and Toad? Who would find Sarah and set her on a clean path? Who would deal with Justin Black and all his manipulative madness?

Who would break the news to the people who loved her?

And who would say all the many words she'd left unsaid?

She deeply regretted her argument with Winter. Her friend hadn't deserved the callous tough love treatment that day. Winter just needed someone who understood.

Autumn did.

And now she was here. Suffocating. Trying with all her might to hold her breath so that the meager bit of oxygen inside the bag would last a little longer.

She couldn't tell Winter she was sorry. She couldn't even say goodbye to any of her friends. Noah. Aiden.

All she could do was witness her own demise as the darkness and dizziness overwhelmed her.

In her fading peripheral vision, Philip barreled into Albert, knocking him aside with unexpected, vicious force. The fleeting hope that she might not be doomed after all assailed her just as her world began to flash in and out of blackness.

Philip approached Albert, taking full advantage of his surprise attack, and punched him in the ribs with a strength Autumn hadn't imagined the doctor possessed. Albert reeled toward the floor, stumbling across the foyer in obvious confusion.

Fighting the thin strips of plastic holding her wrists together, Autumn perceived the rage exuding from his face as he recovered his footing. He charged toward Philip, knocking him into the nearest wall. Three peaceful forest scenes jarred from their places on the shiplap, glass shattering into a sea of shards around Dr. Baldwin's form.

Philip winced, no doubt receiving multiple pierce wounds from his devastated art collection. He struggled to rebalance while Albert paced toward him, gun in hand.

"The time has come to end this," the orderly growled. "You *will* pay for your crimes."

Slipping over the verge of unconsciousness, Autumn yanked with all her remaining strength at the binding encasing her wrists. The effort was futile, as she had known it would be.

The lack of oxygen rendered her feeble. Incapacitated.

Yet there had to be a way to escape this madness.

Growing steadily weaker, she watched through her plastic cling window as Albert regained the upper hand in the brawl. He trained his pistol on Baldwin, and Autumn braced for the impending gunfire. Even if Philip wasn't fatally wounded, he was sure to obtain a serious injury. The fight he'd displayed would naturally diminish.

She *had* to break free of these binds. The fates of Philip and herself could very well lay solely in her hands. Staying tethered to this chair was not an option.

Philip, however, wasn't done for yet. He attacked Albert just as the orderly shot. The pistol flew from Albert's hands and the bullet meant for Dr. Baldwin lodged into the foyer wall.

Albert scrambled toward the gun, but Philip leapt, tackling him to the floor with a passionate yell of fury.

"I never hurt your sister! *I never hurt your sister!*" Philip's scream echoed off the walls.

Autumn thrashed in her chair, a final wave of adrenaline kicking in.

You will break free. You will not die in this chair, regardless of what happens between these two men. You. Will. Break. Free.

But her fiery efforts to break loose made breathing even more difficult and caused an immediate wave of exhaustion that sent Autumn's blurry world spinning. The past and the present melded together in a giant tilt-a-whirl of moving imagery...

"She is your sister now, and you should never hurt your sister! Do you understand me? Answer!" Mrs. Wright's ample chins smushed together as she leaned toward Autumn and Cricket.

"Yes, Mrs. Wright," they answered in unison.

Autumn was only twelve, but she'd figured out how the foster kid game worked all too well. No matter what happened, you didn't argue with your foster parents. It was a very bad move.

Even if you were getting into big trouble for something you didn't do...

Even if you knew the next week would consist of repentant, hard labor in your foster mother's garden under the burning summer sun...

No arguing.

Cricket was only nine and new to the foster system, but he'd followed Autumn's lead ever since arriving at the Wright's home a week earlier. His name wasn't really Cricket, but he'd asked her in confidence to please call him by the moniker.

That had been his nickname back home.

Autumn had wanted to explain to him that the sooner he separated himself from "the way it used to be," the better. Home didn't matter anymore, and holding onto home would only cause him to suffer.

It was better to let go.

Cricket hadn't meant to trip Emily, and Autumn hadn't meant to step on the five-year-old's tiny foot as the three of them collided in the backyard. But that didn't matter. Mrs. Wright favored

Emily. The girl was younger and cuter...easier to love, Autumn figured.

If Mrs. Wright said they'd hurt Emily, then they'd have to accept that they'd hurt Emily. And while this infuriated her young heart, she tempered the feeling with memories of past foster care punishments incurred from her attempts to stick up for herself.

No arguing.

It was better to let go.

Cricket followed her out the back door and toward Mrs. Wright's strawberry patch. They'd earned just three hours of labor today, but only because the afternoon was nearly over. The next few days would be much longer.

Autumn stiffened as Cricket grabbed her hand with his chubby ebony fist.

Unwanted knowledge flowed through her mind.

The boy thought he was going home. Soon. He was pretending Mrs. Wright was his aunt.

She pulled her hand away, resenting the wave of emotion that had drenched her with its disparity. She tried very hard not to wallow in her own pain. Now she had to process Cricket's.

"You don't like me, do you?" he asked quietly, big brown eyes searching her face for softness. She knew all the boy wanted was affection. Someone to trust in this brave, new world.

But Cricket didn't understand that this was all temporary. One of them, or both of them, would be leaving eventually. And neither of them would be "going home."

She put a hand in his black curls and mussed his hair a bit. "I think you're awesome, bud." Three years of age between them, but she spoke to him as though she were a full-grown adult and he a toddler.

"I have a sister. I have two sisters. When I get home, I'll tell them about you. You're my sister now too, right?" Cricket tugged at her t-shirt, wanting an answer.

Autumn swallowed the lump in her throat. She was being

stupid and way too nice to Cricket. If she kept being kind, they'd bond, and she would miss him when they were inevitably parted.

Missing people was awful.

Her real sister, Sarah, was out there somewhere. She missed Sarah terribly, and she knew Sarah's dad wasn't coming back to retrieve her. Maybe he hadn't been lying at the time, but he hadn't followed through.

He wasn't going to.

But when she was old enough, she'd find Sarah. Eighteen wasn't so far away, and surely Sarah would be looking for her too.

Cricket might not ever be going home, but he might see his sisters again, if he was lucky.

Maybe they were both lucky. Maybe that's how they'd ended up here and found each other. And some day they'd find their real families.

Because they were lucky.

Autumn wanted to harden her heart but didn't know how. Cricket's pudgy little cheeks were damp with sweat, and the two of them hadn't even started weeding yet. He was gonna have a pretty rough week living out his first official Mrs. Wright punishment.

"I can be your sister. As long as you know I might have to go to a different house someday. It could be soon. Or not, but you have to remember that I'll be leaving, okay?" Autumn bit her tongue until she tasted the metallic trickle of blood.

Cricket shook his head and gave her a wide, optimistic grin. "You're gonna be my sister forever. You're not gonna leave."

But she had left, and only two weeks later.

Cricket sobbed on the Wright's front porch while her case-worker pulled the car away from the curb, Autumn dutifully buckled into the back seat. Autumn waved out the window and tried not to cry. She rolled the window down just as Cricket's sobs turned to wails.

"Where are you taking her? Bring her back! I want my sister back! I want my sister baaack..."

"You're a murderer!" Albert shrieked, clawing at the floor as he pulled away from Philip's grip. "You killed her! You took her away from me!"

"I! Never! Hurt! Your! Sister!" Baldwin's cry was a roar now. He was crawling toward the gun, but so was Albert.

Please...help me...

The black curtain was falling over her eyes, even as Philip reached for the pistol. The two men clawed and thrashed to gain possession as pain ripped through Autumn's lungs.

The explosion seemed to come from far away...echoing through her body with every beat of her heart. Both men froze, apparently stunned by the violent eruption before Albert slowly sank to the floor. He clutched the wound in his shoulder, howling in maniacal pain.

Philip turned toward her, the gun still clutched in one trembling hand. He hurried to her side, reaching for her throat...

The door crashed open, and Autumn managed to lift her eyelids one last time.

Aiden, Adrienne, Chris, Mia, Noah, Winter...the entire team was here. They'd made it. They'd found her.

Her head dropped in exhaustion, rolling against her shoulder as she glimpsed the agents and officers surrounding Philip, guns raised.

They think he kidnapped me. I have to tell them...tell them they're wrong.

But Autumn couldn't speak or breathe or inform anyone of anything.

Her eyes closed as she struggled to inhale one last time. A scream echoed through her head, pulsing through her body as she dropped farther and farther into the void of death.

Hands clawed at her face and neck, pulling and yanking so hard that her head whipped back and forth. After what felt like hours, a ripping sound penetrated the fog enclosing her. A rush of sweet air ripped through her chest.

"Autumn…"

She inhaled again, the pain of air like daggers ripping through her lungs, but it was the most wonderful pain she'd ever experienced.

With all the effort she could muster, Autumn's eyes fluttered open, and Winter appeared. Her face was pinched in worry, though she visibly relaxed as their gazes met and held. Before she could inhale another breath, she was in her best friend's arms, and they both were crying as someone cut her binds away.

"You're okay." Winter's voice was soothing. "We've got you."

Behind the cooing words came shouts and sounds of a struggle. *Philip.*

Pulling away from her friend, she frantically shook her head.

Winter's eyes went wide. "What?"

Sucking in another great gulp of air, she managed a hoarse whisper. "Not…him."

All eyes turned on Autumn, but it was Winter who understood first. "Baldwin didn't do this to you?"

Relief flooded through her, and she allowed herself to collapse back into Winter's arms. "No…Rice…bad…man."

As the team lowered their guns, Autumn surrendered to the abyss.

33

B *eep. Beep. Beep. Beep.*
Aiden was provided with the assurance that
Autumn Trent was very much alive by the steady rhythm of
the heart monitor machine.

He stared at her regardless, hands shoved deep into his
suit jacket pockets, standing near her bedside in the emer-
gency room of Richmond's Medical Hospital.

Her chest rose and fell with placid, peaceful beats. Bright
auburn hair splayed across the standard grade pillows that
propped her upper body at a slightly raised angle.

All wasn't "well" in the usual sense of the word, but the
situation was okay. Autumn was in stable condition, and the
doctors had assured him...repeatedly...that she would make
a full recovery from the trauma of her abduction.

Close, though. One of the physicians mentioned how
narrow the margin had been between life and death for
Autumn. Her oxygen levels had dipped to dangerous lows.

"I'm not sure she would have made it past another
minute. Not without brain damage of some degree," the
harried ER doctor had told him.

Aiden replayed the words in his head, awed and disturbed that one single minute had made the difference for the brilliant psychiatrist. Her inquisitive, gifted mind would have wasted away in rapid fashion had they arrived at Baldwin's house any later.

One single minute.

He pictured her frozen in a vegetative slumber, kept alive by life support and nothing more, then pushed the image away.

That wasn't the case. They *had* arrived in time. She was safe.

She was going to wake up and everything—

Vivid green eyes met his as Autumn's heavy lashes lifted.

"You're awake." Taken off guard, Aiden's immediate greeting was lackluster at best.

Autumn's mouth curved upward then shot back down. Her eyes grew wide, and she struggled to sit up. "Philip Baldwin's *innocent*. He tried to *protect* me. *Albert*…this was all Albert. You *have* to let Philip go."

Aiden placed a gentle hand on her arm. "Easy, Dr. Trent. Baldwin isn't under arrest."

Autumn stared at him in silence, her brow furrowed with concentration. Unnerved and fatigued, he pulled his hand away. She had a way of making him feel like he was being x-rayed…*probed* somehow.

"You figured the whole thing out," she surmised, relief flooding her features.

His body relaxed as if by osmosis. He'd been unaware of how tense his muscles were.

"For the most part, yes," he admitted, shoving his hands back into his pockets. "The puzzle pieces fit, finally. Albert Rice believed Baldwin was to blame for his sister's suicide. He killed Baldwin's assistant, Mildred, in an attempt to frame the shrink for murder. When that didn't work, he followed him to the hospital to set him up again."

Autumn nodded and smiled, he assumed, at the accuracy.

"He intended to frame Baldwin for your murder as well." Aiden's jaw clenched. "Did I get most of that right?"

"Perfect. I mean, *awful*, but perfect." Autumn laid her head back on the stack of pillows and shot him a small grin. "Excellent deductive reasoning skills, Agent Parrish."

"Thank you. I would have preferred to expedite that genius discovery, but what's life without a few ridiculously close calls?" He wanted to smile and couldn't.

"You were scared," Autumn stated with quiet certitude. "You were afraid the team wouldn't make it in time."

She was correct.

"We were all very concerned for your welfare, Dr. Trent," he admitted, attempting to take the focus off himself. "You have people in your corner who care a great deal about you."

Autumn tilted her head. "I know. I'm lucky."

Aiden didn't know what to say. There should have been words, but he couldn't find them.

"Philip was innocent the entire time," she mused, tugging at a loose thread in her blanket.

"Yes. And I should commend you for following your instincts, especially considering that you had little to no support in pursuing those avenues." Aiden hated himself for not having paid closer attention. He hadn't been convinced that Philip was their guy either, but what had he done to assist Autumn's hunch?

"Zippo," Autumn agreed, meeting his gaze again. "But I'm okay...or at least I'll *be* okay. That's more than I can say for Albert Rice."

Aiden grimaced. "He's in surgery as we speak. A lot of blood loss and possible permanent nerve damage, but he'll recover. Before you know it, he'll be ready for a jail cell and his very own psych eval."

Autumn held up a hand. "I would like to vote for anyone besides myself to take that job on."

Aiden grinned. "I don't think Albert's case will be added to your patient list, Doctor."

"He really isn't a bad person. He lost his sister and life changed. He changed. All he wanted was justice for Colleen. And peace." Autumn bit her lip, and Aiden noted her genuine struggle to stay undemonstrative.

"I have a very hard time empathizing with a man who killed three innocent women and was working on the fourth. Bad person or not, he was seeking solace through murder and deception." He wasn't able to keep the growl from his voice.

Autumn nodded. "I know. I just...I wonder if he would have found that peace had there been an audio feed that proved Philip did nothing wrong. He may not have taken this path or become this person."

"I can't argue with that. Albert very well could have made different choices if the feed existed. But the audio *doesn't* exist, and he *did* kill three women. He'll have to answer for that, peace or no peace." Aiden should have been used to Autumn's giant heart overcoming the greatest of grievances, but she continually surprised him.

Albert Rice had attempted to *kill* her, and she wasn't even angry. Her ability to empathize was uncanny. Aiden figured the unique gift was one of the key ingredients that made Autumn such an asset to the BAU.

She forgave all, regardless of the outcome, while still managing to do her job. He certainly couldn't say the same for himself, or for the masses of humanity in general.

He only worried that her sensibilities might continue to throw her in harm's way.

Worry about that tomorrow. She's here, alive, and undamaged. For the most part.

"He just wanted his sister back," Autumn murmured, staring out the tall windows of the room.

Aiden swallowed. He was familiar with the longing and knew Autumn was too.

"Well, I'm just glad the murder spree is over. Maybe he'll get better. That does happen on occasion," Aiden allowed, immediately thinking of Justin Black.

Occasionally. But not always. And not often.

Autumn turned back to him and flashed an optimistic smile. "I really hope he does. And I guess, bottom line, I should thank you for showing up in the nick of time. It was close. It was *so close*." Her smile faded.

"It?" Aiden pressed, even though he already knew. Saying the words out loud would take some of the horror away.

"Death. The Grim Reaper. The last train. The big sleep—"

Aiden held up both hands. "Stop. I get the point." How many close calls had he witnessed in his career with the Bureau? Too many to name.

But this one had hit him with a severe jolt, the likes of which he would not be quick to process.

"Anyway. Close but no cigar." Autumn chuckled weakly. "I'm sorry. Last one. And really...I mean it. Thank you for saving me."

Aiden glanced over his shoulder, giving an imperceptible nod. "Well, I certainly didn't come to your rescue by myself."

Mia and Chris entered the room.

Agent Logan rushed to Autumn's bedside. "I'm *so* glad you're okay. You're one tough cookie."

The women smiled at each other, and Parker rolled his eyes dramatically.

But Aiden knew the man had been shaken.

In a rare moment of comradery, Chris clapped his hands

together. "You are my hero, Dr. Trent. When I grow up, I want to be just like you."

Laughter emanated from the four of them. Aiden pondered the possibility of Chris Parker being halfway like-able were he able to stay in this "never-before-seen" pleasant mode forever.

He'd be forced to get a haircut, of course. No one could befriend that assemblage of blond blasphemy.

Two more figures entered the room. Winter and Noah approached Autumn slowly, as though they were scared she might not be real.

Aiden wasn't the only one who'd been fighting the sands of time to reach their sweet doctor.

He watched as Noah gave Autumn a cautious bear hug. "You are not allowed to disappear ever again. Your new curfew is seven o'clock sharp, and I expect you to obey the rules, young lady."

Autumn sputtered into vivacious laughter, and Aiden realized that the familiar sound was an element of his daily life that he refused to go without. Dr. Trent wasn't allowed to die. Not on his watch.

"Well, as you can see, I'm not on my knees."

"Yes, you are."

Adrienne's scrutiny was yet another issue for a different day.

Winter and Autumn seemed locked in an affectionate stare down of sorts, and their need for privacy was glaringly obvious to Aiden.

"Okay, Agents. How about the rest of us step out and let these two alone for a bit," Aiden suggested, leading the way.

Everyone, aside from Winter, acquiesced, following him into the hallway.

He caught a glimpse of Noah clapping a brotherly hand

onto Chris's shoulder. The interaction was double-take worthy.

But why. Why did something horrible have to happen before people who were on the same side to begin with could come together?

There was a better way, he was sure. But he also doubted that mankind would change anytime soon. Human nature wasn't going anywhere.

Petty arguments would continue on, cold brick walls of indifference would be built then rebuilt, and important words that hung from the tip of the tongue would go unsaid.

Shake it off, Parrish. You've got work to do. Compose yourself.

Aiden closed the door gently, keeping his eyes down. He steeled himself against the myriad of emotion still running rampant through his mind and strode away from Autumn's room.

He refused to look back.

For now.

34

W inter stood at Autumn's bedside, gripping the side rail of the hospital bed. As the adrenaline wore off, she faced the terror that had wreaked havoc on her psyche.

"You don't understand. Your head was off to the side, all *limp*. And the plastic was so tight…like another layer of skin sucked to your face. The bag was *in your mouth*. Not just over, *in*." Winter's lip trembled as she recalled her first sight of Autumn when they stormed Baldwin's house.

She hadn't meant to provide Autumn with a play-by-play recap of those terrible few moments, but they also wouldn't stop spurting from her traitorous mouth.

Autumn patted her friend's hand. "And you ripped that sucker off my head. I'm *here*. I'm fine."

Winter sputtered an embarrassed laugh. "I'm the one who's supposed to be comforting you." She took Autumn's hand between both of her own. "I was so scared."

Autumn's smile was gentle. "I know. Me too. I'm fine, I promise."

"Fine?" Winter raised a skeptical eyebrow. "Is that the official clinical diagnosis from the doctors?"

"Okay. Maybe not fine, but alive. The doctors have to admit that much." Autumn grinned up at her, unbelievably composed considering the events of the day.

Winter drew in a deep breath, needing to calm herself. "Stop reassuring me. I'm supposed to be comforting you. You're supposed to just, I don't know. Lay there and moan like a good 'I survived attempted murder' victim should."

With great artistic flair, Dr. Trent flopped back on her pillow, closed her eyes, and let out an incredibly convincing snore.

Something about the amusing pose was too reminiscent of the scene they'd discovered in Philip Baldwin's country home for Winter to digest. "Okay. You're hilarious. Stop it."

Autumn popped her eyes open in obedience but continued to rest her head. "Honestly, I know I'll be fine, but I'm exhausted in a way I can't even explain."

"Well, you've never been deprived of oxygen before, so I suppose this was an educational experience," Winter quipped, causing more laughter.

"Indeed. And I should thank you for actually tearing the bag off. I guess the men were all too busy measuring their dicks to save my life." Autumn's eyes glowed with mischief.

Winter lowered her chin in mock despair. "Yeah. Why do women always have to do the grunt work?"

"Ha. You're asking me?" Autumn closed her eyes for a quick moment. When she opened them, they were brimming with tears. "I'm so, *so* sorry, Winter. That fight was stupid. If those had been the last words I said to you—"

"They weren't. And I'm right in the same boat with you. I'd never forgive myself." Winter fidgeted with her keychain. "I should apologize, because you were right. You were right about Justin."

Autumn's eyebrows raised, but she said nothing.

She's being cautious. She doesn't want to say the wrong thing.

Everyone is always so scared of saying the wrong thing about Justin...

"He *is* dangerous, and I *do* need to be more careful. I know what he's capable of and being his big sister doesn't rule me out as his next victim. I get that." Winter forced the words out, hating the sound of them hanging in the air.

He could hurt me, but he won't. I won't allow that to happen.

"I understand how hard that must be to come to terms with. You've found him but you..." Autumn's fingertips drifted up to touch her lips, and she didn't finish what she started.

She didn't have to. Winter knew.

"I haven't *actually* found him." Winter handed Autumn a tissue and took one for herself. "I know. And even with that knowledge, I want to be there for him. He's my brother. *Someone* has to be there for him..." Visions of Justin's feral eyes and blood-covered face flashed through her mind. "He's still a human."

I know you're still in there somewhere. I'll never stop trying to find you.

"Of course." Autumn grabbed her hand and gave a firm squeeze. "I never meant you should abandon him. I just don't want him messing with your head. You're so hard on yourself already."

Winter clasped her friend's hand tighter. "I'll use better judgment from here on out. I'm not going to get caught up in his lies and manipulations. I promise you."

She meant that promise. Losing others was too easy. Her parents and her brother had been stolen from her in the blink of an eye when she was only thirteen. She refused to lose herself as well.

"You'll have to be sure and tell him that I'm sorry for missing our appointment again." Autumn smacked her palm to her forehead. "I'll reschedule as *soon* as I'm able. Barring more elevator zombies and kidnappings, I should actually make it to our appointment this time."

"Don't beat yourself up. I'm not the only one who's hard on myself," Winter admonished, sitting on Autumn's bed near her feet. "I'm just glad that you'll be working with him. He needs to know that there are people in this world who refuse to bend over backward for him but are still *there* for him. People who won't run away no matter how hard he pushes."

"I don't think I'm running anywhere anytime soon, really." Autumn's eyes fluttered shut for a moment. The woman needed, and deserved, some sleep. "I know you can do this, Winter. I know you can love Justin and still keep your wits about you. You're strong and you're smart."

"Ha. Keep that list going. I kind of like it." Winter laughed at her own humor. "You're exhausted. We all know you didn't just return from a lounge chair in the Bahamas. You can admit you're spent."

Autumn cringed. "Admitting defeat is the worst, but I'm still a bit shaken by everything. That's natural. At least I'm in one piece, right?"

"Exactly." Winter nodded vehemently. "And you need to stay that way. The team needs you, Justin needs you, and I need you. I do."

"We don't always see eye to eye, but you have to know I'm never going to let you down. Never," Autumn repeated, her eyes glassy with emotion.

Winter knew this was true. She pulled Autumn into a gentle hug. "Right back atcha, Doc."

"I wonder if anyone will be there for Albert. His family is *gone*." Autumn frowned, biting her lip as her eyes welled with fresh tears.

Winter pulled back, her finger wagging in Autumn's face.

"Please tell me you're not considering visiting Albert Rice in prison."

Autumn slapped the finger away. "That's not what I meant, although I do hope he receives some quality treatment. He spoke a lot about his sister while Philip and I were trapped at that house. More than anything, the man is just heartbroken." Autumn's voice cracked with empathy.

Winter hurt for her friend. Autumn's heart was so big and so open. That quality made Autumn who she was, and Winter loved that person dearly.

But she couldn't deny the quiet fear that rested on her shoulders regarding her sweet friend. Big, open hearts were a wonderful phenomenon.

But just by being herself, Autumn left a door slightly ajar for danger.

Winter intended to be the guard dog stationed at that door. Forever, if necessary.

She hugged her again, firmer this time. "You rest up, okay? That is your official assignment for right now."

Autumn waved a hand in the air. "Psh. You're not my boss."

Laughing again, Winter stood and prepared to leave. "I love you."

Autumn's eyes grew shiny with tears again. "Love you too. And Winter…"

Winter tensed from the change in Autumn's tone. "What?"

"That little talk we just had? You need to have the same talk with Noah, and you *know* I'm right." Autumn crossed her arms and stared at her, waiting for the statement to be challenged.

And the award for best Judge Judy impersonation goes to...

Winter wrinkled her nose in protest but nodded reluctantly as she walked toward the door. "Doctor's orders, right?"

"Yep. You have to be transparent with the man you love," Autumn declared in a haughty, professor-like voice. "Relationships 101."

"Says the single invalid on the hospital bed." Winter pressed her lips together, fighting off the laughter.

Autumn whistled. "Ouch. Low blow, Black."

They met eyes, and the laughter nearly doubled them both over this time.

"Okay, okay. I have to go now." Winter attempted to pull herself together. "But I have to admit that I have a really good feeling about the future. For all of us."

"Me too." Autumn clasped her hands together with a satisfied sigh.

"I'm going to head to the hospital and check on Justin. I'll let him know you'll be meeting with him soon. Assuming you can enter that building and not walk straight into some freakishly horrible situation that deters you." Winter winked at Autumn and grasped the doorknob. "Again."

Autumn shot her a bird. "Catch ya soon, Agent Black."

"Absolutely, Dr. Trent." She flashed one last affectionate smile at her friend and entered the ER hallway.

She *did* have an overwhelmingly positive premonition about the things to come. In fact, Winter couldn't remember a single time throughout the whole of her life when she'd felt this optimistic.

She was going to make the best of what life had given her and be the absolute best sister that she could possibly be, regardless of Justin's ever-changing reactions and attacks. She wouldn't hide her head in the sand, either. She would simply be there for him, insanity and all.

The one thing that she knew for sure was Justin couldn't say or do anything now that would shock her or send her running. They'd already reached rock bottom as far as sibling interactions went. The only direction their relationship could go was up.

Winter made a silent plea to any god who might be listening that Justin didn't prove her wrong.

35

Autumn gripped her hospital discharge papers and pulled her bag over her shoulder. The doctors had released her, with explicit instructions to do nothing but rest for the next seventy-two hours.

Peach and Toad were going to love the quality cuddle time.

Janice, the cheerful nurse on shift who was tasked with wheeling her to the front doors, had agreed to first wheel her down the hall toward a different door.

Before Autumn could leave, she wanted to check on Philip Baldwin. The man had been dragged through absolute hell over the last few days.

And he had saved her life.

He'd been transferred to a regular inpatient room on the same floor she'd been moved to from the ER and listed as stable, but he wouldn't be going anywhere for a day or so.

At least, that was the update she'd been given by Janice, who was more than happy to check at the nurse's station for her.

Autumn felt ridiculous being wheeled around, regardless

of what she'd experienced that day. She was excited to step foot outside the hospital and be in charge of herself once again. Bedrest or not, she certainly wasn't an invalid.

And three hours in the hospital was three hours too many.

As they reached the numbered doorway of the room Philip was assigned to, she breathed deeply and squared her shoulders. Checking on Philip was the right thing to do, but that didn't make the undertaking enjoyable.

"Could you knock please? I wouldn't want to disturb him." Autumn gestured toward the door.

She was damn sure getting permission before entering this time.

Her upbeat nurse gave two taps and waited.

"Come in," Philip responded, his voice gruff and weak.

"I'll only be a minute," she told Janice quietly, opting to stand and enter on her own, sans the wheelchair. Janice nodded her nurse's consent, but Autumn could tell the woman wasn't moving an inch until she'd come back out of the room.

As she pushed the door open and entered, she wasn't sure of what to expect. Up until this morning, Philip had seemingly hated the very sight of her.

To be fair, she harbored no particular fondness for him either.

But today, her regard for Philip had shifted into a much softer light. After what they'd been through together, she figured he couldn't help but to at least not hate her quite as much as he had when he woke up that morning.

Philip was sitting up, but angled backward, supported by the adjusted hospital bed. His wavy hair sat in rebellious disarray. Autumn guessed he was also none too pleased to be sporting the light blue hospital gown that was much more exposé than his usual tailored suits.

"What do you want?" he grumbled, eyeing her warily.

Autumn approached his bedside. "I had to come by and thank you. You saved my life."

Philip snorted. "Don't seem so shocked. I've insisted I wasn't a killer since the moment you people arrived."

"And if you'll remember, Dr. Baldwin, I told you that I believed in your innocence on more than one occasion." Autumn offered him a pleasant smile and waited for his typical argumentative response.

"You're correct." He winced and placed a cautious hand to his side. "Perhaps I shouldn't have dismissed you so easily. But I still hold that there was an endless number of reasons for me to disbelieve you."

"Ribs?" Autumn tried not to picture Albert's ruthless kicks to Philip's body.

"Four broken, two dislocated. Extensive internal bruising. Concussion." Philip recited his injuries with flat indifference. "Lots of pain killers and bedrest are the apparent magical solution."

"Yikes. That's rough. I was worried there might be internal bleeding. I'm very relieved that's not the case." Without invitation, Autumn pulled a padded plastic visitor's chair toward the bed and sat.

"Dear god, please tell me you aren't planning on staying long." Philip held his hands up in protest, but a slight grin revealed the man had a sense of humor after all.

"Just a few minutes." Autumn found herself smiling back. "I'm a little wobbly on my feet right now. I have no idea why that would be."

Philip lifted a shoulder a fraction. "Strange. A true mystery to me."

Autumn laughed, though what they'd endured was far from funny.

Humor is paramount in this line of work.

Philip sobered, his gaze dropping to his lap. "I can't stop thinking about Colleen. I *do* remember her. She was so incredibly broken. I should have done better by her some-how...prevented that ending."

Autumn's heart squeezed in sympathy. She wanted to save everyone too. "You couldn't have predicted the choice she would make." Her opposition to his self-criticism coated each adamant word that flew from her mouth. "You're being too hard on yourself. She was very unstable, and there's no magic wand or crystal ball in our profession."

Philip shifted in the bed and groaned. Autumn pitied his obvious discomfort and adjusted the multiple pillows behind him to better support his wounded body.

"Thank you." He glanced at her, his expression revealing how awkward and uncomfortable the current situation was to him. Autumn understood that Dr. Baldwin wasn't used to being the patient. He probably struggled to ask anyone for even the slightest bit of help.

"No big deal. I owe you. You handled yourself very well considering the danger we were in. Impressive." Autumn hoped she wasn't ego fluffing the already arrogant man. But he deserved to be told that he'd done something good, some-thing *brave*, after all the hell they'd put him through with the murder accusations.

Philip blushed deep red. He appeared to be much more accustomed to handling insults rather than compliments.

"If you ever want to talk..." now that she'd started the invitation, Autumn wasn't sure how to finish, so she just plowed on, "about your fear of confined spaces. I'd be more than willing to lend an ear."

Philip's head whipped up sharply, his features contorted into a mask of absolute horror at the suggestion. "No. No, thank you. I have all that under control. I don't need a shrink. I *am* a shrink."

Autumn was aware that she'd overstepped a boundary, and in doing so, had ended the moment of comradery between them. She sighed and stood from the chair. "Didn't mean to offend, Dr. Baldwin. I'll leave you to rest now."

He said nothing as she walked to the door. She should have known that Dr. Philip Baldwin could only be civil for so long.

"Wait. Come back." His usual deep voice was more of a quiet mumble.

Surprised, Autumn made a prompt return to his bedside. "Yes?"

He gazed up at her, his eyes beaming a silent apology. "I haven't...I've just never talked to anyone about that before. Not once."

"I understand, Philip." Her heart squeezed for the man as he trembled, his embarrassment visible. "The majority of people suffering phobias keep their fears to themselves for their entire lives. You know that as well as I do."

Philip closed his eyes. "My father had a habit of locking me in the coat closet when I misbehaved."

Autumn ached for him. She knew a thing or two about traumatic childhood experiences involving closets. Those memories were stored tight in a box marked "foster care nightmares" somewhere deep in her psyche. Most days, she felt that she'd processed those wounds pretty thoroughly before filing them away.

But occasionally, a random mental souvenir reared its ugly head.

"The abuse never went further than that. He never hit me, but I don't think I've ever fully come to terms with the trauma those punishments caused. I'm a grown man..." Philip twiddled his thumbs together, appearing more like a little boy than he may have thought possible. "How silly to be so afraid of something so juvenile."

Autumn grabbed his hand, her sympathetic nature making it impossible to not follow through on the impulse to comfort the man. "Not silly. You were mistreated, Philip. Memories of abuse don't disappear when we turn eighteen, and neither do their effects."

Currents of goodness and fragility flowed from Philip's hand. She sensed the noble heart that had been on display when he came to her rescue. No amount of grumpy Dr. Baldwin-isms could change what she knew to be true of him. Not now.

"Did *you* have a happy childhood, Dr. Trent?" The boldness of the question surprised her. In fact, it seemed to have surprised them both.

A troublesome flash reel of memories played through Autumn's mind as she struggled to reply. "There were happy parts."

Philip cocked his head. "That's a bit telling. You know, my door is always open should you need to talk." He followed the offer with what Autumn interpreted as a smartass yet genuine grin.

"I'll keep that in mind, Dr. Baldwin. My offer still stands as well."

Philip nodded. "Duly noted."

"I'll let you rest," she proposed for a second time. "I can't ever thank you enough for what you did. Not ever."

Philip met her gaze, his green eyes shadowed and worn. "And I can't ever thank you enough for helping me clear my name. Albeit in a rather roundabout, haphazard way that nearly got us both killed but…"

He smiled, and Autumn joined him.

What a day we've had, Dr. Baldwin.

Autumn headed for the door, remembering that she, technically, was also supposed to be in bed and resting up.

"Dr. Trent?" Philip called out to her as she opened the

door. "You should know that I got a call from the board of Virginia State Hospital. They're giving me my job back."

Autumn processed that for a moment. She had resented Baldwin's way of running the hospital so much. Was she glad that he was given the chance to be the hateful dictator she first met?

She decided it didn't matter. One thing she knew for sure was that she'd never want to be in that position.

Autumn gave him a firm nod of approval. She had been more than a little worried about what Philip would do without the job he was so invested in. "Congratulations."

He rubbed the tip of his nose. "They're working on the video equipment installation as we speak."

Autumn held up a finger and grinned. "Audio too?"

He gave his eyes a dramatic roll. "Of course. What idiot would forget audio?"

"Good point, Dr. Baldwin. I'll be meeting with Justin Black soon. Maybe I'll run into you at your hospital." The thought wasn't nearly as revolting as it had been less than twelve hours ago.

"Do you think you can actually enter my hospital without bringing a dust cloud of chaos along?" Philip's comment was snarky but somewhat fair.

"I'd like to answer your question to the affirmative, but I'm not sure I could promise you that. I have a way of walking into absurd situations." She winked at him and left the room.

She wasn't even sure she could get out of *this* hospital before the bells of madness tolled once again.

36

Justin Black had envisioned killing Victor Goren so many times that he was becoming bored with the daydream. In all honesty, Victor wasn't even worth the level of creativity that Justin was capable of.

Killing is art. Victor is a fart.

Justin sputtered out uncontrolled, high-pitched giggles.

Victor stopped whatever mind-numbing, monotonous sentence he had been stumbling through and peered at Justin with caution from his safe distance across their table in the common area. "Did I miss something?"

He enjoyed the instant hint of fear in his public defender's voice. Was there anything more lovely in the entire world than a human's blatant terror?

He didn't believe so.

The rush of adrenaline, which usually played prologue to some of his most intricate kill fantasies, coursed through him. Such a wonderful sensation.

He wished he were in his room so he could daydream in peace.

But no. He was sitting like an obedient little lamb at a

table in Virginia State Hospital's common area, letting Goren babble on and on and on about the hospital murders.

They'd caught the killer…blah blah blah. Baldwin wasn't losing his job after all…blah blah blah.

The only piece of information Victor gave him that he found worth ruminating over was that Albert Rice had turned out to be the murderer.

Justin wasn't particularly surprised. Rice was shady as hell, always making deals with the inmates to sneak in illegal contraband. And the man had been quiet. *Too* quiet.

If anyone could sniff out a killer, Justin could.

What sucked was that he'd used Albert's services to smuggle in a phone and a few other favors. He always reimbursed the custodian for his unfailing ability to deliver with bitcoin payments.

Both parties had been happy, and the operation ran with seamless efficiency.

But not anymore.

Until another whitecoat showed their true hideous colors and took up where Rice had left off, deliveries were at an ultimate standstill.

Goren's droning voice was just a background of white noise as Justin considered his new obstacle. He did fairly well at blocking the man out altogether when he wanted to.

He surveyed the installation technicians hard at work, fitting out each room with hordes of video surveillance equipment. Justin stared at the cameras, hate stirring deep in the well of his stomach.

"There's going to be a lot more security in this place from here on out. You'll be able to trust you're safe again, Justin. Secure." The genuine concern in Goren's eyes was absurd.

Had the man forgotten he was speaking to a verified, soulless serial killer?

Did Victor think he'd been living in terror for the past few days because of a couple strangulations?

Those barely even counted as murders.

Justin scowled at the cameras.

"What's wrong? I think you have a lot to be happy about right now. You're helping the BAU, and as an asset to their unit, you'll likely be kept at the hospital for the long haul." Victor studied him, obviously wanting some type of praise for doing nothing at all aside from being a giant piece of shit.

The fuck I'm going to be here for the long haul.

"Well, that does beat prison, Vic." Justin stared past the attorney. Those installation men were going on about something. If Victor could shut up for two seconds, Justin might be able to assess what all the fuss was about.

The one highest on the ladder appeared the most perturbed. "You mean to tell me we rushed to set all this up, and it ain't even gonna run today?"

The technician on the floor shrugged. "Ain't *my* damn fault. Some type of glitch with the system. They still need hung regardless. Fully operational come tomorrow morning, so get your panties outta a wad."

Justin considered this information. Tomorrow morning. Starting tomorrow morning, every single thing he did would be on video.

The time had come to act.

"…if you can continue to behave…keep ahold of yourself and—"

"Thanks for the assistance, Victor. I really do believe my life is taking a great turn. I'm gonna go back to my room and take a nap." Justin left the table without waiting for or caring about Goren's response.

The door guard eyed him closely when he exited the commons, and the hall guard shadowed him until he'd returned to his room and shut the door.

There. I'm locked in again. You can relax.

An annoying truth of being a serial killer was that everyone assumed you were going to attempt murder at any given second, right in front of the general public. Justin's IQ was much too high for that type of riffraff nonsense.

In fact, many notorious serial killers had impressively high IQs.

That was his bunch. The thinkers. The planners.

The artists.

Justin went straight to his bed, pulled his knees close to his chest, and began rocking. He even stuck the thumb in his mouth for added effect should anyone glimpse him through the door's observation window.

He rocked methodically, keeping a soothing rhythm that helped him brainstorm. Back and forth, back and forth, back and forth...

Rice was gone. His link to the outside world was gone. And once the sun rose on the next day, his privacy was gone.

Of course, many had escaped hospitals and psych wards of this sort even when under constant video surveillance. Dumb as dirt hillbillies escaped *actual* prison all the damn time.

But that was such a messy way to go. He'd have to kill every single person who tried to stop him. And although he'd enjoy that immensely, he'd lose entirely too much time in the process. And energy.

Time and energy were two tools he couldn't afford to waste. Getting out of the building was only the beginning.

Exhausting himself with multiple slaughters simply wouldn't do.

He had to move fast.

Back and forth, back and forth, back and forth...

Think. Think. Think.

His plan came to him in one clear chunk. No scrambling. He knew what he had to do.

The facility was currently understaffed. Some employees had gone on strike until the all-powerful strangler was revealed and thrown behind bars. Others were suspended for information they had leaked, subtle or otherwise, to the press during the Baldwin witch hunt.

And then of course, there were the two employees who'd been murdered. Those two sure as shit weren't taking on any extra shifts this week.

Even the nurses and guards who refused to abandon their posts were severely rattled by the murder spree.

No one was operating at one hundred percent on this shoelace staff squad. That made now the perfect time for a getaway. And the impending surveillance about to invade his life in the early morning hours made now the *only* time for a getaway.

What he needed to send his plan into action really wasn't beyond the realm of possibility at all. He needed a visit from his sister.

If Winter intended to keep her word and check on him frequently, she'd show her face before the sun went down. And after all the effort he'd dumped into playing that "you abandoned me" card, he doubted she'd be able to disappoint him.

She was already incapable of forgiving herself, which was funny, considering she'd forgiven *him*. While his moments of tender-hearted sibling time were all a hoax, he knew Winter meant every word she said.

She wanted to have a relationship with him. She wanted to be there for him, whatever that meant.

He didn't think her decision to meet with him so often painted a very inspiring picture of her intelligence. Even her dipshit, off-brand Captain America boyfriend knew she was behaving like a moron.

Just further proof that the female species is unequal to man.

The fact that they'd both received fifty percent of their DNA from the same woman was unbelievable. An *insult*, even.

"Weak, simple-minded, hooker-faced bi—"

Tap-tap. Tap-tap. Tap-tap.

Justin turned toward his door and swallowed the urge to scream with unabandoned glee.

As if he'd willed her to appear, Winter stood at his window, smiling and waving through the glass. He returned the grin, but for a much different reason.

Winter's happiness to see him was genuine. She *loved* him.

She was, hands down, an idiot.

Her timing, however, was absolutely perfect. The sight of her appearing, just when he needed her most, warmed his blood. He was elated, in fact. Blessed.

"Thank you, Grandpa," he whispered before waving for his big sister to come into his room.

The time had finally come to make his move.

How nice of Sissy to help him out.

The End
To be continued...

Thank you for reading.
All of the Autumn Trent Series books can be found on Amazon.

ACKNOWLEDGMENTS

How does one properly thank everyone involved in taking a dream and making it a reality? Let me try.

In addition to my family, whose unending support provided the foundation for me to find the time and energy to put these thoughts on paper, I want to thank the editors who polished my words and made them shine.

Many thanks to my publisher for risking taking on a newbie and giving me the confidence to become a bona fide author.

More than anyone, I want to thank you, my reader, for clicking on a nobody and sharing your most important asset, your time, with this book. I hope with all my heart I made it worthwhile.

Much love,
Mary

ABOUT THE AUTHOR

Mary Stone lives among the majestic Blue Ridge Mountains of East Tennessee with her two dogs, four cats, a couple of energetic boys, and a very patient husband.

As a young girl, she would go to bed every night, wondering what type of creature might be lurking underneath. It wasn't until she was older that she learned that the creatures she needed to most fear were human.

Today, she creates vivid stories with courageous, strong heroines and dastardly villains. She invites you to enter her world of serial killers, FBI agents but never damsels in distress. Her female characters can handle themselves, going toe-to-toe with any male character, protagonist or antagonist.

Discover more about Mary Stone on her website.
www.authormarystone.com

Connect with Mary Online

facebook.com/authormarystone
goodreads.com/AuthorMaryStone
bookbub.com/profile/3378576590
pinterest.com/MaryStoneAuthor
instagram.com/marystone_author

Made in United States
Troutdale, OR
03/10/2025

29630864R10186